# OUTSTANDING I
# TOM DEWEESE AND ERASE

I think ERASE maybe the most important political novel since 1984, Atlas Shrugged, Brave New World and State of Fear." *Jay Lehr, Ph.D. The Heartland Institute*

Must Read Book: Tom DeWeese's ERASE Like Atlas Shrugged and the Left Behind series Tom DeWeese's ERASE presents a fictional path through a dystopian future. However, in ERASE every single policy presented in the book, from the use of technology to change our culture; to the use of the public school classrooms to eliminate true knowledge; to the destruction of Christianity in a drive to meld all religions into one powerful tool for government, is all true and happening at this very moment. *Richard Viguerie's Conservative Headquarters*

"Once in a while you read a book and say this is truly timely. ERASE is that book for today. It is believable. And it should be because much of what is in it has actually happened or is currently happening across the country." *Kathleen Marquardt, author of the best selling book, Animal Scam.*

"Tom DeWeese has mastered the art of story-telling and sounding the alarm in such a way, that while we are being entertained, we are also being enlightened. This is not only a suspenseful political thriller … this is the warning bell." *Debbie Barth host of On The Grid Internet Talk Radio/ author of The Promise Book; Tell Someone*

# What other readers have said

"I am reading Tom DeWeese's new novel ERASE which has all the flavor of the late Michael Crichton's State Of Fear and Rand's Atlas Shrugged."

"ERASE… in my opinion, is a 21st century version of George Orwell's 1984."

"DeWeese ties the Global Agenda into a fictional, fast moving, interesting story that would make anyone understand what is happening to our Country, even if they'd not been paying attention for the past 20 to 30 years. This will be a best seller shortly."

"Murder, greed, tyranny, Agenda 21, and New World Order, all tied up in a package of deceit ... and lying at the front door of the White House. You are going to love this one."

"It is eye opening, it is necessary, it is suspenseful, it is just well written. The characters are faced with the same fears, the same trying to stop it, the same helplessness, that many of us are facing daily as we fight to stop such a dark demon from destroying our real lives"

"I think the author did an excellent job in tying in all aspects of the world we live in today. Everyone should read it. It is in story form for the benefit of those who can not wrap their minds around the world today. Factfiction I guess you would call it."

"ERASE gives me hope, that everything wrong will be corrected, that good triumphs over evil."

"Erase is so incredibly believable; I guess that is because most of the things in it really happened or are happening now in America. It is so good to have it in a novel -- it makes for easier reading and a lot more fun. Thank you Mr. DeWeese for writing this. Can't wait for your next book."

"You are a terrific writer. It really flows…"

"It is eye opening, it is necessary, it is suspenseful, it is just well written."

"I highly recommend the book, both as an excellent suspense novel and maybe one that will open some eyes to a real threat."

"We finished Erase. WOW!! We really enjoyed it!"

"I'm working on Erase - great so far."

"I finished your book and it really had me thinking, that's the point right!"

"I am also enjoying your book."

"Oh it's good."

"Exciting read! Each chapter makes you look forward to the next. Relevant to today's America."

"I didn't want to finish it because I didn't want it to end!"

# Forward

I think ERASE may be the most important political novel since 1984, Atlas Shrugged, Brave New World and State of Fear.

## ERASE

### By Tom DeWeese

### Reviewed by Jay Lehr, The Heartland Institute

It has been many years since any writer has attempted to take on the downward spiral of our government in a fictional story that tells the whole truth and nothing but the truth with names chosen to protect the innocent and deprive the guilty of the ability to sue for slander.

Perhaps it started with Aldous Huxley's Brave New World, then George Orwell's 1984, followed by Ayn Rand's

Atlas Shrugged and most recently Michael Crichton's State of Fear. Tom DeWeese may not go down entirely in the company of the aforementioned authors, but he has written a delightful easy to read novel that accomplishes the very same things these four icons did. His advantage is that he has written a "historical novel" when the period of history he is dealing with is "today".

His book ERASE has all the ingredients of a mystery thriller including murder, mayhem and intrigue, villains, heroes and heroines, but all placed in a framework of to-day's reality only slightly exaggerated for impact.

It is often said among writers that there are only 13 original plots and that every one creates a variation on one of those themes. DeWeese borrows from all four of the great dystopian scenarios mentioned above. If you have not read any or all you might put them on your reading list as they are truly classics.

Atlas Shrugged has a mysterious hero whose name is written all over in graffiti "who is John Galt". In DeWeese's ERASE the mystery hero is just known as "H" and his mes-sages are potently described in graffiti all over government buildings in Washington, DC. In "1984" the government rewrites all of history in a language called "newspeak". De-Weese's nefarious government is able to rewrite everything when books disappear and all information comes through a government controlled iPad in everyone's hands. In Brave New World the populace is controlled by a daily dose of a simple little "soma" pill. In ERASE control is implemented through a federally controlled school system with a "Common Core" like curriculum. State of Fear keeps the public in a state of alarm through fraudulent environmental scares. DeWeese does the same herding the population into cities in order to "protect the environment."

The exciting difference in DeWeese's book is his development of the evil doers personalities and how they managed to take over society. But the book is far scarier than its predecessors. It has no hint of futuristic science fiction dystopia, instead it describes "today" with every detail in the book involving actual existing public policy with much of the dialog taken verbatim from recent events. Our nation is being changed before our eyes in much the way ERASE describes. And, just as DeWeese depicts, there are dedicated patriots racing to stop it. In ERASE the ultimate heroes do indeed succeed.

In California, a year ago 1500 farmers were deprived of their irrigation water to insure that smelt, a river fish, had adequate water. In ERASE a team from the Army Corps of Engineers systematically destroy irrigation systems eliminating water flowing from the Mississippi River to adjacent farms. In addition, dams throughout the country are dismantled flooding homes where families are reassigned to cities.

The plot expands to Churches as their pastors are encouraged, in order to maintain their positions, to tell their parishioners that Man is the lowest life form on earth and he must be removed from most of it in order to preserve the earth. Private property is to be eliminated so as not to enslave the land. The new leaders declare that capitalism is destroying the earth.

DeWeese quotes the Czech born French writer Milan Kundera at the end of ERASE, from the "Book of Laughter and Forgetting" which may have been influenced by his colleague Milan Hubl: "*The first step in liquidating a people is to erase its memory. Destroy its books, its culture, and its history. Then have somebody write new books, manufacture a new culture, invent a new history. Before long the nation will begin to forget what it is and what it was. The world around it will forget even faster.*" That is the basic plot of ERASE.

To preserve freedom, DeWeese intones, it is the duty of every American to learn and understand these dangers. That is why true education, in particular, the teaching of history, economics and philosophy are so vital to preserving a free society.

# ERASE

## Tom DeWeese

American Policy Center

Also by Tom DeWeese

Now Tell Me I Was Wrong

Agenda 21:
The Wrenching Transformation of America

ERASE

Edition 1.4, September 2017

Copyright © 2017 by Tom DeWeese

ISBN: 978-0-692-74802-2

This book was printed in the United States of America.

This book is a work of fiction. Names, characters, places, and incidents either are products of the author's imagination or are used fictitiously. Any resemblance to actual events or locales or persons living or dead is entirely coincidental.

You can continue to receive Tom DeWeese's latest writings by reading his monthly newsletter The DeWeese Report: americanpolicy.org

To order additional copies of this book visit: EraseNovel.com

Cover Illustration and Design by Kelly Reed

This book is dedicated to the rare few Americans who see the awful truth of how our nation is being transformed. Just normal, everyday people with children to raise, jobs to work, and taxes to pay. They are afraid. They don't want to stand out. They don't want to take risks. But they understand that freedom is too precious and too easily lost if they do nothing. So they do it. They listen and learn. They attend the city council meetings. They write letters. They make phone calls. They withstand ridicule and threats. And they do what they can to help preserve our nation. To them all Americans owe a debt of gratitude.

# Prologue

---

The call came early that day. It had transferred through the usual secured channels. The right security codes confirmed it was legit. There had been several such calls lately and he had answered them all, carrying out the detailed instructions to the letter.

But there were two details that made this call a bit different. First, the assignment it described was for tonight. Usually he had more time to prepare. Second, this one promised a much bigger fee than the others. That was nice, but it made little difference to him. A job was a job, and he was good at his work.

To not waste precious time, he began preparations. He was supplied the address and the subject's expected time of arrival. Apparently this one was very predictable in her comings and goings. Good. That made it much easier. While he could deal with surprises should they arise, who needs 'em?

Early that afternoon he traveled to the address, just to check it out. First, he drove past the building. No sign of anyone outside. He turned around and passed by the building and then turned again to park a short distance down the street where he had a straight line of vision to watch it.

After parking, he got out and casually walked toward the apartment building. As he passed he could see it more clearly. Good, no security lock or code on the door. He walked into the lobby. No one was there.

She lived on the third floor. That made access a little tougher for him. He walked down the hall. Her apartment number was 309. He walked past it. Then turned and walked back to her door and knocked. No sound came from inside. Good. No dog. And no neighbor seemed to take notice of his knocking sounds. That was good, too. No nosey neighbors.

Leaving the building, he turned to look up at her window. There was a fire escape. Well, that's just too easy, he thought. He'll just turn the window lock.

Nothing to do now but wait. She was due home in about two hours and darkness would fall soon. He walked back to the car and took out the cup of coffee he had brought with him and slowly sipped, thinking about the best way to complete the assignment. Keep it simple was his motto. No need to get cute.

Two hours later a blue Ford Explorer pulled into the space in the parking lot marked for apartment 309 and Terri Miller got out, walked to the back of the vehicle, opened the hatch, pulled out her well traveled suitcase, and went inside the building.

Terri was glad to finally be home after days of travel. Speaking tours in multiple cities are exhausting. A different hotel room every night. Packing and unpacking. Sometimes the hosts don't even think to feed you and you are left to your own creativity for a meal. Many times she just went out to the vending machine in the hotel hallway and bought potato chips, a candy bar, and a Coke.

But her work, the mission, was important. America was changing. Freedom was being challenged.  She was doing everything she could to sound the alarm and expose the threat. Uncomfortable as the travel might be, she knew she had to be out there waking people up.

It was good to be home with a fridge full of her favorite foods. She liked simple, comfort food. Her friends thought she was crazy. She loved to carve up an apple, cut some cheese, and throw a bag of popcorn into the microwave and then smother it with butter. When it was prepared she brought it all out to the sofa in the living room to relax with her feet up.

Tonight she was especially anxious to read a new book she had just downloaded onto her e-book. Actually, it appeared to be more of a report than a book. It had been hard to find. It was apparently a rare document that couldn't be found in any of the few remaining books stores in the nation. That's why she had gone to the Internet.

She had spent hours searching all websites that could possibly deal with such a document. Nothing was found. With each failed attempt, she bore deeper into the hidden corners of the World Wide Web, determined to find it. Just before she left on this last speaking trip to Kansas, suddenly there it was, virtually hidden in an unexpected place online.

This one had been a challenge. But she had been told by an associate that it was urgent that she read it. Why was this book so important? That's what she hoped to find out by reading it tonight.

With only the light from the lamp on the small table beside the couch, she sat comfortably, intently reading. Suddenly there was a stir behind her. Rough hands grabbed her throat and strong arms picked her up off the couch and flung her across the room. Before she could react, a large shadowy figure moved like lightning to her sprawled body. The rough hands grabbed her again and with one powerful squeeze, snapped her neck, and everything went dark as life left her body.

Looking down at her as if admiring his work, he let a shallow smile cross his face. After a moment he quickly turned, walked over to the couch where Terri's e-book had fallen to the floor. He snatched it up, put it inside his coat pocket and disappeared out of the apartment as quickly and as silently as he had appeared.

# Chapter 1

**"The Power of One."** The words were scrawled in red fluorescent spray paint. Brad Jackson snorted in disgust as he saw the graffiti defacing the wall of the metro station in the crisp coolness of the early morning. Everywhere he looked anymore, there seemed to be words scrawled in red paint. The words would just appear overnight. Everyday another surface was defaced with new words, on buildings, on sidewalks, even on the sides of buses and cars. **"The Law," "Freedom," "Liberty."** One day the words **"Moral Absolutes = Liberty"** had been scrawled along the walls inside the metro station. That location seemed to be a favorite spot. What in the world did it mean, Brad wondered.

Brad certainly believed in free speech and freedom of expression. He knew there were desperate people with no voice. But he had never been one to make waves about an issue. He voted. He did express his opinions. But some people just go too far. They think they have to get in your face and scream. There are other, more peaceful ways, to express oneself, he thought.

Who are these idiots who have so little regard for other people's property that they feel the need to make it their personal toilet? What are they trying to say? And who are they talking to? The whole world seemed to be changing. Grace and manners were disappearing. Respect for the property of others was discarded. Nothing seemed clean anymore. Nothing was orderly, as if everything was just done for the moment with no thought for tomorrow.

But that graffiti -- it seemed like a cry for attention. Desperate. Why? Who?

Brad shuddered and felt a little chill run through his body. He kept walking and his disgust was quickly pushed to the back of his mind. Now he was approaching the steps to the high school. As he got closer, another ache started in the back of his head. It was that feeling of dread or perhaps a bit of despair as he prepared for another day in the classroom.

As he quickly ran up the steps to school, students scattered about, some stamping their feet in the morning chill, trying to get warm. The usual few were again leaning against the statue of Lincoln, the school's namesake. Their slovenly, almost menacing manner seemed to make the statue their own private domain. Brad got the feeling there were things going on that he didn't want to know about. This wasn't a crowd to mess with. Other students were just impatiently waiting for the school doors to open.

What struck Brad most about the scene each morning were the students' careless draping of sloppy, shapeless clothes, backward hats and untied shoes. Then there were the outrageous colors of their hair. purple, bright red, and green seemed to be the most popular. Brad thought perhaps it was a cry to be noticed, to stand out from the crowd, to declare some individuality. The only problem was, when they all did it, the individuality was gone and they all looked the same. Why don't they tie their shoes, he usually wondered. How can they walk? But, then again, how can they do anything with their clothes literally falling off their bodies?

There wasn't much of the chatter or laughter you would expect from young people. Each day as he rushed past them, few would even acknowledge him. A couple of nods were all. It didn't used to be that way. He loved coming into this building. Then, there was enthusiasm from the students. Lots of talking and joking. Good-natured ribbing. Now everything seemed to be quiet. A kind of foreboding seemed to grip the whole school.

Remember the days of school spirit, he thought. There had been signs and banners hanging in the halls saying, "BEAT THE BULLDOGS!" referring to Friday night's game against the school's rival. Everyone attended. Now, few bothered to go to the games. Being at school seemed to be at the very bottom of their interests. Little else tended to break their concentration on their iPhones and incessant texting. Their thumbs seemed to get all of the exercise allotted for their bodies.

Brad quickly made his way up the steps into the front door of the school and threw his briefcase on the X-ray machine as he passed through the metal detectors by the armed guards. Just another day at school. A few teachers were in the halls, hurrying to their classrooms before the bell would ring to announce the official beginning of the school day. Brad noticed that the Principal and his staff were already busy in the school office as he passed.

He could hear his heels clack on the empty hallway floor as he headed to his own classroom.

As he entered, he felt overwhelmed. Again, the atmosphere in the entire school seemed oppressive. For years he had loved to teach the kids. It had always been a thrill to see it in their eyes – that day, that moment, when the recognition came to them. When they actually got what he was trying to teach them. There was no greater moment of satisfaction for a teacher.

Yet, it was getting harder to achieve that reaction. The rules for teaching kept changing. There were endless meetings with the administration and with the teachers' union. Everything now was about proficiency tests. Test them again, and again. When the kids didn't seem to respond as expected, there was a big flurry of activity and major announcements about "new standards." "This," said the powers in charge, "would finally grab the students attention and raise their proficiency!" There was that word again.

The other term that kept popping up in the new curriculum he was now required to teach was "global ethic." What the heck was that? Everything seemed to be focused on "global" now. Global citizenship, global economy, global achievement standards. These words were pounded into every corner of the curriculum.

It was all so complicated and, frankly, Brad felt it was a bit mind-numbing. And if it was for him, he felt it had to be for his students as well. The kids today just didn't seem interested. He'd always felt confident that he knew how to motivate the students and help them learn. Now that seemed to be changing and he wasn't sure why.

To him the atmosphere in the school felt more like an exercise in psychology than academics. The halls of the school were covered with posters with simple-minded messages. "Think Green." "The Earth is Your Mother." "We Are All In This Together." It seemed designed to pound a constant message. About what, he wasn't sure. Brad thought it seemed a bit like brainwashing. Did he really need to use such strategy to trick the kids into learning, he wondered. No, I'm a teacher. My children will learn. Catching their attention is the secret.

Yet, now at his desk now in the empty classroom, he thought back to his early teaching days so many years ago. His specialty had always been the ability to muster his passion for the subject. Back then he could feel the students join him in the excitement as he talked about the Founding Fathers and their struggle against the overwhelming odds of fighting the mother country.

The way he taught American history wasn't just through memorizing a bunch of dates to remember for a test. To him, every moment was alive. A moment of monumental importance. The actions from the past told where we came from and why. Where did our ideas for government and families and business come from?  Brad believed that if a nation forgot its roots, then it had no ability to see its mistakes, and more importantly, the way forward. He thought of the Roman Empire -- once great and all-powerful. But its success led to its downfall. Why? It was important to know.

He had always been able to relate that to the students. His complete command of the subject had allowed him to share the personal tragedies and victories of a people determined to control their own destinies. Where did they get the courage to stand so firmly for their convictions?

The students felt it too. They asked questions. They used their imaginations to think through how they would handle a situation.

And Brad, always with a gavel in his hand as he conducted the class (it was his trademark), led them to new ideas. Sometimes his enthusiasm would grab hold and he would pace back and forth in front of the class and up and down the rows of desks, pushing them into seeing the battles, smelling the smoke of the guns, describing the heroics. Sometimes, as a student would shout out an idea, he would actually jump into the wastebasket beside his desk, waving his gavel in the air and shout, "Yes, that's it!"

What was the driving force behind the war for independence? What did the Founders mean by Freedom? What about the Civil War? Why did the Southerners fight against such overwhelming odds for their states? Was it really about keeping people in slavery? How were American interests served by getting into World Wars I and II? How had it all changed our world?

And now, today, America's place in the world was changing. We weren't as respected as once before. In fact, we were the focus of much hatred. How would that endanger our future as a nation? Would we even be a nation in a few years?

To understand and find the answers to such questions required teaching philosophy as much as historic facts. And Brad loved both. He believed a well-rounded academic approach was vital to assure they not only learned the details, but understood the circumstances. If they could relate, then they would remember. That was his motto.

And he loved sharing it all with his students – seeing them suddenly grasp what he was telling them. Watching as they began to debate the issues in class as different opinions and opposing sides formed, just as in real life. His classroom was a bastion of free thought with his encouragement to the kids to freely speak their minds. Above all he was teaching them to think for themselves. That was how academics should be taught; Brad had no doubt.

Students seemed to love his class. He had heard them say so over and over again. He had won teaching awards year after year. Parents came up to him at ballgames and school functions to tell him how their children talked about Mr. Jackson and his great class. That was only a few years ago.

But now that kind of enthusiasm appeared to be fading. As the years passed, Brad couldn't help but notice that a change of attitude had come over the students. They just didn't seem to relate to stories of heroics and sacrifice for a cause anymore. Beyond that, the importance of history and how vital it was to our current lives just wasn't sinking in. They were bored, disengaged, and perhaps even resentful of his attempts to get them involved. They simply had no interest. No motivation. They barely paid attention. Their interest in even the most rudimentary knowledge of American history, let alone an interest about history anywhere else in the world, just didn't exist.

Here they were, in their last year of high school – a time when they should know about civics and some basic economics, and at least the name of our first president. "How do I reach them?" The thought kept him awake at night. More importantly, why had this change taken place? What was the root of this complete lack of interest in academics?

"Who's on the one dollar bill," he suddenly asked in class one day as his patience began to run out. There was silence.

"Nixon," someone shouted out. "

"Who's Nixon?" another asked.

"Who cares?" shouted another.

"Just so it spends!" They all laughed. Everything was reduced to the status of a mindless joke.

Brad had watched many times in utter frustration as Jay Leno, on the old Tonight Show, did his "Jaywalking," taking a camera out on the streets of Los Angeles to ask average Americans basic questions about what he considered standard knowledge. "In what year was the War of 1812 fought?" Silence.

"Uh, 1776?"

"Who did we fight in World War II?"

"Vietnam?"

"What is the Star Spangled Banner?"

"Um, Lady Gaga's dress?"

And on and on it went. It was as if the responders had some vague remembrance from way back in their minds, but they were now resorting to simple word association to struggle for answers. If the question was about a rap song, or about beer, or a video game, they got it. If it had anything to do with academics – no interest.

He found himself yelling the answers at the television. His wife told him to calm down, that it was just funny. "There's nothing funny about it. This is our history. This is where we come from. There are reasons why we have to know this stuff. If we don't know our history, or our nation's economic system, or the ideals that motivated our founders to create this country, then we will lose it," he insisted.

Knowledge was the center of his life. There was a power, he felt, in just having the ability to observe a situation or a policy that was being discussed on a news report and knowing some history behind it. He felt it eliminated that feeling of doubt or even fear.

That's why he revered the classic books that lined his shelves in his library at home. Some were valuable antiques. Here were the thoughts of some of the most brilliant people who ever walked the earth. Just reading their words would enlighten you. Teach you. Make you stronger. To shut out such wisdom and knowledge forces us all to start over. Civilized society collapses without knowledge, he said to himself not for the first time.

These days when he stood in front of his class and the silence grew louder when he asked a question, he began to see the dullness in their eyes. It was as if they were starting to revert back to cavemen where a grunt served as communication. Look how they relate to anyone other than those in their pack. They looked down at the ground. They averted their eyes. And they grunted a greeting, if offering one at all.

Stop it. Don't think of your students as animals. Something is wrong. Something is causing this. But what? Why don't they care? Why have they given up?

Brad was startled from his thoughts as the bell rang and the noise in the hall made by the mob of students announced the beginning of another school day. "OK," he thought, "here we go again."

. . . .

John Lloyd was a proud man. He had worked hard all of his life. Hard work, his father taught him, was the secret to success. While still in elementary school, he started working in the back room of his father's small printing business, sweeping floors and taking out the trash. Later, as he grew, he was given more responsibility. After he got his driver's license his dad let him drive the company van to pick up printing supplies and paper. Soon he was delivering the finished jobs to the customers.

Finally the day came when young John was taught to run the printing press. It was a simple machine -- an AB Dick 360 press. Just one circular drum and a chain driven system that shot the paper through the press. He loved the smell of the ink and the slap, slap rhythm of the paper running through the press gave him an energy he couldn't explain. His father said he had printer's ink in his blood.

And so he worked. The printing business eventually led him to the publishing industry, where his talent began to bring him success and, eventually, monetary power.

It hadn't been easy. He first had to work his way through the system, taking a series of beginner jobs at various publishing houses. Coming from the experience of his family-owned business into the corporate structure of major New York-based publishing houses was like entering a whole new world. There he had to struggle to stand out among the hundreds of employees. He had to deal with those typical fellow workers who seemed to plague every office, they saw every employee with ambition to be rivals and a threat. And, in Lloyd's observation, they were the ones who always sat in low-level management offices with some sort of a controlling position over others. He constantly wondered why top management tolerated these people who so obviously held back the success of the company.

Lloyd had ambition and thus always seemed to be involved in confrontations with lazy oafs. It cost him a few jobs. But he kept pushing forward, learning the trade. He became a major producer with a natural eye for finding the best authors and their works. Within a few years he was responsible for producing nearly half of the agency's output. That's when he decided to strike out on his own.

Today, John Lloyd stood at the head of the world's largest publishing house, Mega-World Publishing. It operated from its own building in the heart of downtown New York City. It was a skyscraper and the letters, MWP, shone in gold leaf from the top to announce Lloyd's world-wide publishing empire.

Lloyd was tall, tanned, and had sandy brown hair. Decisive blue eyes pierced through anyone standing in his sights. He had married the daughter of the owner of a rival publishing house and eventually was able to combine the two, creating a powerful force in the industry. As a result, his years of self-made leadership had given him a confidence that now translated into an aristocratic air about him. While he was soft-spoken, his voice commanded attention. In his book publishing empire, he wielded almost absolute power. The best authors jealously guarded their relationship with him. A book published by Mega-World almost guaranteed success.

Or so it used to be. Today, as he sat in his palatial office overlooking the most powerful city in the world, John Lloyd had a problem. It was called LEAP.

The latest sales reports had just been dropped on his desk. They weren't good. The sales of printed, published books - his empire's lifeblood - were plummeting. Many people apparently had little interest in buying printed books. The second page of the report showed that more bookstores had gone out of business over the last quarter than in all of last year. There were fewer and fewer outlets left to sell his books. Of the two major book outlets that thrived just a couple years ago, only one now remained in business. Local mom and pop stores were shutting their doors rapidly. About the only real outlets left were the bookstores in airports, but they too were showing a major decline in printed book sales.

The reason for the drop in the sale of printed books was technology -- e-books. Everyone was rushing to them. Printing was becoming expensive and outdated. With the e-book all one had to do was download the latest manuscript as soon as it came out, at a fraction of the cost. Better yet, you could now keep your entire library in the e-book. Any book you wanted was right there, anytime you felt like reading it. No need to take up a whole room in your house for a massive library. And you could also have your newspaper and magazine subscriptions right there in the e-book as well. Talk about convenience.

Worse for Lloyd was that his best writers were starting to leave his publishing company, going instead to that new upstart called LEAP. That's because they not only were publishing through e-books, but LEAP had used its growing financial firepower to buy up nearly the entire platform of electronic book manufactures and put them under one umbrella of technology.

As a result, LEAP now had the once unimaginable technical capability to provide audio, video, and even interactive graphics, quizzes, and communications. So now LEAP books could give the reader, as he read, the entire fantasy experience as they read to see, hear, and feel what the author intended. LEAP was driving towards complete dominance of the publishing industry.

Even more impressive, LEAP could actually monitor what the readers were focusing on and know what they enjoyed or disliked about the story they were reading. That meant that authors could reduce their creative energies to a surefire formula to keep pumping out variations of the same story line, all to a pleased and hungry audience. It was money in the bank.

But John Lloyd was old school. Publishing was what he knew and commanded. To him, technology was a whole separate animal. He had adamantly resisted jumping into the e-book craze, continuing to publish his books exclusively through print. The very idea that real books could actually be eliminated was simply unimaginable to him. But now technology was about to destroy him.  He had to find a way to take back control. There was one man that might help Lloyd in his fight to change the playing field.

He picked up his phone and dialed. "Mr. Arter, John Lloyd here. We need to talk."

# Chapter 2

It was just after 3:00 a.m. when Mack Richard's phone rang, dragging him out of a sound sleep. The voice on the other end was that of Jeff Buchanan, and he was obviously upset.

"Mack, they just found Terri's body," he said with a quiver in his voice. "She was murdered in her apartment, apparently two days ago." For a few seconds all Richards could do was sit there, unable to react.

Terri Miller was his right hand. She had helped him found the Voice of Adams and was its most effective recruiter. She traveled the nation, speaking, sounding the alarm, rallying, and organizing new people to the cause. He had wondered why he hadn't heard from her over the past few days. He knew that when traveling and speaking around the country Terri sometimes just got so wrapped up in things that she didn't always communicate with him. He was used to it and so hadn't thought her silence was unusual.

"Tell me what happened," Mack finally was able to say.

"Well," said Buchanan hesitantly, knowing how much his words were going to affect his friend, "I just got a call from Fred, one of our guys who works for the Gaithersburg Police Department. He said they got a call from one of her neighbors because she hadn't been seen in two days, but her car was in its parking place. The neighbor tried knocking on the door, but no one answered. So she called the police. They went over and forced their way in and found her on the floor. Her neck was broken. There was little evidence of a struggle and no sign of forced entry and nothing appears to be missing," said Buchanan as he finished his report. "I'm sorry to call so late, but I knew you would want to know right away."

What Mack Richards did know was that her death was a devastating loss, to him personally, and to the movement they had founded together. Terri was much more to him than a partner and fellow activist. After years of living alone since the death of his wife, Terri was the first woman he truly related to in a personal way. She helped him to feel alive as they shared ideas and dreams and laughs. She had changed his world.

Mack Richards was a former U.S. Marine, and had been elected and reelected five times as county sheriff in his hometown of Tampa, Florida. He believed deeply in the ideals of freedom in the United States and took his oath to protect and defend the Constitution very seriously. "A Marine," he was often heard to say, "is forever Marines stand tall physically and mentally. They can always be counted on, no matter the threat."

As a county sheriff he believed that he had the responsibility to be the most important law enforcement authority to the people. Someone needed to be strong enough to stand up for the citizens to protect them from an overpowering government. During one of his reelection campaigns he declared, "I am not a bureaucrat and I'm not going to answer to one! I'm your employee and I exist to serve and protect you in all matters."

He became a fierce defender of local control and on more than one occasion refused to allow federal agents to confiscate property or arrest his citizens without due process. "The Constitution, is a higher law than any appointed bureaucrats with their own courts." That's why his people loved and reelected Mack Richards multiple times. They felt safe with him in office.

Eventually he wanted to do more on a national level as he saw growing threats wherever he turned. The nation was changing drastically, almost overnight it seemed. The economy was in great danger of collapsing. Individual freedom of choice over one's own life was systematically being replaced by an ever-growing nanny state. And government was growing larger and more intrusive in everyone's life. Surveillance cameras appeared to be on every street corner and in every shop and apartment building. Some were now discovering cameras and monitoring equipment inside their televisions sets and in personal computers. Even cars had devices implanted in them to record every mile of travel and what speed you were driving. The location and action of every citizen seemed to be monitored by what some feared to be unseen forces inside the government.

Worse, private property rights were under assault. People were losing their land to Washington agencies. Always the excuse seemed to be the environment. Under that same excuse, whole industries were disappearing along with their vital jobs for the people. The economy was in danger of collapsing. It seemed there was a growing threat of more and more government takeover wherever Mack Richards looked.

As a sheriff, he was becoming increasingly concerned about the growing militarization of the nation's police forces. "Policemen are not supposed to be soldiers," he said, "they are supposed to protect their neighbors from harm."

Yet, he was alarmed to see more and more incidents occurring of unrestrained police violence against common citizens. On the nightly news there were numerous reports of police guns pulled on citizens in routine traffic stops. Cameras caught one cop brutally slapping a citizen simply because he asked why the cop had to search his car. Home-owners had been shot in no-knock raids on the wrong house.

In one such case, two elderly homeowners lived through a terrifying night they never thought could happen in America. They were rousted from their bed, watched their family dog being shot while they were forced to sit on their couch in their underwear as they were questioned by heavily armed federal cops. As the night wore on the cops actually had a pizza party in their living room. They laughed and joked while the couple sat as prisoners in their own home. Then, the cops suddenly discovered they were in the wrong house and simply left. They didn't clean up their mess or even say they were sorry. And the government never reimbursed the homeowners for their loss of damaged property. "That doesn't happen in a free society," a furious Richards declared.

Just as alarming, there was a new threat from inside the government against those who spoke out against such policies. People were actually being threatened with arrest for having opinions contrary to the government's policies.

Property owners, seeking to ask questions at city council meetings about new regulations that might affect them, were often denied the microphone to speak to their elected representatives. Incredibly, some were bodily removed from such public meetings by armed guards. Richards observed that more government power was leading to more government corruption. And it was happening across the nation.

Richards fully believed that control of speech and thought was a terrifying force inside the nation that was supposed to be the freest on earth. What he saw was an absolute unwillingness by the government to compromise or even discuss the growing control of the people. His worst fear was that the nation was becoming a police state. "That must change if freedom is to survive."

People, were feeling a growing nervousness, not fully understanding what was happening in their nation or to their personal lives. Mack Richards saw a desperation coming from the people as they realized that the government no longer cared about their wants, needs, or dreams for their own lives.

So he now felt an urgency to take action. He decided to not run for reelection. Instead he began to travel the nation speaking to audiences, describing the danger of the threat of a government growing more and more out of control as an oppressor of the people.

Now his thoughts turned back to when he and Terri

had first met at one of his public talks. "The ever growing expansion of government at every level is usurping individual freedom," he had passionately told the audience of about 100 people.

"We need patriots to stand up and shout from the rafters, NO!" he cried. "NO! to policies that infringe on our liberty. NO! to massive waste of the tax payers' hard earned money. NO! to political leaders who grab power, endanger the election process, and corrupt the system with illegal search and seizure of private homes and property."

"No American," he said, "should ever grow to fear their own government. Americans should live in confidence that government's only purpose is to protect our ability to pursue our own happiness. That is its only purpose. We need to force our elected representatives to keep the oath they each swore to when they took office – to defend, uphold, protect, preserve, and obey the U.S. Constitution as the law of our land," he concluded to a strong ovation of approval from the crowd.

Terri Miller had rushed up to talk to him as soon as he came off the stage. She was young, slight in build, her big blue eyes full of fire and excitement. She was moved by his speech and wanted to talk.

She was a local volunteer for a variety of political causes and could always be counted on to help with petition drives, fundraisers, and in organizing rallies for candidates. Terri even worked at the polls on Election Day. She believed every citizen had a duty to be involved in the operation of their community.

Then, as she listened to Mack Richards explaining the

dangers he saw facing the nation, she was transformed, barely able to sit another minute. She felt the need to take action.

After the meeting they had gone into the bar of the hotel and talked for hours about what could be done to put his ideas into reality. It was her idea to create a national organization to fight the growing tyranny they saw building across the nation. "Government is out of control and we need to stop it or freedom will die," she said, her expressive eyes almost pleading for a solution.

Richards suggested that the new group should be the voice of the people. "No," she declared with a huge, excited smile on her face, her eyes dancing with an idea that had just come to her. "It should be the Voice of Adams!"

"What do you mean?" asked Richards.

"Samuel Adams, the man who started the Sons of Liberty during the Revolutionary War. The man who was more responsible for getting America to overthrow British tyranny and establish American independence than any other Founding Father."

She almost giggled with joy as she thought of the possibilities. "We can organize to reestablish those ideals of freedom that drove the first Americans. We can motivate patriots to rebuild the Republic! The Voice of Adams will be our banner, our battle cry – the name of our new organization!"

And so was born, The Voice of Adams. Now, at their national headquarters in Washington, D.C., hung a banner in the lobby that said, "*If ever a time should come, when vain*

*and aspiring men shall possess the highest seats in govern-*
*ment, our country will stand in need of its experienced patri-*
*ots to prevent its ruin."* Samuel Adams.

That was their motto, their goal, their reason for being
– to prevent the ruin of the Republic that was called the
United States of America. All inspired by the spirit of Sam
Adams.

It had all been Terri's idea. Her passion and her leadership had made it a driving force in the political landscape.
There were now a few Congressmen who were starting to
listen to Voice of Adams' warnings. Even more importantly,
there were now a growing number of state legislators and
even local officials who were starting to call for legislative
action to rein in the growing power of central government.
"Fighting from the local level up is how we will counter
their power and put things right," said Terri.

Now, Voice of Adams leaders addressed congressional
hearings, worked inside state legislatures to help create
policy, and appeared on national news shows, carrying the
message that government was raging out of control. They
organized rallies across the nation with the banner of Sam
Adams always prominently displayed. In fact, slowly Sam
Adams seemed to be emerging as the symbol against opposition in a renewed rebellion across the nation. And the
number of people attending those rallies was growing.

Of course, Terri and Mack knew their success really
only amounted to mere baby steps in the fight to restore
the Republic. They needed thousands more to stand up and
speak out. But they were satisfied that they were making
progress down a long, difficult road and they were dedicated
to seeing it through to the final victory.

The best part, Mack thought, was how Terri was able to keep everyone motivated, keeping their eyes on the ball. She understood that even the smallest victory was indeed a victory to be celebrated and used as fuel to reach for the next. She was an amazing force!

But there was another element to the Voice of Adams, perhaps more important than even the legislative arm. Across the nation, they provided special training programs in which locally elected sheriffs were taught Constitutional law, learning that they were the last legal line of defense against an out of control government.

Mack Richards taught the sheriffs to serve the people just as he had. When faced with illegal actions or threats from federal government agents, Richards taught the sheriffs that they had the legal right to stop them in their counties. He believed that, someday soon, with enough trained sheriffs around the country, there would be no more cases where defenseless Americans would be forced to stand alone, helpless, as central government agents, armed in military fashion, simply forced their will at the point of a gun. As Mack Richards liked to say at these training sessions, "There's a new sheriff in town!"

To keep on top of the situation so that there could be no surprises, the Voice of Adams also had a sophisticated computer operation manned by a staff specifically trained to scan through the proposals and policy documents in every agency of the federal and state governments. Using key words such as "population," "transformation," even "land use" and "community planning," the system was able to root out new federal dictatorial polices designed to control private property in local communities. These policies, believed Voice of Adams, were the key elements in the vast growth of government intrusion into the lives of the people.

Richards knew that being informed of government actions was vital in a free society in order to keep the people in control. Government, especially one bent on growing and enforcing centralized power, liked to operate in the dark. He was determined that the Voice of Adams would always be the lighthouse and the gatekeeper to sound the alarm and take action at the first sign of any such covert activity. In the current atmosphere of the nation, this was no idle threat or paranoia. People were losing their lives and their liberty.

And now Terri was one of those victims. Had someone in authority decided to push back against Voice of Adams? Had someone decided to fire a warning shot against them? Was this the reason why Terri was targeted? Voice of Adams obviously had enemies. But who, specifically? Mack Richards was determined to find out.

Oh yes, Mack Richards had one other very compelling reason for finding Terri's killer. He had been deeply in love with her for some time. And she with him. They were both very passionate people and that was a combustible combination between two such highly charged individuals.

The love affair had burst into flames during one of their long speaking tours shared so often in lonely hotel rooms. They had kept it a secret from most, mainly because they valued this one small bit of privacy in their very public lives. God, he loved her passion, her zest for life, the way her eyes flashed when challenged, her absolute lack of hesitation as she rushed into the battle. They had been made for each other. They had planned a future together. They talked of starting a family. They even dreamed of that ivy covered house in the suburbs and vacation trips where they could learn to relax, away from political combat. Now it would never be anything but an impossible dream.

As he hung up the phone, Mack Richards vowed that he would find her killer and he knew what he would do when it happened. There would be no hesitation on his part.

• • • •

Brad Jackson rushed to the platform of the light rail passenger train that took him directly to his apartment on the 15th floor of the Chavez Building. He was late tonight, and if he didn't get his writing done before the nightly energy curfew, the power in the building would be turned down and the computer would be off.

He hated that part of modern society. It was only in the past few years that he had to cope with this power shortage, but it was still hard to accept. Brad understood that is was necessary to conserve energy. Everyone understood that it was important for the environment. The government had issued report after report on the coming environmental disaster if everyone didn't cooperate.  But Brad lamented that there must be some other way than to force the whole city into darkness every night. The streetlights went out, along with the traffic lights, so driving wasn't possible. All homes, office buildings, restaurants, and stores had to turn their lights off from 11:00 p.m. to 6:00 a.m. every day of the workweek. Even the elevators didn't run during energy curfew hours. On weekends power was supplied until 1:00 a.m. so the clubs and bars could stay open.

At least apartment buildings and other housing, and certain businesses like restaurants, were given enough power to keep the refrigerators and heat going – to a bare minimum anyway. Those special meters that the electric company installed in the building last year controlled the thermostats so no one could cheat and use power they

weren't entitled to. "We are all in this together," the government constantly reminded them. "After all, cheaters hurt
everyone!"

This resulted in some very cold nights during the winter
months and some very hot nights in the summer. Everyone
just had to learn to cope. Remember, as a recent newspaper
editorial had pointed out, a hundred years ago people didn't
have indoor heat and air conditioning. That was a new phe-
nomenon of a modern society, said the latest government
report. It added that we were now suffering the consequences of a dying planet as a result of our over-indulgence.

So it was important that Brad get home and to his computer with enough time before the power curfew kicked in.
Tonight he had to write his regular book review blog called
*The Page Turner*. Every week he reviewed a new book and
posted it on his webpage.

His page was actually becoming quite popular and
boasted a loyal readership across the nation. Just a week
ago his readership had hit the one million mark. A positive
review in *The Page Turner* had become highly prized by
authors, literary agents, and publishing companies, which
now regularly sent their latest books for him to read and
pronounce judgment on.

Brad's reviews had even been quoted in the *New York
Times*. They were often used in ads on *Buy Right, Inc.*, the
world's biggest online retailer of books. In fact, these days,
to get a "Best Seller" label on *Buy Right* was almost as pres-
tigious as one from the *New York Times*. And it was much
easier to acquire. A favorable review in Brad's blog could
help an author to quickly achieve such status.

Rushing in the door of the apartment, he was met by the

aroma of Tofurkey roasting in the oven that his wife, Kate, was preparing for dinner. Actual meat consumption was no longer permitted. Government reports had confirmed that raising animals like chicken, turkey, and cattle actually added to the pollution of water, and the flatulence from the animals contributed to air pollution, causing severe climate change. Plus, it was determine to be downright cruel to raise such animals just for the purpose of eating them. It was considered to be nothing short of cannibalism. The Animal Rights movement had worked hard to educate the public to stop eating animals, for the good of everyone and for the Earth.

But Kate had become quite creative in her cooking skills, using substitutes like tofu and soy.

Kate was his second wife. His first wife, Carol, had died after being bitten by a mosquito and contracting malaria. It was a growing problem now that the use of most pesticides had been banned. Bedding nets were now familiar accessories, even in the apartments in the highrises of the megacities. Windows were supposed to be kept closed, but that was hard during the summer now that most central air conditioning was no longer allowed.

Kate was a bit younger than Brad. They had met in a grief counseling group both had joined to deal with the deaths of their spouses. Kate's husband of only a year was been in the military and had been killed while jumping out of an airplane during a training exercise. They had been high school sweethearts and she had never dated anyone else. She was simply lost without him.

After one of the sessions, they started to talk. A couple of weeks later Brad asked Kate to join him for coffee. She accepted. He learned that she was an only child, that her father had died at a young age, and her mother had a hard time making ends meet while Kate was growing up. Her mother had long been in failing health and died just after Kate graduated from high school. Losing her husband just seemed to be the final straw in a very difficult life. She simply couldn't see a way forward; the grief consumed her.

At first Brad viewed Kate as a challenge. He began to think of ways to put a smile on her face. It was such a pretty face but always seemed to wear a frown. As he focused on helping her over the pain, his own grief began to give way. In a short time they were dating. They both learned to love again and to depend on each other. Kate smiled. Brad felt joy. And just two years ago they married.

Now she was carrying their first child. It hadn't been easy to get the permit for her pregnancy since Brad already had a daughter, Tracie, 15, from his previous marriage. Parent licenses were tightly controlled under the government's drive to reduce overpopulation. But the principle at the school where Brad taught had intervened on his behalf with a local official who granted the license – after more than a few dollars passed his palm.

It happened more often than people realized. There was always a way around a law. In fact, an underground economy for many of the banned government items was starting to flourish. Brad tried to remain inside the law, but sometimes it was necessary to do what needed to be done to live in the city's ever-growing population.

The crowded living conditions seemed to be getting worse on a daily basis as the government forced more people out of the rural areas of the country into the cities.

He had read a report just a few days ago that it was more efficient and less taxing on the environment to have everyone living together rather than sprawled out over huge tracts of land. So, slowly, suburban housing, and even whole towns in rural areas were disappearing as the inhabitants made a slow but steady march into the cities.

As he walked into the kitchen of their small apartment, Kate's eyes lit up. "I'm so glad you're home. You're so late, I was beginning to worry. I've been keeping dinner warm for you. But I'm excited. I was actually able to get some fresh fruit at the co-op today. You know it's so very hard to come by out of season," she went on as she proudly held up some plump red strawberries. "I baked a short cake to have with them! I know it's your favorite."

Brad hugged her and gave her a gentle kiss and a bit of a rub on her bulging belly. Only a couple more months until the baby is due. Kate was so excited.

"Listen, Sweetie, I am really running late and I've got to get this week's blog written and posted before the power curfew. Would you mind terribly if I ate in the study while I write?"

A quick look of disappointment crossed her face, but she understood how important this was to him. "Go on in and get started, I'll bring you a plate." Again he kissed her. How he loved this wonderful, sweet, gentle woman. What a joy she had brought to him after the grief that came from losing Carol.

As Brad entered his study, he felt that familiar warmth rush over him. This was his favorite room in the apartment. His huge library covered the walls clear to the ceiling on his hand-built bookshelves. He cherished every volume, especially the collection of antique books. Books were his passion. He savored the words and wisdom of the creative minds of those who wrote them. He loved just holding the books, feeling the pages in his hands, the smell of the leather on some of the better-bound copies.

He had read every one of them over the years. He valued even the ones he didn't agree with because they were expressions of ideas. A mind that only allowed one narrow path of ideas to enter was a dead mind, he believed. To Brad, the very idea of book burning, as had been done in so many totalitarian regimes around the world, was simply a barbaric act.

Sometimes he liked to randomly select a book and start to read it, no matter how many times he had read it before. He always learned something new. Of course, many of them he actually knew almost line for line.

After turning on the computer, Brad performed an act that had become a bit of a ritual. He carefully opened a drawer in his desk and pulled out one of a hidden stash of incandescent bulbs he had collected and horded after they had been banned. Slowly, almost lovingly, he screwed it into his reading lamp.

The government said incandescent bulbs used too much energy and so they had become a victim of the strict environmental regulations. But he hated the new mandatory environmentally correct bulbs; the light was too harsh and gave him a headache as he read his books. It was a small infringement – another small act of defiance on his part. Perhaps he was becoming a radical! Well, it was just a minor thing, and besides, it was important that he was comfortable while he wrote.

Just as he was ready to start writing, Tracie opened the

door carrying his dinner plate. As she put it on the desk in front of him, she looked around at the books lining the walls. "Dad," she exclaimed with a tone of disgust, "why do you keep all of these books? This apartment is small enough, and they take up so much room," she said, waving her hand around at all the shelves. "Don't you know you could put this whole library in one e-book and save all this space?" Old people, she thought. They are so primitive.

As usual, when she expressed her teenage exasperations Brad just smiled and starting eating his dinner. She said nothing more and stomped good-naturedly out the door.

Now to work. Tonight's review was right up his alley! A book on history, specifically the Civil War. This one was a well-researched comparison of the leadership skills used by Abraham Lincoln and Jefferson Davis, the two Presidents who had led the separate sides of the divided nation during the war.

Brad began to write. "The fascination with the American Civil War has generated many books but there's always room for one more, especially if it is as well written and researched as *Vision of Leadership: Abraham Lincoln vs Jefferson Davis – Their War and Peace*. It is a hefty volume of 630 pages that looks at both men side by side, removing the myths and presenting them as complex men with very different, yet some strikingly similar, personal and professional lives."

Brad was in his element. Total concentration on the words he was producing. His dinner now forgotten and growing cold.

# Chapter 3

The jumbo television screen in Times Square carried news 24 hours a day. News, weather, sports – all updated regularly throughout the day.

Today's news hit John Lloyd like a blow to the head.

The excited TV reporter was talking to the in-studio news anchor about an event that had apparently just taken place. Almost breathlessly he told the anchor, "Today, new publishing giant LEAP has announced a massive gift to America's school children. According to LEAP Chairman, Edgar Thornton, every student in the nation will be given one of the new LEAP e-books as part of their educational tools."

"Why is that so important?" the anchor asked.

"Well, Paula, because this will save schools billions of dollars since they will no longer have to purchase printed

schoolbooks. And think of all the trees this is going to save."
"Further, the e-books can be used to actually personalize
lessons for each student's needs. Schools can now update the
e-books instantly with any new discoveries, historic events,
or even to accommodate new teaching methods that may
be developed. All without having to buy new, expensive,
printed textbooks."

"And the new e-textbooks bring an incredible new
technology to teaching, plus they will also allow schools
to monitor student study habits – even to tell if they are
actually reading the assignments. This is a huge new use of
emerging technology to vastly improve teaching techniques
while, as I said, saving billions of dollars for schools across
the nation."

Back in the studio, the news anchor continued the
report, saying, "Here is video from the news conference that
was just completed moments ago." There was the image of
Edgar Thornton, head of LEAP, telling reporters that, "this
gift to schools across the nation will bring a revolution to
the American educational system and our local schools.
This," he said with a purposeful smile on his face, "is a great
LEAP forward!"

As the video ended, the reporter and the anchor, Paula,
engaged in their usual happy talk. The now excited Paula,
finally catching on to the massive significance of the LEAP
gift said, "It is so refreshing to see big corporations sharing
their wealth with the nation and literally saving billions of
dollars for the school systems."

"Giving back, that's what it's all about!" said the reporter.

"It's the kind of thing that makes us all proud to be part of such a unique nation," said Paula. "Now, for more good news, here's the weather."

A stunned John Lloyd quickened his stride toward his now urgent meeting with Peter Arter.

• • • •

In the early morning as Brad stepped off the train onto the platform just outside the school grounds, there it was again – more graffiti. The bright red paint in big, bold letters – it appeared to him to be almost a desperate cry for attention:

**"Check Your Premise… all is not as it seems!"**

Once again, he thought, what does that mean? Who are these people? He seemed to ask himself these questions with every new blast of graffiti. What do they want? While the previous messages had seemed smug or matter of fact, this one had a feeling of growing desperation -- as if someone was urgently trying to warn us – but about what?

Check your premise? What premise? What is not as is seems? WHO ARE YOU? Brad wanted to scream as he hurried out of the station to the safety of his classroom.

• • • •

Scott Jacobs was devastated to learn of Teri Miller's murder. "It's my fault," he thought as he remembered their conversation. "I told her where to look for that report. But I warned her to be careful. This is my fault," he said to himself over and over again.

He had been in her audience in Salt Lake that night. After her talk, Jacobs felt a need to approach her. He was now a member of the local school board, but he had retired from the U.S. Marshal's Service after 30 years of putting away some very bad people. Jacobs was actually glad to leave the service because it seemed the new leadership was moving the agency in a different direction, one he wasn't comfortable with.

To the Service, fighting crime didn't appear to be as important anymore. He felt the real focus now was on pleasing the higher-ups for promotions rather than arresting bad guys. In fact, he had seen cases involving powerful, but guilty, people simply ignored. These influential friends of those in power had the idea that rules were for everyone else, but not for them. He knew of a couple of cases in which they had literally gotten away with murder.

When he confronted his superiors about some of these cases he was told to just let it go. He did let it go as he decided to walk right out of the Marshal's Service forever. But he kept in touch with some of his old colleagues, so he would hear about new developments around the nation and in Washington. DC. He knew things that most didn't.

He had listened to Terri's speech on the dangers facing America. She had told the audience about the growing expansion of government at every level. She explained that the innocent, positive sounding policies operating under the name of "Planet Protection" which they also called the "Spirit of Rio" (where the plans were presented to the world) were much more ominous than people were led to believe.

Because, as Terri warned the gathering, it wasn't really about Planet Protection; it was about changing our way of life and even our form of government, and not for the good. The economy and people's personal lives were being drastically affected. "And," she warned, "the more powerful government gets, the more corruption there is. Our government is no longer answerable to the people – to you. A government that is free to do as it pleases is nothing short of tyrannical," she said with conviction.

She told the audience how shocked she had been when one of her college professors has stood in front of his class and revealed the real goals behind the massive changes that were being enforced across the nation. What was it he said? "Global Planet Protection requires the deliberate quest of poverty, reduced resource consumption, and set levels of mortality control." In his passion, he had nearly shouted at the class, "You've got to learn to live on less!"

"What?" she thought back then. "These people posing as heroes to save the planet really mean to destroy our economy, make us live in poverty, and control who lives and who dies? That," she told her gathering, "was what started her down the road of no return." She had to find out who these people were. Who was in control? How could they be stopped before they destroyed America?

As she looked across the nation, she was shocked to find how far they had already come in changing everyone's way of life. "Manipulation of the system of government," she warned, "was leading away from local representation to more of a backroom system of appointed bureaucrats. That was the real danger," she said. "That's how they are making changes without a vote of the people."

"Locally elected representatives, whom the people had put into office, were slowly losing their power to those all-powerful, non-elected shadows in the backrooms." She implored the audience to get involved with their local government and restore the power of duly elected local representatives of the people and get rid of the shadows. "They have no business being there."

"Bring them out of the dark of the backrooms, unseen and unknown to most of the community. If the people don't take such action, then everyone's lives will change, as we all fall under the influence of the true agenda of a few powerful radicals that made it their mission to alter the very structure of the United States of America. That," she warned, "would lead to nothing less than a new Dark Ages of misery and sacrifice affecting every American."

Jacobs was familiar with Terri's very impassioned writings and many television appearances, though they had not yet met in person. He had done some work with Mack Richards and was familiar with the Voice of Adams. Terri was so close to the truth, Jacobs thought, but she was missing vital information. She needed details that would help her fill in the blanks and make her presentation much more powerful with indisputable facts.

Jacobs knew some of this information himself and he wanted to get it out to the public, but he didn't have the means or the credibility to expose it. Terri and the Voice of Adams did. Jacobs believed that, if Terri were armed with such facts, she and the Voice of Adams would be much more valuable to him and his own goals. But he also knew that she needed to discover those facts herself. Without the full knowledge of the agenda they were fighting, he believed that Terri and her group were just stirring up the wind.

That's why he decided to approach her. His face grave,

he told her that she was missing a huge part of the puzzle. That he was aware of a much bigger agenda involving power and people that she could only imagine. She needed the details if she ever hoped to put together a successful opposition.

"What do I need to know? What am I missing?"

All he said was, "Find a copy of a report codenamed ERASE. I'm told that it contains everything you need to know." His last words as he turned to leave were, "Be careful."

Did she find it? If so, would that explain what happened to her? She would not be the first to meet such a fate because of that report. According to confidential reports he had seen, there was a trail of dead bodies in its wake.

Jacobs, himself, had been aware of the existence of the report and the secrets it contained – ever since that strange man in the dark alley had told him to find it. "All the details, all the names, all the answers are in that report," he had said. Then he seemed to just disappear into the dark night. Since then Jacobs knew of at least three other deaths connected to that report, apparently including its two authors. They had tried to send a warning to Congress and had paid with their lives.

He only wished now that he had stated his warning to Terri more forcefully. He should have known that nothing would stop her if she were on the trail. Now she too, was one of its victims.

# Chapter 4

Peter Arter reached out his hand in greeting as John Lloyd entered his office on the thirtieth floor of the Rachael Carson Building. It was a bit of a shock to have someone of Lloyd's stature and reputation seeking him out for assistance. Lloyd wasn't known for his warmth or friendship.

Arter was the head of an innovative marketing firm, *Buy Right*. Over the last ten years his company had developed cutting edge concepts for promoting and delivering goods to consumers across the country. He had, in fact, changed the very structure of retail and wholesale buying. *Buy Right* was a shopping mall via the Internet and the mail. The fact that he didn't need to maintain expensive stores to sell his customers' products allowed him to provide everything for much less.

Instead, *Buy Right* had four massive warehouses, one in each section of the nation, from which all the products were shipped. Each was equipped with the latest robotic technology by which items could be located, selected, packed, and made ready for the parcel shippers without a human touching them. It was a technological marvel that Arter had created from scratch and was the reason why he could operate so cheaply and why *Buy Right* was now a huge industry unto itself.

Of course it hadn't always been that way. Arter had lived a life of challenges, just like most successful entrepreneurs. In high school Arter was considered by some to be a bit of a character. He was always industrious, creating new ways to make money. While he was still in school, one of his most successful ventures was a little procurement business. He could find anything anyone wanted. Students and teachers began to seek him out when they were looking for a special gift, or a hard to find auto part. Somehow he always came up with it. Customers were happy to pay him a finder's fee.

Some of his classmates could still remember how excited young Peter became when news about the creation of the personal computer was announced. "Do you know what this means?" He asked anyone who would listen. "The way we operate businesses will change. This is a new age!"

Most of all Peter Arter wanted to be Bill Gates and Steve Jobs. He spent hours trying to design his own personal computer with a feature that was eerily close to the modern computer mouse. It never worked for him.

Then he tried writing his own software for business purposes. He called it an office system. Of course, in those days software wasn't downloaded into the computer. It was placed on a big floppy disc and inserted into the slot on the computer. It wasn't a bad system that he had created, it was just a bit ahead of its time. There was also the problem of capital; he couldn't find anyone to invest in his "ahead of its time" product. Eventually, Gates and Jobs did it better.

So Peter was a bit discouraged that he wasn't able to join the ranks of the big boys, but he kept trying. In the end, he returned to the idea of his most successful venture – procuring. He decided to take that talent of finding hard to locate items and mix it with his deep interest in computers. He started small, but eventually the concept for *Buy Right* was born.

Now, some fifteen years later, *Buy Right* sold nearly everything, from clothing, to cars, to books, all delivered right to the purchaser's door. In fact, with all of the retail bookstores closing across the country, he was now one of the biggest marketers of published books. He even had his own bestseller list, coveted by authors as much as the New York Times bestseller list. And it was much easier to become a *Buy Right* bestseller because of the way he broke down the book categories into more specialized groups. Cookbooks had their own category, as did political books, and mystery novels. They didn't have to compete with other categories to make the bestseller list. And any author who gained the title, "best-selling author" retained it forever. It was a huge boost in getting the next book published for a nice advance.

Naturally, Arter was now interested in pursuing the new, technology-driven concept of e-books and was looking for an effective e-book product that could compete with the new e-book giant, LEAP. That's exactly what John Lloyd was looking for, too. Still, to have a corporate giant like John Lloyd reaching out for Peter Arter's help was a thrill and perhaps vindication that he had finally made it to the ranks of the big boys.

Lloyd didn't waste any time getting to the point of the meeting. "Mr. Arter, my industry is in grave danger of being destroyed by this LEAP bunch. They are moving to control the whole industry, but the danger is much more than just new technology to replace an old one.

"There is a powerful force growing here that, if allowed, could control the published word through every source. And that is a very dangerous thing. It would control ideas, innovation, even the whole concept of free speech, all under the command of one entity. If LEAP is not somehow checked, it could impact all of human progress."

"Do you grasp that fact?" he asked Arter. "Do you understand how it can be done?"

Arter squirmed in his seat. He understood competition. He thrived on it. It gave him a rush to find a new way to get the better of a competitor, to spoil their day, so to speak.
"Tell me what you're thinking," said Arter. In fact, Arter had already experienced some of LEAP's heavy-handed practices and wanted to see what Lloyd knew.

Lloyd settled in with his subject. "LEAP is systematically buying up major retail outlets of published books and closing them. There is only one major outlet left, Banner's Books. They have outlets in most airports and at some major shopping malls across the country. If they go under then, aside from your operation, I'll have literally no national outlet for my books."

"Well," asked Arter, "why do you need printed books? Why not just go to e-books?"

"That's the problem, LEAP has nearly cornered the

market on e-books. And they have refused to publish my catalog of titles. I'm losing authors. If it continues, LEAP will decide what gets published. Did you hear their announcement this morning? They just destroyed the entire educational book publishing industry," Lloyd said with a bit of a quaver in his voice.

Arter began to understand Lloyd's point. He was having trouble of his own with LEAP. For years, the e-book industry had been divided into a variety of platforms. Some offered the basic book. Some offered sound. Some offered the ability for the reader to interact with the story. The latest breakthrough was about to offer virtual reality inside the e-book stories.  Until now, no one had been able to bring all of these platforms together into a single product. But LEAP was moving rapidly to achieve it. They were somehow grabbing up all of the patents and that was making competition very difficult.

Arter had been working on a solution for the past year, but LEAP seemed to be ahead of him at every turn, blocking him. His group of researchers, inventors, and engineers kept coming up with ideas, but before they could file a patent, LEAP beat them to the punch. Then, almost by accident, he discovered the reason why. He found that his chief designer had been quietly working for LEAP all along, passing his secrets on to them. Arter fired him and now the spy was openly working for LEAP, but at least he wasn't giving Arter's designs to them now.

"It seems to me that the three major factors in successfully competing are the quality, cost, and availability of the product. I've built my business by making sure we offered all three. At the same time, you, Mr. Lloyd, have dominated the book publishing business by offering the best authors and the largest catalog of books. It seems to me that by combining our efforts we could give LEAP a major run for the money."

There was a moment of silence as each man thought about that statement. They were both successful business-men. Giants in their fields. There was no reason to panic. Combining their forces would indeed create a powerful force. Lloyd smiled because he knew his instincts had been right. He had chosen the right man to link up with.

"OK," Lloyd finally said, "let's take these things one at a time. You have a built-in distribution system that is the best in the world. So we have that advantage. LEAP won't have access to it. Since they refuse to offer my catalog of pub-lished books, we can promote it as a classic book collection unavailable anywhere else. And we can introduce the whole catalog as available for the first time on e-books," he said, as he started to get excited about the prospects. "But, how do we offer a product for less than LEAP?"

Now Arter was getting excited. "We keep it simple. A standard e-book without all the fancy bells and whistles. Cheaper and with wider distribution. Let's create a product that appeals to a bit older audience that usually struggles with all this new technology. Let LEAP have the younger audience at this point. The older consumers have the cash."

"That's certainly a good start," said Lloyd. "But there is still another detail that is hurting me in a big way. LEAP is stealing my authors by offering more money and distribu-tion. I have to deal with that. And I think I know exactly how to hit LEAP right where it is most vulnerable. And, at the same time, we can counter their intimidation tactics."

"How?" asked Arter, suddenly sitting up to attention.

"Two approaches, both aimed at LEAP's credibility and business practices. First, some of the e-books they publish aren't accurate."

"What do you mean?"

"Well, I've looked through some of their books as they have published them, classics like the works of Edgar Allen Poe, *Last of the Mohicans,* even some of the works of Shakespeare. Those stories have been changed. They aren't accurate. Words have been changed, even whole story lines are sometimes left out, changing the entire meaning of the book in some cases. This even includes a few books by Hemingway and F. Scott Fitzgerald. And you won't find any of the books written by authors like Michael Crichton, one of the biggest selling authors of all time. And none of the Founding Fathers writings are even available to download."

A puzzled frown came over Arter's face.

Now a cynical smile crossed Lloyd's face as he continued, "I have friends in the media that I can call on to publish some stories about LEAP's e-books and cast some doubt about them. Can't hurt!"

"OK, that's an interesting idea. But how does that affect their ability to twist arms and force things their way?"

"Well," said Lloyd, "that's my second approach, how about contacting some friends in Congress to start an investigation into possible RICO racketeering violations by LEAP? They are interfering with free trade and putting out a deceptive product."

In a sudden charge of excitement, Peter Arter stood up.

"I know just the man," He almost shouted. "Albert Morris. He is Chairman of the House Committee on Intellectual Property. It's a subcommittee of the Judiciary Committee and Albert is a personal friend of mine!"

"Excellent, so we have a plan. We create a superior product with a strong marketing plan, and we give the competition a taste of their own medicine by playing some hardball ourselves! Let's show these upstarts how it's done."

With that, the two men, smiling, shook hands with firm grips and mutual respect. "I'll be in touch," Lloyd said as he headed for the door.

"I'll call you as soon as I talk to Congressman Morris," said Arter. With that, Lloyd was out the door, confident that this meeting was the turning point that he had needed to save his publishing empire.

As he watched the door close, Peter Arter turned and picked up his phone to place a call to Capitol Hill.

• • • •

It was billed as a gathering of religious leaders from across the nation and they were meeting at one of the largest and most historic cathedrals located in the heart of New York City, St. Paul, The Redeemer.

The chief sponsor for this major religious conference was the Religious Partnership for Justice. The purpose of the meeting, said the invitation, was to find common ground among the many religions in the nation.

The Partnership was pushing for a formal agreement

among four of the nation's largest religious organizations
as an effective means for "addressing poverty and Protecting God's greatest creation, the Earth." The Partnership
believed the issues were interrelated and that the religious
community would be a powerful force in creating solutions
to both issues. "Our nation will self-destruct unless we can
bring human civilization under control," said the invitation.
"Moreover, religion is beginning to recede as a major force
for good in our society. Working together, we can change
that!"

The Partnership had been traveling the country, meeting
with local pastors, priests, and rabbis to teach them new
ideas to bring the many religions together into a powerful
force for peace and justice. Now they had established the
Temple of Justice, officially housed in the great cathedral of
St. Paul's.

This upcoming meeting in New York City had taken
two years to pull together, but the effort had finally been
successful as representatives from the four major religions
of the nation were to be there: The American Catholic Congress; the leading protestant Christian organization called
the National Congress of Churches; The U.S. Jewish Association; and the Evangelical Stewardship Network.

In addition, there were to be representatives from a
variety of private groups, Non-governmental organizations
or NGOs, as they were called. Many had recently appeared
on the national scene, promoting religious involvement in
stewardship of the Earth. There would also be representatives of major corporations and even one from the Federal
government's most popular science agency, NASA.

The specific purpose of this meeting, said the invitation, was to bring together the religious leaders along with business and science to find common ground to bring peace and understanding to an ever more violent nation, whose human inhabitants were not only killing themselves in a wholesale manner, but were also destroying their only means of human existence, the Earth. "Our nation will self-destruct and our world will be destroyed unless we can bring human civilization under control," said the invitation.

Pastor Dave Delray was a bit surprised to get an invitation to such a gathering. He was, certainly, a national religious figure. His 6'5" bulky frame, always dressed in a white suit with a brightly colored tie and pocket scarf to match, was a familiar image to many Americans as he appeared each Sunday on his popular television show to preach the gospel. He was best known for his fiery sermons. And lately they had more fire than usual. Not from the fire and brimstone of the Bible, but more out of his own fear. He could feel it. He could see it. The Church was dying.

Religion was being shoved aside in almost every part of society. Christianity's mighty message was being eliminated from government buildings, school classrooms, and even the annual Christmas celebration. "The whole purpose of celebrating Christmas was to celebrate the birth of Christ, for crying out loud," he declared in utter frustration.

Pastor Dave believed that the whole of Western Culture was built on the idea that God created Heaven and Earth and gave man dominion over the Earth. From the Bible's teachings, he knew that Christianity was the root of the ideals of free enterprise, individual liberty, and private property. All of which led to prosperity and freedom. The nation's Founders knew that and they built the nation to prosper under God's Commandments.

"Destroy those concepts," he preached from his television pulpit, "and you not only destroy the Christian religion, but you will destroy the very nation that was built on those concepts. Freedom itself would cease to exist. Read your Bible," he said over and over during his sermons. "Read your Bible! Take heed," he implored his flock. "Renew your Christian teachings and stand and fight for the very soul of God's Church."

As he again read over the invitation, Pastor Dave thought back over his life and his involvement in the Church. He had felt the calling from a very young age. Literally all his life, he thought. Even in elementary and junior high school he had preached the Gospel to anyone who would listen. He felt the spirit. The excitement. The passion of the Word. It meant everything to him.

He remembered one night long ago while he was in the 8th grade. He was with his friend, Allen, who wasn't much of a believer. Dave tried to find a way to open Allen's heart to the Lord. Dave had really felt the presence of the Holy Spirit that night and the preaching just poured out of him.

But Allen seemed a bit bored, not really listening. In total frustration, Dave looked down at Allen's dog which was looking up at him and seemed to be listening intently. "See," said Dave, "Patches understands!" That got both Allen and Dave laughing. But Allen never came to the Lord.

That didn't stop Dave. In fact, it made him more determined. "You can't win them all," he said many times. "But you never stop trying. You preach the word and see where it sticks. Save one soul at a time and in the end you will make a difference." That was his motto and he lived by it with passion and determination.

So now he was excited to receive the invitation. His hard work, his devotion, his effectiveness was, it seemed, finally being recognized by the major religious leaders in the nation.

This meeting just might be the start to bring the nation back to God and His teachings. "We all preach the Gospel of God's love," he thought as he read the invitation. "We all teach our parishioners to love their neighbors, to be honest, to not lie, steal, or kill. And we certainly believe God gave us dominion over His Earth to care for His creations. Why, then was there so much hatred among us? Why couldn't the leaders of these similar, yet different religions, unite for those common goals?"

So, with great hope for the experience, Pastor Dave made plans to head to New York to see what could be done. This just might be an historic opportunity – and he was excited to be part of it.

# Chapter 5

A s he hung up the phone, Peter Arter was not happy with the result of his conversation with Congressman Morris.

The Congressman was sympathetic. He said he understood the concern, he even admitted that he had been watching the growth of LEAP and he too was concerned. "Some of those involved with LEAP are nasty people," he told Arter.

"I would love to do an investigation of them, but to do it, I need to have some hard facts in my hand. I can't just start an investigation into a private business without a reason.  Good Lord, man, did you just see what they announced today? Free e-books for every schoolchild in the nation. The media is playing them up as heroes. How would it look if I suddenly attacked them?"

Arter tried to counter that they were changing some of

the books and their meaning, as Lloyd had told him. Morris shot back in an irritated voice, "That's not a criminal offense worthy of a congressional investigation. It certainly isn't a RICO offense."

Again, Arter tried to bring up the points he and Lloyd had discussed. "What about the fact that they are buying up book stores and closing them?"

"Not illegal. Look Peter, I understand your concerns. I believe there is something about LEAP that isn't right. I personally do not like Edgar Thornton. Something is really off about that guy. I've run into him at meetings and parties and he makes the hair on the back of my neck stand up. But I need something, anything concrete to start an investigation. Get me that and I'll run with it. But it must be something very powerful and the information has to be genuine to make the charges stick, or I'll be a laughing stock. I don't want to be the next Joe McCarthy."

Peter's last shot was, "But McCarthy was later proven to be right."

"Not in his life time, Peter. Get me the goods and I'll see what I can do," Morris said as he hung up the phone.

• • • •

Phyllis Jasper was the Secretary of the Interior. She had only been in her job for a few months, appointed by President Gravell, mainly, she thought, because of her devotion to him and his courageous stand to protect the Earth.

In college she had become a dedicated activist for the cause after hearing then-Senator Gravell deliver a speech on campus. His passion was the key to her transformation. It brought tears to her eyes to think of all the damage that humans were doing to their own planet, as he had described it. Gravell was a master at painting vivid word pictures. There were the polluted rivers and the clearcut forests where the animals could no longer call home. And then there were the vivid images on television of those helpless drowning polar bears, unable to even find land as the ice cap melted out from under them.

It was all too much for a young college girl who had spent so much of her life pampered and unaware in an upperclass household in Cape Cod. Her life had been a series of the proper parties with the proper people in the proper outfits. By the time she was in college she felt a mind-numbing boredom for the people, the events, and their attitudes of privilege. She felt the need to rebel and to actually stand for something.

To make a difference, she organized clean-up parties along local riverbanks, getting her hands and clothes shockingly dirty in public. She protested the local industries (many owned by friends of her parents) to demand they stop fouling the air. She took part in rallies, and eventually even lobbied Congress, including many Members who were in her parents' social circle. Single-minded, outspoken, and rebellious were not the traits of a "proper girl." Her parents feared for her future. Where did such a radical come from and what would become of her?

In truth, she wasn't really such a radical. Phyllis really wasn't against industry, as so many of her fellow activists were. She did have a clear understanding that the country needed what they produced and people needed the jobs to survive. But she just wanted them to be responsible. She didn't consider herself to be a radial tree-hugger. A little common sense was all she asked.

The question of her future was unexpectedly answered one day when a lobbying trip to the nation's capital led her to Senator Eric Gravell's Capitol Hill office. To her amazement she was invited into his private office to meet him. That conversation landed her a dream job on the Senator's staff. For the next ten years she served as a dedicated legislative aide, specializing in environmental issues.

So, when he ran for President six years ago, Phyllis naturally assumed she would be asked to join the campaign. But the call didn't come. And after he won the election no job offers came to her either, not until the Secretary of the Interior, John Ramos, had recently resigned unexpectedly. No one seemed to know why. It appeared to be a very sudden decision. Some speculated that he had major differences with the President over policy matters.

So it was a complete shock when a delighted Phyllis got the call came from the White House saying President Gravell was considering nominating her to fill the position. Of course she was curious as to why Ramos had resigned, and even more so as to why Gravell suddenly picked her. But she accepted the nomination because it meant she was back in the fold, back in the excitement of the nation's power center, back where she could again make a difference.

She was quickly confirmed.

All that had happened just a few months ago. Now, as she sat behind her desk in the impressive office of the Secretary of the Interior, she was troubled. She had assumed there would be regular access to her old boss, now the President. She thought they would have discussions over policy in which she would have input and influence.

But that was not turning out to be the reality she was experiencing. Instead, she had to deal with Steven Daniels. He was middle-aged and not too concerned about his appearance as was apparent from his wild, graying hair and long, scraggly beard that usually contained a few crumbs from his latest meal. His clothes could use a pressing. His tie was always pulled down and usually had a spot of food on it. His shoes were scruffy Earth Shoes worn with white socks. Usually, at least one of the socks was falling down exposing too much of an alabaster ankle. She could accept all of that, but his attitude was one of arrogance that simply did not tolerate questions of his convictions - or edicts.

Daniels was one of the radical Greens she had been forced to deal with during her activist years and when she served in the Senator's office. They were zealots who refused to listen to any opinion other than their own. She had often wondered if they truly were concerned about actually protecting the environment or if there was another agenda hidden behind their cause.

For example, Daniels hated the timber industry. He called them monsters that were destroying the forests by clear-cutting all of the trees and turning the forests into a sea of mud. Phyllis tried to explain that it simply wasn't true, that the timber companies weren't suicidal. She described how they would put themselves out of business if they destroyed the forests. She even showed him pictures of private timberland that was cut and replanted decade after decade. She said they could find common ground to both allow the timber industry to thrive while protecting the environment. Daniels refused to discuss it, saying again that they simply ravaged the forest then moved on to the next area to destroy it. End of story.

Another day they were discussing the Forest Service's new policy of allowing dead trees to simply lie on the floor of the forests, in fact refusing to clear them out. She had tried to explain that the current policy of leaving dead trees on the forest floor created huge amounts of kindling that caused fires to burn hotter, destroying more forestland and even the animals that lived there. It was better forest management, she argued, to clean the forest floor and prevent the hot burns. "Absolutely not," he declared. "It's natural to leave the dead trees there. That's how it was done before humans fouled the landscape."

Who did he think he was, thought Phyllis? The fact was, he was sent over by the White House and he was the one with the direct contact to the President. There he sat in an office just next to hers. She was frequently irritated as he walked into her office, unannounced, whenever he pleased. He was demanding, and tolerated nothing she had to say. He basically dictated what department policy would be, who would be chosen for leadership positions, and what she would say to the media. If she objected he responded in a smug tone, "The White House will decide."

What was going on here, Phyllis wanted to know? She was the one who held the position of Secretary. Daniels didn't even have a title, as far as she knew. White House flunky, she thought with a disgusted shrug.

However, she thought back to what she had learned only last week, and the situation became even more troubling. Just after the most recent meeting of the President's Cabinet, she had tried to discuss the situation with President Gravell.

He just smiled, touched her shoulder and told her Daniels was there to help her learn the ropes and get up to speed on his policies. That was it. No more discussion.

Her frustration must have shown, because after that brief exchange with the President, Felix Johnston, Secretary of Veterans Affairs, asked her to join him for lunch at his office. Over their meal he asked how she was getting along and she unloaded her frustrations about Steven Daniels and her inability to talk directly to the President.

Secretary Johnston had smiled with a little sadness in his eyes as he explained that her situation was not unique in the Gravell Cabinet. He told her that there was a Steven Daniels in nearly every agency of the government, including his. They called the shots on orders directly from the White House. "We call them the Dirty Dozen," he said, with little humor in his voice.

"But why?" asked Phyllis. "I am the one who was chosen to lead my agency. I was confirmed by the full Senate. If they wanted Daniels to run it, why didn't the President simply nominate him?"

"Because," said Johnston as he leaned forward and spoke in a hushed tone, "these guys could never be confirmed. They have very dark backgrounds. They are hired guns for some very powerful forces. I'm not sure even President Gravell has a choice about them. But they need to choose people like you and me, people with clean, open records, to be the figureheads to sit in front of TV cameras and Congressional hearings."

Phyllis was shocked. What was going on inside this government? Who was in charge? Who were these "Dirty Dozen," as Secretary Johnston called them? What could she do? Was I chosen for this position because I was inexperienced and they believed they could control me? She decided to take her time, not rock any boats, and see what happened. Perhaps the President had told her the truth, and Daniels really was here to help her. Time would help her sort it all out, she thought. She would eventually learn the truth, she felt certain. Then she would know how to act on it.

The next morning however, a new development was presented that had her mind racing for an answer. The only thing she could think to do was to call the President and confront him.

Daniels had just charged into her office and plopped a series of Executive Orders onto her desk. "Here are the new orders from the White House for you to put into action immediately. This is vital to the President and must be done now," he said, looking at her with that smug look of contempt that always seemed to cover his face.

"What are these?" asked Phyllis.

"They are new land policy orders that are to be carried out by this department. You and I are going to meet with the Bureau of Land Management, the Forests Service, and the Park Service this afternoon to go over these and put together a plan of action to carry them out. You'd better start reading them so you're up to speed."

As she read the documents her shock grew. Who came up with this, she asked herself as she tried to make sense of it all. Who and what was behind these Executive Orders? If these five Executive Orders were put in place as government policy and fully enforced, dams and entire water preservation systems would be torn down, irrigation systems for farmers would be shut off, ranchers would lose their water rights for their cattle, the timber industry would have absolutely no ability to harvest a single tree, and millions of productive acres necessary to grow food for the entire nation would be locked away in a new land designation process that claimed these private lands to be public wilderness areas. It was a land grab of gigantic proportions, and it would completely destroy the economies of several Western states. Whole towns would die as a result of these policies.

Incredibly, as she read, Phyllis realized that the Executive Orders were much more dangerous than that to the future of the nation. The fact was, she was very familiar with this plan because it had been thoroughly defeated in Congress when it had first been proposed eight years ago. On her strong advice, Senator Gravell had voted against it.

Now, here he was taking the same plan and using Executive Orders to completely bypass any vote by Congress. If Congress simply rolled over and allowed him to get away with it then the government of the United States would be forever changed. Why? Because, by allowing the President to simply issue an order to enforce policy that Congress had expressly turned down meant Congress itself would be rendered irrelevant in stopping an out-of-control Executive Branch. It was nothing short of the creation of a dictatorship.

She quickly picked up the phone and tried to call the President, but was told he wasn't available. She had two options, she thought. One was to openly fight the policies from the inside, and would surely lose her job. She was new. She would be painted as inexperienced and perhaps disgraced.  Or she could resign in protest, causing the President embarrassment and making powerful enemies she wasn't prepared to fight.

Was this why former Secretary Ramos resigned? Then Phyllis Jasper decided on a third option -- to stay for a while, agree to play ball, and see where it all would lead. Now that she was more aware of the game that was being played inside the White House, with more information to guide her, she could more effectively fight it by staying. First and foremost she needed to know who was running things behind the scenes. Was someone or some thing actually holding President Gravell's administration hostage?

# Chapter 6

"Beware! Acceptance of autocracy is blind obedience... Question authority and hurry!"

It was the same fluorescent red paint as all the other graffiti that had been splashed across railroad bridges and on the sides of buildings throughout the Washington, D.C. metropolitan area and its suburbs. Another of the mysterious, cryptic messages that appeared overnight without detection – a bit like the reports of the discovery of crop circles in open fields. No one had any idea of who was responsible or how they were able to spread the messages over such a wide area.

But here was another one. Only this time it was found emblazoned on the front steps of the Supreme Court building. As the city awoke on that cool, crisp fall morning to the reports of the new message, the entire official population of government in the nation's capital seemed to experience a group shudder, and some even felt an unexplained feeling of dread.

. . . .

Outside the great Cathedral of St. Paul the Redeemer, in the late autumn chill, there was a distinct sense of a circus atmosphere as a large crowd took over the grounds of the church in the heart of downtown New York City. Throughout the yard the pounding rhythm of drum circles and clanging finger symbols could be heard. Ancient medieval chants were sung to Sun Gods and the Earth Mother. Incense burned, and the unmistakable smell of smoke from other "natural" substances floated above the crowd. People in the gathering seemed to lose their inhibitions and were now dancing to the drumbeats.

On the steps leading up to the great cathedral, an odd but fascinating ceremony was taking place. A Catholic priest, Father Bonner Martin, was performing the ceremony of the Feast of St. Francis. To receive a blessing, elephants and camels were paraded up the steps to a makeshift altar.

A procession of women clad in long white robes and bare feet, danced to the rhythm of the drumbeats as they carried baskets of compost and worms to the waiting priest. They were followed by a near endless line of parishioners leading their dogs, cats, and other pets, all to receive the priest's blessing.

As the ceremony concluded Father Martin raised his arms above his head and gave an invocation, declaring, "We are now entering a new, exciting era for the world. An era of peace. The era of Earth consciousness. We declare that all of the Creator's creatures are made in His image, not just humans. The world is being called to a new post-denominational system that understands that the Earth is a living being to be worshiped and cared for by us all. Go now and take this new Gospel to your families, to your neighbors and to your churches. Tell them this is a new dawn in America." The crowd cheered and dispersed as the animals were led away.

Pastor Dave, dressed in his trademark white suit and brightly colored tie, was a bit uneasy with all of this strange activity and hurriedly pushed past the throng and climbed the steps to the meeting inside as he remained optimistic that something good, something positive would come out of this day. Once inside, he saw an impressive sight as more than 200 delegates gathered in the hall of the great cathedral.

The elaborate costumes of the religious leaders stood out in a impressive array: the scarlet robes of the Catholic Cardinals mixed with the black robes of the protestant ministers combined with the broad brimmed black hats of the Jewish Rabbis. Next there were the conservative suits of the business leaders and government representatives mixed in with the casual t-shirts and jeans of the representatives of the non-governmental organizations, or civil society as everyone called them. It was quite a diversified crowd.

He was shocked, however to see a very familiar face sitting among the dignitaries at the head table. It was none other than Eric Gravell, President of the United States. "I was right about one thing," thought Pastor Dave, "this meeting is a very big deal."

The Master of Ceremonies was Shawn Trent, chairman of the host committee, the Religious Partnership for Justice.

He had long, thick, black hair, a full beard and mustache. As he began to speak, his voice was deep and resonant. It commanded attention. He spoke in slow, deliberate sentences.

"I welcome you all here today to this historic gathering. This event brings together a formal understanding of four of the nation's largest and most influential religious sects – Catholic and Jewish, along with the more liberal wing of the Protestant religion, represented by the National Congress of Churches, and the more conservative wing, represented by the Evangelical Stewardship Network." There was a brief applause for each entity as the Chairman extended a hand to each sect and their leaders bowed in recognition.

"Along with these powerful religious groups, the RPFJ partnership joins with the strong influence of private business, private civic organizations representing civil society, and the representatives of government to assure our success," he said with obvious pride.

Pastor Dave watched in anticipation. "Could the nation finally be coming together to follow the great power of the Scriptures? he wondered. "All of us working together to assure that the nation follows God's word in religious teachings in setting the direction for each individual citizen for the business community and in the decisions of government?"

As he sat there among some of the most powerful religious leaders in the nation, Pastor Dave thought about how this great nation was founded. It was a meeting much like this one of just such leaders made up of individual citizens, captains of business, religious leaders, and those experienced in government. Each had understood that guidance by God Almighty was the key to their success. This was the powerful message the nation was founded on and why it was so successful from the beginning.

But now, he knew, those teachings had begun to diminish as the nation grew and matured. Consequently, also lost were those bedrocks of morality and prosperity. This was why the nation was running into trouble. Perhaps now the drift could be corrected. Those were his thoughts and his hopes as the Chairman continued to outline the purpose of the Partnership and this gathering.

"Our nation has been adrift for too long," continued Trent. "We are witnessing the wholesale destruction of the greatest creation, as described in the Holy Scriptures - the Earth, our sole means of survival. The Earth, which mankind was entrusted to protect. The Earth, the living, breathing pristine world God provided, now deteriorating under the pall of man's industrial activity. Change has to come, now. Before it's to late to turn back," he nearly shouted, arousing the crowd.

"To that end," said the Chairman, "the objectives of the RPFJ are nothing less than the transformation of our social order into a global society organized around the notion that the Earth itself is the giver of life. And so we must all come to recognize the undeniable fact that it must be protected at all costs, no matter the effect on industry, family, or individual desire," his deep voice was quivering now. "All of human kind, must take responsibility and all must be guided to take action to restore our Earth Mother!"

As the Chairman paused for a moment, suddenly, Pastor Dave began to feel a growing nervousness. He looked around the room to see if any of the other religious leaders shared his concern. He saw nothing but smiles on their faces, looks of excitement and anticipation. Their facial expressions were almost fanatical, a look of hunger in their expressions.

The Chairman continued, "How people of faith engage the environmental crisis will have much to do with the future well-being of the planet and, in all likelihood, with the future of religious life as well."

"Caring for Creation, that is the banner under which our Partnership will march. Through legislation and government policy, we will create a new Noah's Ark to restore the Earth to the pristine jewel we were provided. Two-by-two we will restore whole species. We will re-grow the majestic trees that once dominated out landscape. We will again see the buffalo roam on the open prairies. And we will rejoice as the sky is again filled with flocks of the great birds. The plenty of the Earth will be reborn, the promise of the Garden of Eden rediscovered. The Book of Genesis will again be our guide for man's future." Now the Chairman was warming to his subject as his voice reached a peak.

"Even before this great meeting today, the Partnership has been having a huge affect on our religious foundations. The training for this new religious order has already begun. RPFJ has now provided education and action kits to over 67,000 religious congregations. These will ultimately reach over 100 million churchgoers.

"We are helping to write sermons dedicated to Creation Care so that the good news comes straight from your pulpits. And we are teaching pastors and priests and rabbis to always think in terms of the Earth as they spread their message of love and understanding," he said proudly.

"You will deliver your flocks to our new order of society – a society that will cleanse itself of the destruction of the planet by reducing mass production and learning to live on less of the Earth's resources. Your children will be encouraged to hug a tree in their Sunday school classes to learn firsthand the glory of the creation of the Earth Mother. New scriptures will be added to the Holy Word to guide us in this mission. Our mission is to create a society in which man is just one of the creatures and is kept fully under control for one central purpose – to Care for Creation."

Pastor Dave felt a kind of primal scream building in his brain. "NOOOO," he thought. "This is not the teaching of God. HE is the giver of life – not the earth. You're talking about earth worship, paganism, not the teachings of God. "This is a political agenda! What's going on here?" he wanted to shout out. But he remained quiet. Perhaps he was misinterpreting. He waited to see.

The Chairman was speaking again. "And now, I want to introduce to you a very special guest today, a man who has worked tirelessly behind the scenes to bring this partnership together and who is determined to see our national government implement every part of our Partnership goals. Please welcome the President of the United States, Eric Gravell."

As President Gravell walked to the podium the crowd again erupted into applause. He was in his second term and was viewed as a great unifier. With massive problems facing the nation -- the economy in disarray, cities in turmoil, and the national education system in freefall -- he had skillfully used these national problems to unite a vast array of movements across the nation. With a compliant news media, none dared oppose him for fear of looking out of step, perhaps appearing to be an insensitive, selfish enemy of the Earth.

As a result, groups that had at one time opposed each other now seemed to resist conflict to allow Gravell's programs to take hold. Leadership in Congress, though from different parties, was falling in line to help implement the President's wide-ranging policies, giving the central government a free hand to take whatever actions were necessary to bring what news editorials were calling a "rebirth of society." The unity of such a diverse coalition was a great surprise to political experts.

Gravell's administration was determined to cut the nation's use of energy by a full 50 percent. That was the reasons behind the policy of shutting down power in homes and office buildings at night. He had led the fight to enforce what he called more "livable" cities, reducing the maddening congestion of privately owned cars to be replaced with public transportation and riding of bikes. In fact, he had said walking was the most desirable and healthy policy he could imagine. So his government was now working fast to transform American cities to make them walkable.

Perhaps his most far reaching permutation of society was the effort to stop the wasteful shipping of products and foods by introducing incentives to assure each community could support itself through small community-owned farms. This, he proudly declared, would save millions of gallons of fuel and make each city self-sufficient. "Isn't that the American way?" he asked.

He had taken on industries and forced them to reform or cease to produce. He had begun programs in schools to teach children about the sins of reproduction as over-population destroyed the Earth. He had led the way to reduce the great divide between rich and poor, declaring, "We must all learn to live on less." Now he was pushing to unite the nation's religions into a mighty force for saving Mother Earth.

The delegates fell to a hush as President Gravell began to speak. "My fellow delegates, this meeting is of great historic importance to all of mankind. For centuries religions have been at war over ideology. Today we announce a coming together over common ideals for all of the Earth's inhabitants. No longer will the religions of the world waste their good works fighting each other. We seek one voice and one unified religion to actually enact the promise of the Gospel rather than fight over tiny differences to decide who's right. The Creator, as the Scriptures tell us, gave us this Earth to oversee. And that's what we intend to do," Gravell said, his voice rising. The gathering took to their feet with thunderous applause.

He continued, "We believe a consensus now exists, at the highest level of leadership across a significant spectrum of religious traditions, that the cause of environmental integrity and justice must occupy a position of utmost priority for people of faith. That's why we unite today, to help assure we can bring that about. And we will do it with the great powers of religion in partnership with government, business, and civil society to enact the changes necessary to reorganize human society in unquestioned unity with the Earth Mother who provides for us all." Again there was enthusiastic applause and cheers from the nation's leading religious leaders.

As the delegates wildly applauded their approval, the scream was growing louder in Pastor Dave's head. He began to feel trapped. "What do I do?" he kept thinking to himself. "How can I let this go by? This is a threat to the very heart of the teachings of the Gospel," went the scream.

"My administration is preparing new regulations, to be implemented through several agencies, to remove from use and harm many of our precious lands and natural resources," he declared. "The only hope for the Earth is to withdraw huge areas of the nation from human use in order to create natural sanctuaries from the depredations of modern industry and technology.

"We will identify large areas of rural space in every state in the nation to be restored to a semblance of natural conditions for many species. This land will be restored back to the way it was before Christopher Columbus made his first fateful footstep on this continent and started the white man's degradation of it. Finally, we will reintroduce grizzly bears, the gray wolf, and long-destroyed native prairie grasses, to once again reign over the wild lands.

"Above all, we will declare these areas off-limits to modern human civilization. We will finally give the rest of the creatures of the Earth an equal and fair chance to survive and compete with encroaching humans. These areas will serve as a new Noah's Ark to preserve the Creator's plan," said Gravell, now warming up to his subject.

"We must stop digging under the skin of Mother Earth. Human society must stop selfishly stealing her abundance of natural resources. She is sick and crying out for our help. She is beginning to crumple under the weight of mankind. The human species is not the only inhabitant of the Earth, but its numbers are exploding and must be brought under control. We must protect our Earth Mother at all costs." Gravell paused to let that sink in.

And then he continued toward his dramatic conclusion, "Fellow delegates, we are here today to acknowledge these facts and to plan for what will be a wrenching transformation of human society. It will be hard to give up our luxuries and creature comforts we have grown so used to. But these are destroying the very Earth we depend on and so it is necessary! We must take every action to lead man away from the horrors of the industrial revolution and the misguided religious premise that has doomed mankind. We must prepare for sacrifice. I say it again and again, we must learn to live on less," demanded Gravell, his eyes wide open and darting in nervous energy.

"Above all, the idea that man has dominion over the Earth must be removed from our thinking. That falsehood has nearly destroyed our planet. Today the great religions must all come together under one idea – one fact – one banner. And all of our actions from this day forward must reflect that truth." As he prepared to deliver his most powerful line, determined to bring all of these religious leaders together with him, Gravell paused, and his voice became low, almost a whisper, as he began again. "We must all acknowledge that God is not separate from the Earth."

With that President Gravell stood back, thanked the delegates for their support and left the stage to more thunderous applause.

For several moments, Pastor Dave sat there in utter shock. And then, as the applause began to die down he heard the shout – "NO!" – over and over again in his mind. Suddenly, without realizing he was doing it, he stood up. His great height and bulky framework in his pure white suit stood out in the crowd. Then he heard himself actually shout, "NO!" This time it wasn't just in his mind. It was real. And everyone in the great hall heard it. All eyes were suddenly on Pastor Dave Delray.

He looked back at them for a moment, not sure what to do. Then, seemingly unable to stop himself, he walked to a place just in front of the stage and turned to the gathered delegates. No one made a move to stop him so he began to speak to the gathering. His words came from somewhere deep inside his soul.

"Did you not hear these words just spoken to you? Business is to be destroyed! You, who are representing business, are you here to aid in your own demise?" he asked looking straight at the business representatives.

"Government representatives, I ask you, where in our great government structure is the authority to simply lock away millions of acres of our nation on a whim or the say-so of one man? What you have heard is the foundation for tyranny. Do you not question that?

"And you, who are here today representing science, do you have any proof that this is even necessary for so-called earth protection, that there is any such danger as the idea that man is destroying this earth?

There was silence in the room. Apparently no one here thought to question what he or she was hearing.

But, as the anger and frustration grew inside him, Pastor Dave kept his most direct comments for the religious delegates that he knew best. "You, representing the great religions, everything said here today is not the Gospel of Jesus Christ or even of the Holy Scriptures of the Old Testament.

In fact, it is the exact opposite!

"Do you not know your Scripture well enough to understand that the story of Noah's Ark was not about restoring
a pristine environment. Except for Noah and the animals
gathered to him, nothing was to be spared. God set out to
destroy all the beasts and the birds and the creeping creatures along with all of mankind in the face of man's wickedness." Pastor Dave's voice was shaking now.

He then turned to the delegates from the American
Catholic Congress and said, "Your religion has always stood
for the procreation of man. Yet today you applaud a man
who tells you that the new purpose of your religion is to
eliminate as many of God's children as possible?"

Then he spoke again to all of the delegates. "Have you
all lost your way so badly that you want to help replace the
teachings of God with a pagan political agenda? You are
accomplishing nothing here today but to turn religion into a
tool for government. A very bad, dangerous government."

And then Pastor Dave felt a great strength come over
him as he raised his hand in the air as if giving a benedic-
tion, and shouted, "The earth is not our Mother, God is our
Father. He is separate from all of us. The earth is simply
His creation. But if you turn your back on Him and begin
to worship the creation rather than the Creator, then the
consequences will be much greater than anything you can
imagine. I cannot and I will not let stand this blasphemy we
have heard today!"

With that, Pastor Dave began to walk in determined
steps toward the exit of the great hall. As he approached the

door, one of the delegates from the Evangelical Network shouted to him, "What do you think you can do to stop us?"

Pastor Dave stopped, turned on his heels to face the delegate and said, "The nation and your congregations must know the truth of what you are doing here today. I will tell them." Then, as the room grew silent again, Pastor Dave looked at each and every delegate as he said in a low, powerful voice, "And I will bring down the wrath of God on your heads!" With that he hurried out of the hall into the light of day.

# Chapter 7

It was a rare warm and sunny day for that late in the year, so Brad decided to forgo the school cafeteria and instead take his lunch to the park across the street from the school. It felt good to soak up some sun after all the bleak, rainy days of the past few weeks. Fall had come on in a hurry after a less than hot summer. But today was a welcome break. Indian summer some called it.

He found a park bench under a large old maple tree. He liked looking up into its huge branches. He remembered how, as a kid, he loved to climb trees and just sit in the strong, comfortable crook they made to cradle his body. And from there he could see all over the neighborhood. Sometimes he would see friends walking down the street towards him, unaware he was in the tree. As they passed underneath, he would take out the squirt gun he always carried and start spraying them. He laughed at the memory of what was a great, carefree childhood. Kids didn't seem to have as much fun these days.

As luck would have it, Kate had prepared a lunch for him today, and he began to spread it out on the bench beside him. He placed a large paper napkin on the bench and then took out one of the two tofu-based, fake ham, and cheese sandwiches.

He really wished he could have some of the white bread he ate as a child, but that now was next to impossible to acquire. Apparently the government had determined it was bad for your health and banned it along with all soda products. How he missed a cold refreshing Coke. So, today he had to be satisfied with just water. But the newly approved non-plastic containers kept leaking. Only about half of the water was still in it. What did they make these containers out of anyway, he wondered with more than a little irritation. The good news was she had included some more of those delicious strawberries.

Now, as he began to eat, he was looking forward to enjoying a quiet period of solitude away from the hustle of the school. He had brought with him a new collection to his library. It was called *Saving Monticello*, and it told the incredible tale of the family that had bought Thomas Jefferson's famous house after it had nearly crumbled into great disrepair. They saved it for posterity. It was the perfect book for a history teacher to read while he enjoyed the sun. Digging into such an inspirational story gave Brad the energy he needed to face yet another class this afternoon.

Before starting his reading, Brad sat back a moment and looked around the park. Hanging around a bench just a few down from his was an odd gathering. At the center of a small group of students was an older man. Brad had seen him before in this park. By his clothes he appeared to be perhaps homeless. The man's clothes were worn, yet he had a dignity about him. He wasn't dirty and his clothes weren't wrinkled. It was apparent that he tried to keep them clean and repaired. The clothes look like they had once been of good quality. Perhaps that's why they seemed to hold up now.

On the few previous occasions Brad had seen him in the park he found it interesting that the man was occasionally talking to some of the students. Usually it was just one or two, but today there were eight and they were gathered around him locked in an intense discussion. It was rare for Brad to see the students so involved. They always seemed so distant and uninterested in anything adults had to say. Brad couldn't hear what the discussion was about, but it seemed this downtrodden-looking man had their attention. Then suddenly, as if they were dismissed, the kids scattered back into the school, with smiles and looks of excitement on their faces.

As they left, the man looked over towards Brad and their eyes locked. The man gave Brad a gentle nod. He seemed like a nice man. In fact he gave an air of intelligence and education. Brad wondered what had happened to bring him to what appeared to be a state of homelessness. But times were tough everywhere. Seeing people down on their luck wasn't all that rare.

So, today, as Brad prepared to eat his little picnic lunch, he made a snap decision to postpone his reading and instead called over to the man, "Hi. Would you like to come over and join me? I've got plenty."

The man's head turned as he heard the invitation. He seemed genuinely grateful as he rose from his bench and headed toward the inviting teacher.

"I'm Brad Jackson," he said casually with a smile and an offered hand.

The man took his hand in a firm grip and just said, "I'm Harold."

Brad made room for Harold on the bench and handed him his extra sandwich. Harold accepted it and pulled back the special environmentally-safe, biodegradable wrapping and took a hungry bite. They were engaged in a bit of small talk about the weather when Brad finally asked him, "Do you live around here?"

Harold hesitated, then responded, "Yes, sort of. I don't really have a home, the park is sort of my home for right now," he finally volunteered.

"You live in the park?" Brad almost choked on a strawberry.

"Sometimes, I move around a lot."

"But winter's coming. How will you survive that? Aren't there shelters to go to?"

"The shelters are dangerous. I've been to a few and if it gets really cold I'll probably go into one. But you've got to be careful."

Brad looked closely at Harold, trying to figure him out. There was a manner about him, Brad thought. This man seemed kind, likable, basically non-threatening, but at the same time he seemed a bit closed, hesitant to open up. As Brad had noted earlier, his clothes seemed of good quality. He was wearing a suit jacket. His shirt, while a bit frayed, was clean and somewhat pressed. His hair looked like he cut it himself, but it was neatly combed and seemed clean. Interestingly, under his nails Brad noticed what looked like paint.

"Are you able to work," Brad asked, looking at the paint spots.

"Oh, some. There's not a lot available right now. I take some odd jobs, yard work and handyman type things. I get by."

"I noticed you talking to some of the kids. They seemed to be really interested in your conversation. What was that all about?"

"Oh, I just enjoy talking to them. We talk a little bit of philosophy. Ideas about life, you know," Harold responded with a bit of a dismissive manner.

"Funny, I have rarely seen them talking to an adult, let alone discussing philosophy!"

"Sometimes they just need someone to listen to them. That's what I try to do. After all, I'm not too busy these days. Listening is a pleasure. What do you do?"

"I'm a history teacher at the high school."

Harold suddenly looked interested. "You teach history? Whose history?" he asked, now intense on the subject. The tired look that had been in his eyes was replaced with a fire Brad hadn't seen before.

Brad hesitated for a second before answering. Finally he said "American history."

"Whose version?" he asked, almost a challenge.

"I teach American history. The American Revolution, the building of the nation, our great system of the Republic and how it benefited us to grow prosperous and successful," said Brad, almost in a defensive tone.

Harold thought for a minute. "They let you say such things in the classroom?"

"Well of course. It's history. I love to challenge the minds of my students and get them involved in the great events that made our nation. I love to play devil's advocate and make them think how they would have approached some of the dangers our Founders faced," said Brad with a bit of pride.

Harold listened and thought about that answer. Finally he said, "I'm glad you're still doing such teaching. The children desperately need it. But you won't be allowed to much longer. Teaching basic academics to enable children to think and grow on their own is a danger to the Order. Changes are coming. You won't be permitted to teach such things much longer. Social engineering is the new purpose of education today."

Brad suddenly felt that familiar ache in the back of his head. He knew the school system was changing and there were lots of new rules about how and what to teach. But he had been able to resist it. After all, how could you not teach actual history? It was fact. It had already happened. This little man in the worn out clothes was challenging his passion for teaching. Brad was good at his job and he knew it. No one was going to come into his classroom and dictate how or what he taught. "My classroom," Brad said to Harold with pride, "is a bastion of academic enrichment!"

Harold looked at him as his eyes reflected sadness again. "Mr. Jackson, I can see that you're a good man. I have no doubt that you are an excellent teacher and your students are lucky to have you. But, if you haven't yet seen the changes coming to your classroom, then you are naïve and you'll soon learn that your academic skills are about to become irrelevant." With that, Harold stood, extended his hand and thanked Brad for the lunch and his generosity. "Please be careful," Harold said as he walked away.

Brad sat on his bench for a few moments thinking about the exchange. Social engineering? That's a little far fetched, he thought. Things are bad, but not that bad. Brad gathered his things and headed back to class.

• • • •

Dave Perry, the Speaker of the Ohio House of Representatives was a strong leader and ran a tight ship. One of the biggest problems he constantly had to deal with was keeping his members in the House informed and up to speed with all of the legislation they needed to consider. In addition, there were so many hearings with all the accompanying testimony, plus there was the background information in the modern political world that had to be studied. It seemed no one could keep it all straight. Government was just getting too big to handle.

Now he had just received a solution. That's why he was excitedly walking through the State Capital rotunda and up the marble steps on his way to a meeting with some of his legislative leadership team. He carried information that would revolutionize how future political leadership would be performed.

On the second floor were the many committee meeting rooms. In Room 201, sitting around the large conference table, Speaker Perry found his closest allies in his leadership. "Gentlemen and lady," he said, as he entered the room, "I asked you to join me here because I've got something really great to tell you."

There was immediate attention from the three men and one woman gathered around the table, his majority Whip, Pete Brown; his assistant Whip, Jerry Johnson; Jim Davidson from the Governor's office; and his special assistant, Ellie Bryant. "What's up, Dave?" asked Brown.

"I just got off the phone with Edgar Thornton, the head of LEAP," said Perry. "He made me an incredible offer that I believe will revolutionize how we do business here in the Capital." Perry looked around the room, enjoying the expectant looks on everyone's face. He wanted to savor the moment. No one said anything. Finally he began his presentation.

"What is the biggest problem we have here in trying to keep our people under control?" Without waiting for anyone to answer, he hurried on. "Making sure that we can control the information we share with them so that everyone is on the same page to act as we need them to do." There were nods round the table. He continued, "What if we could assure that all of the members received exactly the same information at exactly the same time as we issued it? With all the committee hearings that every member must attend, how do we make certain all of them get the specific import-

ant testimony that we want them to hear for each bill? And
how do we keep a running vote tally for the bills important
to us so that we know if we have the necessary votes or not?
Gentlemen and lady, I have the answer to all of these questions," he said with excitement.

"LEAP has developed a new e-book with programs
specifically designed for legislative organization and control. Each member of the legislature will be provided one of
these e-books to have with them at all times. That means we
will always be in instant communications with each member. We can instantly forward copies of bills as they are introduced, along with leadership memos, and even testimony
from hearings. We can send out surveys to all members to
keep tallies on where they stand at any given moment," he
explained excitedly.

"We can know where we need to apply pressure and we
can eliminate surprises on the floor before votes. In short,
we can control everything that happens in this legislature.
In fact, members could actually cast their votes from the
e-book without actually being on the floor. This will help
free up a lot of our time. We can even vote while we're on
the campaign trail. In short, we can control the entire legislative process right here from our e-pads." With that, Perry
sat back and waited for comment.

Finally, Davidson asked, "Why did Thornton call you
about this?"

Perry said, "Remember a few weeks ago when LEAP
made that huge gift to the schools to give every student an
e-book? Well, they're going to do the same thing to every
legislature in the nation. And Ohio is going to be the first
to receive it. We are going to help them work out any bugs

in the system before they pass them on to every other state legislature!"

He continued, "Friends, our jobs just got a whole lot easier. The LEAP e-books will be here next week. Let's prepare our strategy on how to most effectively use them," Perry instructed as the meeting focused on the details of this new world of electronic politics.

• • • •

John Lloyd and Peter Arter, two of the nation's giants of commerce, stood in front of a large gathering of reporters to announce their new joint publishing effort.

Arter described his new e-book and its simple, easy to use features. Then Lloyd announced that his catalog of books would be the first featured on Arter's product. What they weren't prepared for was the almost total lack of acceptance or even interest by the press.

"How can you try to compete with LEAP with such a product?" asked the New York Times. "There's nothing special here. There are no new bells and whistles. Kids will be bored with it," went the comments and pointed questions.

Arter tried to explain that this device was aimed at the older generation that didn't want all those extras. Ho hum was the response.

After the disastrous new conference, the two slunk into Arter's office. Neither said anything for quite a while. Then Arter said, "We've failed on both fronts. Congress won't investigate them and our product designed to compete with them is a bust."

Lloyd starred down as his feet and fidgeted with tie. He wasn't used to losing. "We've got to find another way to tell people that LEAP is a fraud. I'm not done yet. Something will come to me," he said, almost believing it himself.

# Chapter 8

The lead story on the nightly news, reported by a grim-faced anchor, was the announcement from Interior Secretary Jasper that President Gravell had just issued five new Executive Orders announcing a wide range of regulations to be enforced in specific areas of certain Midwestern states. The television screen switched to Secretary Jasper detailing the new plans which she said were designed to "protect the native ecosystems and the collective needs of non-human species in areas of certain states, protecting them from being destroyed by human activity and growth."

Continued Jasper, "The President's plan is to reclaim the roads and plowed lands in these areas and unshackle rivers from the chains of the dams that have been placed there. We are going to return large amounts of suffering lands back to their original state of wilderness as they were before man was allowed to foul them."

The news anchor then called on reporter Dan March

who was at the scene of the news conference. "Dan, can you provide some details of what's contained in these Executive Orders and what they will mean to those affected?"

"Yes, Steve, and I can tell you that several critics here in Congress believe these Executive Orders are going to be very controversial. Even though the news conference just ended, I'm told there is already some heavy opposition from a few Members of Congress."

"Why is that?" asked the anchor.

"These Orders cover a huge area of the midsection of the nation where perhaps millions of acres of land will be placed under direct control of the federal government. Some sources on the Hill tell me that the result of these orders will be to actually revoke personal control of private property, perhaps even forcing some people off their land. The Orders will also place strict regulations on some industries, especially farmers."

"What are those areas?" asked the anchor.

"It covers large areas of five states, Wisconsin, Minnesota, Iowa, Illinois and Missouri; specifically areas of those states that border the Mississippi River. They are calling it the Mississippi Preservation Corridor. These Orders lay out specific details that will severely restrict farming along the banks of the Mississippi and place much of that land under the control of the Interior Department."

"What's the point of that?" asked the anchor back in the studio. "Haven't farmers been using that land for centuries to raise crops for the nation's food supply?"

"Yes, and according to the Interior Department, that's the problem. A new study, they say, shows that farming those fields along the river is reducing the amount of native plants and wildlife. They also report that dams, levies, and irrigation systems built to help the farming industry are also responsible for flooding along the river. That, says the Interior Department, is destroying natural habitat of several species and fish that historically make the river their home. So the government is moving in to put a stop to it and protect those endangered habitats. According to Interior Secretary Jasper, that could lock away from human use more than 100 million acres of farmland up and down the Mississippi River. It may even restrict some commercial boating."

"What are some of the specific details in the Executive Orders?" asked the anchor.

"Well, a couple of them deal with how the government will act to accomplish the task, such as creating a system of federal zoning so the Interior Department can control how farming is done, what methods are to be used in farming, and even in some cases, what crops can be grown. The purpose of that is to make sure every aspect of farming is tightly controlled by the government," concluded the reporter.

Back in the studio, the anchor said, "Well, not everyone in Congress is pleased about these Executive Orders. There is a minority view."

The news report then switched to a very red-faced, angry Congressman Rod Barnes from Iowa. "These Executives Orders are a government overreach of epic proportions that will destroy the economy of the Midwest and the lives of the people who live there," he fumed. "Worse, the federal government has already destroyed the beef, pork, and chicken industries by banning most meat consumption. Now, if these orders are allowed to stand, they will severely damage our ability to grow wheat, corn, and soy. What do they expect people to eat if they destroy the breadbasket of the nation? I guarantee that, as a result of this action by the President and the Department of the Interior, every single American will feel the pain as our precious farm lands will dry up and die. We cannot and we will not let this stand."

• • • •

The Ball was a hundred-year-old tradition to honor the 1775 founding of the U.S. Marine Corps. The formal event started with the reading of a special order that had been read by every Marine Commandant since 1925.

The Special Order, Number 47, signed that year by then-Commandant John Lajeune, described the founding of the Marines. It began by reviewing the incredible history of the Marines, from its first combat in the Battle of Trenton, when George Washington routed the British on Christmas Day, to the Argonne in World War I. The Order went on to praise the heroics, virtue, and honor that now signifies every Marine. And then the traditional Order concluded with a pledge that, in the name of that honor and distinction, every Marine, as long as the spirit of freedom flourished, would be a worthy successor to the long line of illustrious men who have served before them as "Soldiers of the Sea."

Special Order Number 47 was read in its entirety every year at the birthday ceremony. Then, in dramatic fashion, the cake was cut by a special two-man team made up of the oldest and the youngest marines present. They used a special ceremonial sword to make the slice. Once the cake was cut, the formal ball began. The sight of those young Leathernecks, dressed in their impeccable dress uniforms while leading their ladies to the dance floor, brought back fond memories to Mack Richards.

He, too, was once a young, dedicated, heroic grunt ready to take on any foe who threatened the security of his nation. And he remembered on several occasions, as he was assigned to duty at the Navy Yard in the nation's capital, his thrill to attend this birthday celebration and observe its age-old traditions of service and dedication. In fact, it was at one of these celebrations as he watched the pomp and tradition, that he had quietly dedicated his life to fighting evil wherever it threatened his nation's security. It was a pledge he had kept right up to this day.

At the head table was Marine Commandant, General Hugo Hollingsworth. Not only was he the head of the U.S. Marine Corps but, as of two weeks ago, he was now Chairman of the Joint Chiefs of Staff. In short, he was the chief military advisor to the President and the Secretary of Defense.

The son of a Marine, he had dedicated his life to the Corps and all it stood for. He was tall and straight and one could see that he carried himself with pride and confidence. A man who tried to do things by the book, but in a few cases he had been known to toss the book aside in preference for just plain common sense. "You can't just follow rules," he once said, "you've also got to think from time to time!"

That way of thinking on his part was fully revealed during the first Middle East war. As a young Colonel, he had been given an order to attack an enemy convoy. But the order had a special exception. When Hollingsworth read it, he actually spit out his half chewed cigar as he shouted

"WHAT?" The order, coming through the Pentagon, but heavily influenced by the State Department, stated that he had to make sure no "innocent civilians" were harmed in the attack.

Later, after his men had successfully destroyed the convoy, a congressional hearing was held to investigate whether Colonel Hollingsworth had broken the rules of engagement by killing civilian truck drivers in the attack.

Hollingsworth had sat straight in his chair in the hearing room and looked directly at each member of the committee as he answered. "Those men were driving military vehicles for the assistance of my country's enemies. It was clearly an act of war against my men who had sworn to protect this nation. My staff and I stood on that ridge, looking down at that convoy that was moving ever closer to our lines. They were bringing in high-powered weapons and reinforcements for the sole purpose of killing my men. As they drew near, one of my staff asked how we could possibly stop the convoy and still avoid killing civilians," Hollingsworth testified. He paused. And then as the committee waited for him to continue, some almost holding their breath in the hushed hearing room, he said in a dramatic tone, saying each word slowly, one at a time, "I could not answer." Again the room was silent.

Finally he continued. "I thought very carefully about my next actions and what they would mean to my men and to my country. Based on that, I made the judgment that whoever had made out that order couldn't possibly have understood what it's like to stand on the front line, facing an enemy determined to kill you. This was not a police action. I didn't have the luxury of arresting them and then determining who was guilty and who was INNOCENT. Why would I give up the advantage on the battlefield? To what end? I considered it a stupid order so I made the decision to ignore it and face the consequences later. My men destroyed the convoy. I saved lives and I accomplished my mission. And now here I am, at your mercy, and I ask each of you to decide just what you would have done in the same situation," he concluded with a flourish.

The vote that day by the Committee had been unanimous. Without question, the Committee had determined, Hugo Hollingsworth was a national hero, not a scapegoat for incompetent bureaucrats at the State Department. It had been a victory for the military and a major setback for what some called the "surrender mentality" of official Washington.

Now, years later, here was Hollingsworth, awarded the highest position of any military officer in the land. Mack Richards had known the Commandant back in those early days. In fact, he had been on that line to stop that convoy. However, it had been years since they had talked.

Eventually the music changed from the formal fox trots and cha-chas to something a little more modern and to the tastes of the young Marines who entered the dance floor to take up the beat. That's when Mack Richards headed over toward the head table.

"General Hollingsworth, it's good to see you, sir," Richards said as the head Marine turned his way.

"Captain Richards, it's been a long time." "But I see you've been keeping things stirred up. What's the name of your group of rabble-rousers? Voice of Adams? That's got a nice ring to it," joked Hollingsworth.

"We do what we can."

Then Hollingsworth turned serious as he said, "Wasn't that one of your people they found murdered?"

"Yes," said Richards quietly, "It was Terri Miller, my second in command."

"I'm so sorry to hear that. Have they caught whoever did it?"

"No, And no leads. But I'm working on it."

"Well, I wish you luck and please let me know if there is anything I can do. I've heard too many stories like that of good people just turning up dead with no clues lately," said the Marine.

"Well thanks, but I do want to ask you about something that affects you," said Richards.

"Oh?" asked Hollingsworth, tilting his head to the side that way he always did when curious.

"Yes, but maybe we should take this out in the hall, out of earshot."

"OK," said the Commandant.

When they had found a private spot on some chairs in the corner of the reception area, Richards leaned forward and said quietly, "Sir, you have always stood for the good of the nation. You have fought enemies outside and inside to assure security and to uphold our nation's principles of freedom, haven't you?"

"Yes, I've always tried to do that," said Hollingsworth cautiously.

"Then why," asked Richards, his voice getting a bit louder, "are you sitting back, actually serving in this government without taking action to reign in this President and his gang of thieves?"

Hollingsworth stood up, his tall, thin frame actually towering over Richards. "What do you mean, gang of thieves?" he asked, now openly upset.

Richards didn't give an inch. In fact, he too stood. "This President is literally changing our system of government right under our noses." He is bypassing Congress and simply issuing his own orders to make laws. It is a violation of the separation of powers. He is destroying our system of representative government. He is setting himself up as a dictator. Some of us are beginning to wonder if he will go so far as to declare martial law and even suspend the upcoming elections to further build his drive for power" concluded Richards.

"Mack, those are serious charges," said the General. "That's a charge of treason. Do you have any proof to back up your charges?"

"Well, of course I do," said Richards. "His federal agencies are dictating policy in every community in the nation. He's appointed judges who have actually overturned votes of the people. Did you see what he just did to those farmers in the Midwest? He is going to starve us all if he cuts off our food supply. He has suspended attempts in every state to clean and verify legal voting rolls. He is making secret deals with foreign countries that Congress isn't even allowed to read. And he has ignored the Constitution in every case. My sources say Gravell is moving to declare himself a dictator," Mack almost shouted, his voice cracking from his emotions.

The General made no response. There was a moment of quiet as the two stood facing each other. Then Richards just shook his head and said quietly, "Why am I alone in this? I provide proof of the evils of this government every day. I give details, provide direct quotes, and even show you the devastating results of these policies across the nation. But you don't listen. You still doubt me. General, you of all people know that I'm right."

Hollingsworth, noting his former Marine's passion, backed off a bit. "Mack, treason is a pretty serious charge. One has to be very certain of his ground before taking action to enforce it. I am certainly no friend of this President. He's a dangerous man and I'm just as concerned as you about his policies. I see those stupid orders his bunch constantly send over to us in the Pentagon that make no sense for defending a nation. I fight what I can. But the fact is, he is the Commander in Chief. We have a Congress that votes on these appropriations. They are supposed to keep him reigned in. If they fail to do that, what can we do except to try to elect the right people in the next election to stand up to him?"

"Sir, if you know he's dangerous then it's your duty to act. I am receiving information every day that we are witnessing nothing short of a complete takeover of our government by forces hiding in the background, unseen by most. I'm quite certain that you are receiving much of the same information. I firmly believe that Gravell is secretly doing their bidding. I'm doing everything I can to expose and stop it. I repeat, General, why won't you act?"

Again, Hollingsworth was silent, as if he were reviewing in his mind all that Richards had said, looking for an
answer. He knew that Mack Richards was as good a man
as any who had ever served under him. He admired his
passion and dedication to saving the freedoms his nation
represented.

Then Richards continued, saying, "Sir, I don't have the
official capacity that you hold. My God, Sir, you are the
most powerful military man in the nation. You've dedicated
your life to protecting our county and you've stood up to
bad leadership and bad decisions your entire career. It is
your sworn duty to protect the Constitution and the nation
it outlines.  That's why I have come here to ask you this
question. Will you now stand back and watch this man destroy all you have sworn to preserve or will you take action
to stop him?"

After a few moments Hollingsworth said quietly but
forcefully, "Mack, I will make this pledge to you. If you have
positive, actionable, proof of what you're charging, and not
just political opinion, then bring it to me. I promise you
that with such proof in my hands, I will move with all of the
authority and power I can muster to stop this president and
his cohorts. But it has to be undeniable proof."

As Richards left the party his mind raced. "How do I
find such proof? Where do I look? Terri was searching for it
and maybe that's what got her killed. What am I up against
here?"

• • • •

Missouri farmer Jimmy Armond had a fairly successful
business growing wheat and soy on his farm just outside St.

Louis. He and his son spent a considerable amount of time building and repairing the elaborate irrigation system they had designed to supply water directly from the Mississippi river onto his land. The crops thrived. There were over a hundred farmers like Jimmy in the area. None were really politically active. Their passion was farming and they kept the local economy thriving. Each fall the farmers filled their trucks and hauled the grain to the local mill for processing and distribution to the national system of food manufacturers, groceries, and dinner tables across the nation.

• • • •

Yesterday, Armond had discovered a team from the federal government's Army Corp of Engineers systematically destroying his irrigation system, blocking off the water flowing onto his land. They had an official notice which they dutifully handed to Jimmy saying he could no longer use the waters of the Mississippi to feed his land, by order of the U.S. Government. As Jimmy stood there staring at the document, the agents completed their task and moved on up river to the next farm.

# Chapter 9

A t last it was Christmas and Brad had a full week of vacation from school, clear through New Year's Day, to spend with his family. He was looking forward to it. Kate would be ready to give birth to their new son in about two weeks. So this quiet time together over Christmas would be their last for a while.

Tracie would be sixteen in the coming year. That meant a more active social life, school dances, boys, dating. Life in the Jackson household was about to drastically change. That was for sure.

The artificial tree was up, the presents were wrapped and Kate, in the eighth month of her pregnancy, was doing her best to prepare a special Christmas dinner. It wasn't easy considering the growing shortages of many fruits and vegetables. What she would give to have just one big, fat turkey to throw in the oven instead of pretending that the tofu molded into the shape of a turkey was a proper substitute.

Brad came into the kitchen to help with the preparations. His brother Mike was coming for dinner. That always meant a lively discussion around the table. Mike was involved in some sort of political movement. Brad wasn't sure what it was all about, but Mike was usually a bit argumentative. It wasn't always pleasant to have him around, thought Brad with a sigh.

"Where's Tracie?" he asked Kate.

"She's up in her room wrapping your present. She is very excited about that gift and can't wait to give it to you."

It was their tradition to not open presents first thing in the morning like most families did. Instead, they preferred to wait until the dinner was over and everyone had time to relax and appreciate the gifts in leisure.

As the dinner preparations continued, there was a knock on the door. Brad threw it open to see his younger brother standing there with the usual crooked grin on his face. "Hey Brother," he said with a bit of merriment and a hug. Mike wasn't married and had no other family than Brad, Kate, and Tracie. He was, Brad decided, a bit of a playboy, never settling on one girl for more than a few weeks, then on to the next. So, Christmas at Brad's was the main family get-together for the brothers.

As Mike entered the apartment he turned to Kate, gave her a hug, sidestepping her swollen belly, and handed her a bottle of wine. "I hope this goes OK with your dinner," he said.

"Thanks Michael," she said. "Merry Christmas."
"Oh," said Mike, "you still say that? I thought the proper,

accepted greeting this time of year is to be "Enjoyable Winter Solstice," or some such neutral nonsense."

Brad laughed and said, "And so it begins… time to bring politics into the mix, eh!"

Mike grinned, put up his hands in a defensive manner, and said, "Hey, I didn't do it. I'm just trying to make sure I'm a proper citizen with all the proper attitudes that we're told to observe. Sure wouldn't want to insult anyone. After all, it is the sacred Solstice season when our beloved Mother Earth freezes everything in place while she rests," he said with mock concern.

At that point Tracie bounded into the living room and threw her arms around her Uncle Mike. "Hey gorgeous," Mike said to her playfully. "Have you got any lucky guy on the string yet?"

"I've got some possibilities," Tracie smirked. "But you know that dad keeps this tight leash on me. I might as well be a nun," she said in a mock pout.

"You're too young for boys," shouted Brad, himself laughing at the banter.

"Daaad," said Tracie whining.

Just then, Kate managed to break up the debate as she called from the kitchen that dinner was ready and everyone filed in to take a seat at the table.

As they ate, the discussion progressed from updates on the family, the hospitalization of Uncle Carl, the divorce of Aunt Jeannie and Uncle Paul, and the news that cousin Lori was going to graduate from college this year. After Kate had proudly presented her prized hand-made apple pie, still warm from the oven, the meal concluded and all moved into the living room to open presents.

Brad and Kate took their usual seats on the comfy couch with Mike in the armchair, as an excited Tracie rushed to the tree and grabbed a neatly wrapped package with a big red bow handing it to Brad. "This is for you, Dad It will change your whole life!"

Brad was intrigued as he began to carefully tear at the colorful paper. Pulling it away revealed what looked to him like a small laptop computer. In the corner was a red log that said LEAP. He looked up at Tracie as she moved toward him saying, "It's an e-book, Dad. I know how much you love to read and now you can access every book in the world! This will be a huge tool to help you write your blog," she said, giggling with glee!

Brad looked at it with a bit of a frown on his face. His nose crinkled up a bit as he handled the thing gingerly, like he was afraid it would bite him. What was he to do with it, he thought.

Tracie saw his look. She knew he wasn't very much into technology. He was such a cave man, she thought. He just doesn't understand what he has in his hands! She tried to explain. "Dad, you can take every one of your books in that library of yours and download them into this one tiny box. You can take your precious books with you wherever you go. Isn't that cool? And look at all the space you can save in your office," she said, almost pleading. "Don't you under-stand?"

He tried to perk up and put on a good show for her.

She was so excited. The last thing he wanted to do was hurt her. So he smiled, and said, "Oh, I see. OK. I get it. That's very nice, honey," and he leaned over and kissed her cheek. "Tomorrow you can show me how to download a book on it, OK?"

Tracie smiled. "Absolutely. I'll help you. Wait until you see what all this thing can do. You can interact with the story, even add sound and animation to some books, just like watching a movie," she said happily.

Great, thought Brad. Just what I always wanted to do. But he said, "Wow, that's really something, honey. I can't wait to see it in action." Satisfied that her gift was as special to him as she had hoped, she proceeded to pass out the rest of the gifts to everyone.

Later, after all had been opened and the rustle of paper subsided, Brad and Mike sat back and began to chat. As they talked about various current events, Brad mentioned his strange encounter with the homeless man in the park a month or so ago.

"He said the strangest thing to me, that I wouldn't be able to teach academics in my classroom much longer." "Where would he get such an idea? That's such a strange thing to say, don't you think? I mean, educating without academics is an oxymoron. What else is school for, but to teach reading, writing, and arithmetic?"

Mike smiled. "Brother, you do live in the past, don't you?"

"What do you mean?"

"Our world is changing, Brad. The ideal of the individual as an independent force is slowly being replaced by the common good of the collective," said Mike, with a bit of a smug look on his face. "At least that's what our government tells us on a daily basis. Look around you. What individual decisions can you make in the course of a day? For example, can you choose to take a drive in the country if you like? No. Why? Because government has decided that driving a car is bad. So they have you living in this city where you can either take the train, ride your bike, or walk, but only as far as the city limits."

"But," said Brad hesitantly, "we had to get rid of the congestion. It was hurting the environment. The news is full of the disaster that is facing us unless we take drastic measures."

"Really? Have you seen the proof of those claims?"

"Well, not specifically. But it's obvious that we have been consuming too much. You can see it everywhere. The Earth can only stand so much. I know it's harder, but is seems these changes are good for us. They are protecting our planet, cutting back on consumption, and making us safer and healthier. I read a report on that just last week. But I'm not a scientist. Why would they lie?"

"Because," said Mike, "Fear is an easy way to gain power and control. Using that excuse of environmental degradation they now control your movements, your water usage, they turn off your power at night, controlling how you spend your evenings. And look at the meal we just ate for Christmas dinner. Kate did a find job of preparation with what she had to work with. But the fact is they now control what we eat. I repeat.

What individual choices do you have left to make for yourself?"

"Oh my God, Mike" shouted Brad. "Where do you get that crap? That is absolutely ridiculous. That's just a paranoid conspiracy theory!"

"Brad, I remember when you were younger, in school you were so full of spirit and ideas of rebellion and freedom. Do you remember when you used to debate with other students about the differences between the ideas of Locke and Rousseau? You marveled that they both advocated freedom, but one advocated that freedom could only be achieved through government power and the other said it would only be achieved if government was tightly controlled. Back then you sided with Locke. Check your premise, Brad," Mike said with arms raised in the air.

The words, "check your premise," made Brad pause. Where had he heard that phrase before? "Mike, "where do you get such information? Where do your ideas come from?"

"Have you ever heard of the Voice of Adams?"

"No, should I?"

"It's an organization I belong to. In fact, I'm this state's field coordinator. We are organizing in every state now. We believe that every individual is born with the right to choose their own path, to follow their dreams, to achieve what they are capable of achieving. And we believe it is government's job to protect those rights. But there are forces now working to use government to control us and we aim to stop them. They have been achieving that goal through scare tactics to gain control of every part of our society. As I said, they dictate where you can go, what you can eat, the kind of home you can live in. But, the most powerful tool they may hold over us is the ability to control knowledge. People thinking the wrong way, they say, is a threat to society. I refuse to live in such a world and I will do everything I can to stop them. That's the whole reason for the Voice of Adams and why I joined."

"I'm sorry, Mike, I don't buy it. I teach in my classroom. No one can control knowledge. It's everywhere. Books are everywhere. The teachings of ancient societies are right there for anyone to see. Controlling all of that can't be done."

"Brad, let me ask you some questions. Are they listening? Do they care about these books or are they bored? Have you noticed what is happening to the children today? Have you seen a change in them? Can they answer even the simplest questions about anything that happened before last year? Have you ever seen them pick up a book to read on their own? Look at your precious books in your expansive library, your classics. Who will ever read them? Kids can't comprehend what those books are saying. Do you know why?" Not waiting for Brad to respond, Mike hurried on, "Because they haven't learned the historical references or been made familiar with the literature. So they can't relate to the stories of the Iliad or the Odyssey, or even the reasons why this nation was founded. Knowledge, my dear brother, is disappearing before your very eyes."

• • • •

His iPhone chirped the special code ring. He knew it was a message for another job. Time to get ready.

Vito Mangreen was from pure Italian stock. His first ancestors had come from the old country in the 1890s and they landed in Cleveland, working mostly in unskilled, hard labor jobs. But his grandfather was a master bricklayer. He and his crews built half of the homes in the upscale neighborhoods surrounding the city.

Vito's father was a local Teamster president in the city. He was a tough disciplinarian and he practiced it on Vito. "Just shut up and do it," he directed young Vito whenever the boy showed any sign of reluctance to perform a task, be it homework or yard work. "No excuses," he told Vito with his teeth firmly clenched. "Get the job done and move on."

But it wasn't easy for young Vito. He didn't get along well with the other kids and had no boyhood chums. From an early age he was much bigger than other kids. He was tall, about 6'2" by the time he entered junior high school. And he was heavy. Big arms and a big stomach gave him a stocky look. Worse, he was flat-footed which caused him to walk with a strange, forced gait, with both feet pointed outward at an odd angle.

However, his most noticeable trait was his strange way of looking at people. He didn't look straight at someone. Instead, he tilted his head to the side and looked out of the corner of his eye. And as he did, his head shook a bit from side to side, like a tremor.

His strange appearance and personal tics assured that he was not appealing to women and mistrusted by men. So it was hard to find a job and nearly impossible to find love, though he desperately searched for both. Growing up, his only close relationship was with his father. His mother had died while giving birth to him and he had no siblings. He worshipped his father, the only real human contact he had. But his father was rarely home, instead staying busy with union meetings and contract negotiations. So Vito Mangreen grew up to be a loner, quiet, with a tendency to stay in the shadows, just watching everything around him.

Yet, his neighbors did notice him. And they felt a great uneasiness when they observed some of his actions. It seemed young Vito had an anger that was growing into a cruel streak. He especially seemed to enjoy taking his anger out on helpless animals. The neighbors still talked about the day a baby bird fell from its nest high up in a tree. It dropped helplessly into the middle of the street. As it lay there frantically chirping for its mother, the neighbors were horrified to see Vito on his bicycle, speeding straight at the bird, an evil grin on his face. He deliberately ran over it, laughing loudly as he sped on down the street.

In another incident, some neighbor kids saw him trap a squirrel in a hole in a large tree where it had built its nest. As he blocked the squirrel's escape, Vito nailed a screen over the hole. There the squirrel screamed until it died, unable to escape from its prison. Few in the neighborhood would talk about the way he tortured a pet duck with a pencil.

Then came that horrible, freezing cold night in December. Vito's father had been skimming money from the local Teamster pension fund. Of course it was discovered and the real union bosses, those who hid in the shadows, came to collect.

Vito was down in the basement, unobserved, as the two

thugs smashed in the front door. They grabbed his father and tied him to a kitchen chair. One held a gun on him as the other began an interrogation in a very violent way. Every time Vito's father failed to give them the answer they desired, the thug hit him in the head or on the arms with a baseball bat.

Slowly Vito opened the basement door and got on his hands and knees and crept unnoticed into the kitchen, shielded by the table. On the counter, just over his head was set of very sharp kitchen carving knives. As the man continued to beat his father, the thug with the gun stood with his back to Vito. Very quietly, Vito reached up and felt the wooden handle of one of the knives in his hand. Like lightening, Vito leapt up and stabbed the startled hoodlum in the back. As the man fell, Vito, without hesitation, charged forward and cut the other man who was swinging the bat. The bat fell to the floor while Vito stabbed him repeatedly.

Vito was surprised to feel a rush of pleasure run through his body as he saw the knife slice into the thug's flesh again and again. He saw it happen almost in slow motion, but in a matter of seconds both men lay dead on the kitchen floor.

He rushed over to tend to his father, cutting the tape that bound his hands and body to the chair. His father, bleeding heavily from his head wound, hugged Vito and held him tight.

"Thank you, my son, thank you," he said, his arms around Vito's stocky body. "You saved my life, but this isn't over. In fact, there's probably another one outside waiting in the car. We need to get out of here."

Before they could get out of the house, a gunshot rang

out and Vito's father fell dead on the floor. Vito hesitated for a moment, looking at his father. Then, with a burst of speed he rushed directly into the shooter who stood in the doorway. Vito knocked him down and was out of the house and running through yards and out of the neighborhood. No one there ever saw Vito again.

He knew the mob would put a price on his head and keep looking for him, so he made his way out of Cleveland and headed for New York City where he thought he might be able to blend in, hiding among the teeming crowds.

Within six months of Vito's arrival he learned to live on the streets of New York City. Eventually he found a room in a flophouse, where one took whatever bed could be found. There he would lie next to other dark shadows that no one noticed.

He tried to find odd jobs to provide some food and to pay for the room at night. Eventually, when no work could be found, he learned new ways to survive. Snatching a purse or mugging some Wall Street banker, were his favorites. They always seemed to have a lot of cash in their pockets. He never tried to hurt them. He just needed the money.

One night, as he was searching for such a victim while hiding in a doorway, he saw something flash past him. He looked up in time to see the dark figure grab another man. The attacker leapt on the victim, knocking him to the ground, and was preparing to take a knife to him.

In an instant, Vito reacted. He rushed over to the attacker, grabbed him by his collar and spun him around. The attacker charged Vito with his knife. He first sliced the air then, in a back-handed swing, cut Vito on the neck.

As a small river of blood began to trickle down his old, grimy shirt, a familiar rage grew in Vito and he charged, even as the attacker again sliced the knife across his arm. Vito pushed harder, knocking the man to the ground, and snatched the knife from the attacker's hand. Now, with his heavy knee on the attacker's chest, Vito took the knife and slowly sliced across his neck in a deep cut that almost severed the man's head. And Vito smiled.

As the attacker made some final gurgling sounds in his death throes, Vito stood and turned to the victim who had watched the whole thing in shock and amazement. "You saved my life," said the man. Vito said nothing. He was wondering if perhaps he should finish the job and take this guy's wallet. Judging from his clothes he was obviously well-heeled.

Before Vito could decide what action to take the man began to speak again. "You didn't seem to be afraid. You just rushed in. Are you a professional?" he asked.

"Professional what?" asked Vito, startled by the question.

"Who do you work for?" asked the man, even more persistently.

"I don't work for nobody," said Vito quietly. "I just work for me."

"Well, I've got work for someone who can handle himself as well as you. You would just have to be willing to follow my orders to the letter. Could you do that?"

Vito looked at the man out of the corner of his eye as his head shook in that annoying, trembling way. The man was short in stature, his clothes were impeccable, a sharp crease in his pants and a bowtie around his neck. He had an air of authority about him. Vito got the impression that people did what this man told them to.

The man's penetrating blue eyes studied him, waiting for an answer. Finally, Vito thought, maybe this could be interesting for a while. Why not? "Yes," he said. "Sure, what do ya want me to do?"

From that day, Vito had been employed by the man. He just called him the Boss. They didn't meet. They communicated via a sophisticated system. When the Boss had a job for him he received a message with the details. He did the job and waited for the next assignment. He was well paid. He had a decent apartment. And the part he liked most was that the Boss left it up to him how best to do the job. It was a good partnership.

Now his tickler system had just alerted him to a new assignment.

# Chapter 10

Scott Jacobs had made the trip from Utah to his old office at the U.S. Marshal's Service in Washington. He met with his former boss, Jim Gallagher. As they sat around Gallagher's desk discussing old times, Jacobs asked, "Have you guys done any more investigations into those mysterious deaths surrounding that secret report?"

"What do you mean?" asked Gallagher, acting as if he didn't know what Jacobs was talking about.

"Come on Jim, you know what I mean. Last year before I left the Service, we were discussing the strange deaths that had occurred and they all seemed to be tied to that report."

"Oh, Scott, those were just rumors. A nutty conspiracy theory. We never found any substance to it nor did we find any such report. There's no investigation," he said with a dismissive tone.

"How can you say that, Jim?" asked Jacobs, a bit of alarm in his voice. "We discussed this several times as we investigated those deaths. There were two government employees who turned up dead. It was believed that they had written a special Whistle Blower report detailing some scandal in the government. Then there was a Congressional staffer found dead in his office. It was reported that he had been looking for that report. And most recently Terri Miller of the Voice of Adams was found dead in her apartment just a few months ago. I have personal knowledge that she was looking for that report."

"Scott, there is no such investigation. We never found any substantial evidence to link those deaths with such a report. In fact, I received direct orders telling me to not pursue that investigation. There just is no evidence to follow."

"Who told you to drop that investigation?"

"I got that order directly from the Attorney General's office about six months ago. In fact, I was told that order came straight from the White House. So, it's a dead issue for us."

"Jim, why don't you make it a priority to find that report and then force it on them over at Justice and demand that the investigation be reopened?"

"It's not going to happen, Scott. I'm surely not going to risk my neck after the White House said no."

Jacobs left the meeting, shaken and deeply troubled. Who had reason to want such an investigation stopped? When he was still working for them, the Marshall's Service had been certain that there was a connection. The White House gave the order?

Troubling, very troubling, he thought.

On the plane ride back to Salt Lake, Scott Jacobs had only one thought. He must find that report, see what it revealed and give it to the Marshall's Service to demand they reopen the investigation. Terri Miller's killer needed to be brought to justice.

The theory was that the report could be found somewhere on the Internet. Perhaps ERASE was a secret code or an encryption. Finding a document deliberately hidden on the Internet could be a daunting task. You needed the exact code it was filed under. And you needed to know what dark corner it might be stored in. Things hidden on the Internet could be removed from one server and then distributed automatically across a dozen others. Along the way the encryption code could also change. That's how things could remain hidden forever.

It was early in the evening when Scott Jacobs began his search. At least he had been given some training in Internet encryption when at the Marshall's Service, so he had some idea where to start. He typed in ERASE. Nothing. He tried a variation of the word. Rejected. Added some extra numbers, dates, common codes and passwords. Dead end. Hours passed. Rejected, NOT AVAILABLE. Denied.

About 3 a.m., as he wearily typed in yet another series of codes, suddenly he heard a click, and on the screen there it was, ERASE. Seventy five pages. He began to read. There before him were all the details he had been looking for. Shocking information. Names. Dates. Details. Who. What. Where. How. Here were the details that the Marshall's Service needed to reopen the investigation. This was damning information. Heads were going to roll. Big heads! He was sure of it. And Scott Jacobs was going to make it happen.

His first thought was to simply email the file to Gallagher. But he thought better of it. With the Justice Department watching, the file could simply disappear again. He couldn't take that chance, especially after just reading the explosive details the report contained. He needed to personally place this report in Gallagher's hands. Quickly he hit print and the pages began to pour out of his printer. He carefully encrypted the file and parked it on a little known storing service for his own safekeeping. He knew he would need it later.

Jacobs called the airlines to check on flight availability and found there were no flights from Salt Lake City to Washington, D.C., until the next afternoon. He would just have to wait.

Late the next morning, he prepared to head to the airport for his trip to Washington. He climbed into his car and started it, ready to back out of the garage. Suddenly in his rear view mirror he saw a large head, slightly twitching as the eyes looked at him in a sideways glance. The lips were a mixture of a pout and a grin. Before Scott could react, he felt a strong arm around his throat, pinning him back into the seat as a razor sharp knife cleanly sliced his throat from left to right. Scott Jacobs slumped into the seat behind the wheel of his still running car.

Vito Mangreen picked up the envelope containing the printed report, shut off the engine, closed the garage door and carefully but quickly disappeared down the street.

• • • •

As the New Year began, life in the nation was changing.

The streets, once bustling with commuters and shoppers, were almost empty. There simply seemed to be no jobs available. Manufacturing was suffering from heavy new regulations that made it nearly impossible to operate, and thus production was down. Layoffs were commonplace. Wages were falling. Across the megacities in the mighty high-rise apartment buildings, where most people lived, there was a kind of malaise of hopelessness sinking in. There was no reason to leave home. Young people stood on street corners, idle, desperate for something, anything to happen. Eventually that led to trouble including drugs and fights, even shootings.

The winter was especially cold, but government now controlled the thermostats and kept the houses cold and uncomfortable. Just keeping warm became a challenge, especially for the elderly and the sick. In fact there had been several reported deaths of some elderly and sick folks who were simply unable to tolerate the cold.

Of course, no one drove a car anymore. There was only public transportation, buses and trains to get people to work. But more and more these days, there seemed to be annoying breakdowns in the once reliable subway service. Buses always seemed to be late. It was way too cold to consider a bicycle. And few could afford to go to stores anyway. Most just stayed home wrapped in blankets, hoping for an early spring.

But growing food shortages were the real threat to human survival. Lines of hungry people were becoming commonplace at groceries as people waited for fresh deliveries of much needed staples. The supplies were growing smaller and scarcer. Bare shelves were becoming the norm. When new products finally arrived, before they could even be put on the shelves the gathered crowd descended on the boxes, pushing others out of the way, and grabbed all they could afford to buy – which wasn't much.

Meanwhile, though the major news outlets didn't report on it, rumors were growing of actual food riots taking place in many cities. On New Year's Day there had been major demonstrations by farmers in Wisconsin, demanding that regulations be pushed back to allow them to prepare to plant their spring crops.

In a new twist to the food saga, the government had confiscated seed supplies the farmers needed, claiming they needed to be protected to assure there were enough seeds to supply the nation. So the seeds were locked away in storage facilities for safekeeping, as the government stated it. Yet the very people who needed them, argued the farmers, were, of course, the farmers! Finally, in an act of desperation and near panic, the farmers gathered in front of the facilities and demanded access to them. When the government still refused, the farmers spontaneously rushed the storage facility and broke into the grain bins and took the seeds. Several arrests were made and the leaders were set to stand trial. Meanwhile, the waters of the Mississippi were still denied to the farmers.

Frightened Americans began to write letters and make phone calls to Members of Congress demanding an investigation of governmental policies that were creating the food shortages. Overwhelmed Congressional staffers stopped answering the phones.

Voice of Adams' President, Mack Richards, took to the airways on major news talkshows to put his own pressure on Congress to find a solution to the growing crisis.

On the widely watched CNS news network, in exasperation, Richards looked into the camera and said directly to President Gravell, "By blocking farming along the Mississippi, you've taken out the aorta of the nation's breadbasket and you will starve us. Whole towns are dying, Mr. President. You tell us that all of this misery is necessary for your misguided attempts to protect the environment. I ask you Mr. President, when the lights go out in the greatest nation on Earth, will the American people feel enlightened and gratified for your actions, or will they just be cold, hungry, betrayed, and dying?"

In response, Interior Secretary Phyllis Jasper was forced to go on the news programs herself to call for calm. "Please understand," she pleaded to the American people, "that we are working to preserve precious resources for our future generations so that your children can rely on having an abundance of nature resources, just as all of you have had. If we continue to rape the land as in the past, the Earth will die and none of our future generations can survive."

When the news anchor remarked that people were hungry and there was great danger in the nation's cities of possible widespread starvation, Secretary Jasper could only look into the screen and say, "We are a nation of abundance. This is just a temporary situation. The winter has been more severe than was predicted. There are efforts underway by your government to establish reliable food sources. Please stay calm. This will pass."

After Jasper was out of the studio and back in her office, Steven Daniels walked in unannounced to tell her she had done an adequate job defending the government policy. Jasper looked at him with uneasiness as she said, "I warned you. These policies are destroying the economy and the ability of people to feed themselves. We have destroyed a huge section of the nation's farming industry. How can those left be expected to feed the rest of us?"

Daniels' face turned fire engine red as the anger built in him. He got very close to Jasper's face and spit out, "Small, independent farmers are a relic of the past. The future is for government run farms to produce the food we need in a proper process that will protect the environment – free from the drive for profits. We have a plan to make every city totally self sufficient with their own locally-grown food – enough to sustain every city."

As Jasper backed up toward her desk, staring at Daniels with a disgusted look on her face, he continued his tirade. "It is just plain selfishness for some people to insist on living in these far out rural areas, forcing our very limited food and energy resources to be stretched to the breaking point. In this day of seemingly perpetual crises we all need to learn to sacrifice and live on less. These people need to accept the government's leadership on this and help us help them by coming into the cities where there are adequate services to maintain a healthy lifestyle. President Gravell has a very clear vision for feeding the people and you had better get with the program!"

With that Daniels turned on his heels and strode out of her office. Jasper began to shake with a growing anger and frustration. She fought to hide it. "I can't go on like this. This is not what I signed on for. I've got to find a way to reach the President. She could not tolerate the outrage of having her office controlled by a lackey like Daniels much longer.

• • • •

"Mack, did you see the news?" Jeff Buchanan asked as they met in the hall of the Voice of Adams offices.

"No, what's up?"

"Do you remember Scott Jacobs?"

"Yes, we've met a few times. Good man. What about him?"

"He's dead," said Buchanan, almost in a whisper.

"Tell me the details, what happened?"

"He was found in his car in his garage out in Salt Lake. After I heard the news report I called one of our people out in the Salt Lake police. He told me Scott had a nasty razor cut from ear to ear. Looks like someone attacked him from behind. No other marks. A professional hit it seems."

"Didn't he work for the U.S. Marshall's Service?"

"He used to. He retired about a year ago. That's the interesting thing. Apparently Scott was just in Washington last week and met with Jim Gallagher. Jim told my friend Pete Hook that Scott was raving about a series of murders connected to some kind of government report."

"What kind of report?" asked Richards.
"I don't know, but he brought up Terri in connection to the report and said it was the cause of her death. Then Scott flew home and a couple days later he is dead.

"There's one more thing, Mack."

"What?" asked Richards with a look of dread.

"Well, you know, one of Terri's last speeches was in Salt Lake."

"Yes, so?"

"Well, Paul Diamond, the head of our Utah chapter told me that he saw Scott and Terri engaged in an intense conversation after that meeting."

Mack Richards just stood there for a few seconds, before responding. Finally he said, "Do we know anything else?"

"No, that's it. I asked Hook to let me know if there are any new developments.

"OK," said Richards. "Keep me posted."

He walked back to his office and closed the door. He just wanted to be alone. What was going on? What am I missing? Something. Something is just out of my sight.

• • • •

The lead story on the nightly news was about more than just the destruction of property. Said the reporter, "The words found in the graffiti seem to carry a dark and disturbing, some may say dangerous, message of hate and disharmony. That's why government officials announced today that they are starting an official investigation to find if it's just an individual or perhaps if a subversive group may be responsible."

The reporter then turned to videotape of an interview he had just conducted with Herb Wright, head of the Department of Special Citizen Security. "Officer Wright, what can you tell us about this graffiti and why the concern?"

"Well, for almost a year now, these messages have been showing up over night. They appear on the walls of train stations. Lately they have been found on the sides of government buildings. Just last week a message was actually scrawled on the side of the U.S. Supreme Court, of all places. And they aren't contained just here in the city. Similar messages and methods have turned up all over the Maryland/D.C., metro area. That's why we think it may be an organized effort rather than just a single individual. And that's why we've started an official investigation."

"Why the concern about these messages?" asked the reporter. "Is it because it is damaging public property?"

"Well, of course that's a concern that every citizen should be upset over because removing the markings takes taxpayer money. It really is vandalism. But we believe there is more to these messages. We believe there may be a hidden code that could be a signal, perhaps to a terrorist organization. Perhaps even an instruction to strike at pre-selected targets," reported Wright.

"What sort of messages?"

"As you know, our government has been working for years to end the strife between diverse cultures so we can harmonize our society. We face such incredible challenges to assure everyone is fed and cared for. We've made great strides in our efforts to guarantee housing and salaries are equal. We seek a nation in which no one is better or richer or more privileged than the next. That's how we can stop jealousy and envy. And only in that way can we create harmony in our cities and stop the killing and violent crime. We can do that only when everyone begins to realize that we are all in this together and that we must all push forward together," said Wright with a punch of his fist in the air.

"Yes," said the reporter. "We all certainly accept that very important premise for everyone. But how does this graffiti undermine or threaten such a concept?"

"Each of these messages has focused on promoting self-ish individualism, such as 'The Power of One,' that appeared several months ago. Now this one has popped up on more than 25 buildings here and in Washington, D.C., just last night."

As Wright talked, the camera panned onto the latest graffiti in bold letters, scrawled in the usual bright red paint, **"Beware the Trojan Horse. Submissive Cooperation over Individual Action.  Handcuffs on the Mind."**

"We see this as a direct challenge to our government's policies. If people begin to question cooperation and simply demand their own selfish wants, our entire well ordered society could come crashing down into chaos and violence. Surely you remember the old days when there were riots in the streets, deadly shootings on every newscast, until we were able to turn it all around with our national 'Hug Your Neighbor' program.  Peace has been the driving goal ever since. But this message and the other graffiti we have seen are designed to undermine that. "That's why we are deter-mined to find the  person or group that is doing this and stop it before it's too late," concluded Wright.

"Well, thank you, Officer Wright. We certainly wish you a speedy success in finding the perpetrators who are clearly

working to undermine our government's efforts to bring
peace, harmony, and good health to our society. Back to you
in the studio, John."

The news anchor thanked the reporter for the story
and turned to the camera to directly address the audience.
"Viewers, be on the lookout. If you observe it, report it. If
you witness someone placing such graffiti on public buildings call the Department of Special Citizen Security. Their
number is on our screen. 468 WATCHER"

# Chapter 11

Brad Jackson sat behind his modest desk in his study staring at the LEAP e-book Tracie had given him for Christmas. It had now been two months and he still hadn't tried to use it. She kept asking him, "Did you download a book yet?" He always had an excuse about being busy, but would soon, he promised.

And it had been a very busy time. Just a month and a half ago Kate had given birth to a beautiful baby boy they named Jeremy. He rarely cried and seemed to like to lie in his crib, cooing and smiling. He watched everything Brad did. Sometimes Brad liked to put the crib in the study with him as he worked. It gave him comfort and provided Kate with a bit of a break. Right now, Kate and Tracie were out shopping as Jeremy lay next to Brad's desk, sound asleep.

Here he was on a quiet Sunday afternoon with no more excuses. Tracie had shown him how and where to go on the Internet to find books he wanted to download. Finally, with a sigh, he picked up the e-book, switched it on, and started a search.

What book should he choose? He thought about one of his favorite book series that, as a history teacher, had give him such pleasure as it chronicled the history of the nation's founding, John Jakes' *Kent Family Chronicles*, or as many called the collection of stories, the "Bastard" series, that had been published at the time of the country's 200th anniversary. Its eight volumes would give Brad plenty of reading pleasure. Plus it would be nice to relive the joy he had experienced when he first read them.

Brad typed in the title of the series. Up came the response, NOT AVAILABLE. As a bit of disappointment crept in, he thought, well, this technology is new. Maybe they haven't downloaded everything yet. So he thought of another book. How about the collected works of Tom Clancy? Again came the response, NOT AVAILABLE. *The Time Life collection on the Civil War.* NOT AVAILABLE. Winston Churchill's *History of the Second World War.* NOT AVAILABLE.

OK, he thought, maybe they don't do literary collections. He typed in the title of the book that had sold more copies than any other in history except for the Bible. Ayn Rand's *Atlas Shrugged.* NOT AVAILABLE. *The Law*, by Frederic Bastiat. NOT AVAILABLE. *Thomas Jefferson, an Intimate History*, by Fawn Brodie. NOT AVAILABLE. Finally in exasperation he typed in, *The Declaration of Independence.* NOT AVAILABLE.

"What books are available?" he shouted at the screen and then checked himself as he heard Jeremy stir in his crib. Calming down, almost as a joke he typed in Saul Alinsky's *Rules for Radicals*, one of the most revolutionary books ever written. Available. Al Gore's, *Earth in the Balance*. Available. *Silent Spring*, by Rachel Carson, Available.

This is nuts, he thought. Why do they have these very radical books, but not classics that deal with American history?

OK, let's go in a different direction, he thought, now determined to find something, anything that he wanted to read. He typed in the titled of one of the all time classic books, *Huckleberry Finn*. To his amazement it popped up and downloaded. Satisfied that it was a start, Brad settled back and began to read.

About two hours later Brad began to frown. What he was reading just didn't seem right. First he noted the omission of certain words. Injun Joe was no longer an "Injun," now he was just Joe. Worse, the word "nigger" had been replaced with the word "hipster." What in the world did that mean? The author, Mark Twain, had written the book in his time. The references and racial slurs were common then. To remove them changed the tone and misrepresented the times. Could they have made less egregious substitutes like "Indian" or "Black?" At least those would have been semantically correct, but "hipster" for a negro – that's just ludicrous. How could people today appreciate and understand those times if the books have been cleansed of any historical verbiage?

But the worst change was that the entire story line of Jim, the slave, had been eliminated. It simply wasn't there. Consequently there was no story, no purpose for the book. Huck Finn was just paddling aimlessly down the Mississippi with no direction. It was simply incomprehensible.

Who had done this? And why? He took a deep breath, calmed himself yet again, picked up the e-book and decided to try another title.

There was a book that, as a history teacher, he knew very well. He had actually taught from its pages. It was the *History of Plymouth Plantation*, written from the original manuscript by the Pilgrim Governor, William Bradford. The book detailed the forty years of struggle to establish the Plymouth colony. This, Brad knew, was vital American history that every American should know, explaining some of the nation's most important foundational roots.

Brad typed in the title. Available. He was ecstatic. Wonderful, he thought as he downloaded the book into his e-book. Again he began to read. But, again he was soon troubled and his head began to ache.

As he read the historic document, he became aware that important references to God were eliminated. Brad knew that the Colonists had placed great faith in God as they suffered through some of the most difficult conditions ever faced by a settlement. Belief and faith in God was literally what got them through the worst of the hardships. It was vital to tell the reader, he thought. Without those references there simply was no way of understanding the Pilgrims and their heroic struggle.

Then it got worse as he continue to read. Brad was well aware of the historic fact that a great deal of the hardships in the colony, bordering on starvation, were the fault of the economic system that was first enforced. They had original-ly set up a communal system to rule over the colony. It was called the *Mayflower Compact*. Under this system, no one owned the exclusive fruits of their labor. Instead, everything produced went into a central pot for all to share equally. Of course, on paper, the idea had sounded grand – so fair for all involved. But eventually, human nature took over. As everyone shared equally, regardless of how much, or how little effort they put into the work, the producers began to notice they were working harder for an equal share with those who didn't work as diligently. So the producers simply slowed down their production to the point that the colony was on the verge of collapse. It was purely human nature, thought Brad.

As described in the original manuscript, in a last desperate effort to save themselves, the leaders threw up their hands and decided it was to be every man for himself. Whatever you produce is yours, they declared. It was almost miraculous to observe how production of food suddenly began to improve to incredible success. In celebration of their bounty and to give thanks to God, they organized a feast. It is still celebrated today, known as Thanksgiving. The lesson, as Brad taught in his class, was that the first Thanksgiving was a celebration of free enterprise winning over Socialism.

To Brad's horror, that entire part of the story had been removed from the e-book version. Now he became very concerned. There seemed to be a troubling pattern to his efforts to download a book. It appeared that any book that centered on individualism, freedom, free enterprise, or the concept of limited government, family, or Christianity was either NOT AVAILABLE or the message of individual freedom was deleted from those that were available. Could this be true?

What was it his brother Mike had said on Christmas Day? "The children can't relate to the classics because they don't have historic references to understand their meaning." Well, Brad had to admit, if what he was seeing here was any indication, Mike was onto something.

If you change the books, thought Brad, you destroy history, culture and, God forbid, knowledge. Barbarians destroy knowledge, was the thought that screamed into Brad's head and wouldn't go away. Was this a deliberate attempt to erase history? Why? What monster would do such a thing? Surely this was a misunderstanding. These e-books were new. Not perfect. Maybe he had downloaded the wrong version.

But he was troubled. As he thought about the possible consequences of a changed culture through the destruction of knowledge and history, it all seemed so impossible. How do you kill knowledge?

Yet, he couldn't shake off the memory of a conversation he had with Tracie just recently. Brad had asked Tracie about her schoolwork. "I was given an assignment a couple of weeks ago to write a paper and I got an "A" on it," she reported with some pride.

"Really," said Brad. "What was it about?"

"Well, we were assigned to compare the writings of Karl Marx with the Book of Acts from the Bible."

Asked Brad, "What possible comparison could you come up with between the Bible and Karl Marx?"

"Oh, it was very relevant. As you look through the entire Book of Acts, it tells of the early church of Jesus and how his followers, in the name of Jesus, shared all of their material goods with those who had nothing. They even sold possessions and gave the money to the church. But in one case a man sold his possessions but kept a profit and the church said it was a sin. Jesus talked over an over again about sacrifice for the common good. That's exactly what Karl Marx taught. So my conclusion in my "A" paper was that Jesus was a communist," Tracie concluded with a tone of triumph in her voice. "My teacher loved it. Even read it out loud in class."

Brad sat there, not moving. He was dumbfounded, not wanting to believe that his own daughter had said this. Just as he had witnessed in the students in his own classroom, there was something radically wrong with the thinking of today's children. Now it seemed to be influencing Tracie. How could that be? He had shared many father/daughter conversations with her and, as she grew up, he tried to influence her to read, research, and get to the truth. What was this new influence that now caused her to think such twisted thoughts?

He shuddered a bit then tried to shake off the memory of that conversation. He was tired and just didn't want to think about it anymore. Kate and Tracie had returned and were busy fixing dinner. So he picked up Jeremy and headed to the kitchen. Later in bed, he spent a restless night before having to go back to his classroom on Monday morning.

# Chapter 12

State Representative Guy Marshall was furious as he stormed into Speaker Perry's office in the Ohio State House. Perry's secretary tried to stop him but he just brushed her aside and threw open the door.

Perry was just hanging up the phone and said with a mixture of alarm and irritation, "Guy, what's wrong?"

Marshall tossed his LEAP e-book on the desk. "What are you trying to pull Dave, it's gone. It's all gone," he shouted even louder.

"What's gone? What are you talking about?"

"The testimony for my bill, it's not here."

"Calm down, Guy, and tell me what you're talking about?"

Marshall took a deep breath and started to talk slowly to

make his words deliberate and understandable. "Yesterday we had a hearing on my Bill, #564. You know, Dave, the one to free local communities from federal and state regulations that force them to create central government-directed development plans to reorganize their cities. My bill is intended to protect local governments from too much federal overreach."

"Yes, I know the bill you're talking about. So, what's wrong?"

"Well, we had several experts testify. Some were from the federal government who said their planning was necessary to control development and protect the environment. They said growth of cities had to be controlled in order to protect the natural habitat of animals and cut back on energy use. And I can tell you, they were not too happy with my bill and said so in very strong terms."

"Well," said Perry, "those plans are being enforced all over the nation. We have to do it. All the official reports are emphatic that, unless growth is controlled, massive sprawl will run out of control. So I'm not surprised that the Feds don't like your bill."

"But, I also had representatives from over ten communities testifying that they were drowning under these regulations. They said they were being forced to create regulations that were damaging homeowners and businesses and they wanted a way out of the oppressive regulations. More than that, the city representatives said the real danger is from the federal money they are being forced to take to pay for these plans."

"Well that's a strange complaint," said Perry. "It's free

money to them. The government is simply returning their own tax dollars to them."

"You're missing an important point. Those grants are forcing specific policy on the communities; they are dictating where and how the communities can develop. They tell them what land can be used and what has to stay undeveloped. One of the people testifying, Mayor Peterson, from down in Marietta, testified that so much of his community's land is now locked away from use that it's destroying his tax base. A whole section of town has been depopulated and even farmers are starting to suffer from restrictions on how and where they can raise their crops. These development plans are a disaster and we need to free the cities and allow them to control their own growth."

"Well, if these arguments are sound, the legislature will support your bill. So what's your problem, Guy?" asked Perry with a little more irritation seeping into his voice.

"The problem, Dave, is that today, none of the testimony from the cities supporting my bill is there in the record. It's all gone," shouted Marshall. "You gave every member of the legislature one of these e-books and you said we could free up our time by not having to attend all of these meetings and hearings because they could read all the minutes and testimonies right here in the e-books. That's why there were only a couple of members of the committee at my hearing. But now I discover that none of them have the proponents' testimony. Just the attacks from the feds. What happened, Dave?"

Speaker Perry simply looked up at Marshall, trying to muster a reply. But he had the look of a child who just got caught in the cookie jar. Finally, he said weakly, "I don't know what happened, Guy. It's a new technology. I'm sure it has some flaws. Perhaps one of the clerks simply missed loading it into the file."

"Well, you'd better get it fixed. I demand that the entire legislature hear the testimony of my expert witnesses! If that doesn't happen, and soon, I'm going to demand that we ditch these worthless e-pads and return to the old way where people actually talked to each other. "

As Guy Marshall left his office, Perry picked up the phone and called Jim Davidson in the Governor's office. "Jim, Edgar Thornton isn't going to be happy."

• • • •

**"When people reject absolute truth, they lose their standard for reality. They will believe anything in their futile search for something."**

It was the newest blast of graffiti from the unknown writer. This time it was spread across the walls of the Department of Justice in the Capitol City.

RJ Stevens was fascinated by the graffiti he saw popping up on the sides of so many buildings lately. Like many others who observed it, he wondered who did it and what message they were trying to convey.

RJ knew that even the feds were looking into it to try to find who was doing it. They think it's a terrorist group. RJ didn't agree. He believed it was something else, but what? Terrorists, he thought, didn't quote Founding Fathers.

Sometimes the message was simply a quote from one of the founders. Other times it sounded like a warning, as if there were a hidden message, a puzzle that needed to be solved. "Check your premise." "All is not as it seems." "The power of one."

Yet today's new message painted on the side of the Federal Department of Justice seemed to be a new kind of message, perhaps a major piece to that puzzle, thought RJ. "When people reject absolute truth …". Hmm. Very curious.

RJ had a special reason to be interested in the graffiti. He was 19 years old and was a master of Internet marketing. More importantly, he was the IT guru at the Voice of Adams. Mack Richards depended on him for nearly everything related to computers and the Internet.

RJ had to laugh when he thought about it. Mack was of the generation that really couldn't quite comprehend computers. He knew how important they were, but knowing how to even start to find answers he was looking for using the computer, was beyond his ability. "How do you know that?" Richards constantly asked him.

RJ's reactionary response (which he always kept to himself, unspoken) was, "well I'm older than twelve and younger than thirty."

RJ had created the Voice of Adams' website and the marketing program to sell Voice of Adams' DVDs and books, along with building the group's outreach on social media. He also spent a great part of his working day researching government policy.

As a result of RJ's efforts, the Voice of Adams was now

able to reach several hundred thousand people in an instant over the Internet. Those emails informed supporters of new government policies or actions that might affect them. And they provided a call to action when necessary. It was helping make the Voice of Adams a potent voice in their fight against what it saw as an ever-growing oppressiveness over the rights of the people.

But what were these graffiti messages and who was behind them? Some people had written into the Voice of Adams asking if the group itself was behind the messages. Or was there a rival organization working underground to destabilize the government?

It was a puzzle indeed. No one had ever seen anyone painting the messages. They just seemed to appear overnight.

RJ typed in all the known messages that had appeared and, using a new publishing software, he visually cut each message into separate pieces. Now, on the screen, they were scattered in front of him as he moved them around, changing their order, trying to see if there was a pattern to their meaning.

"All is not as it seems." "Check your premise." "When people reject absolute truth…" Clearly the writer was trying to send hidden messages. Did he mean someone was lying? If so, today's message was very intriguing. This one seemed to be directly related to current policy statements coming out of the federal government. Did the past hold the key to the future, or was it the other way around?

"I don't know what the message means specifically, but clearly someone is trying to tell us something," thought RJ.

He kept staring at those pieces. Now he was anxious to see the next message. What would it tell him?

Would he be any closer to understanding what they mean?

• • • •

It was a Sunday evening as Brad Jackson settled in front of the computer to write a new installment of his weekly book review blog, "The Page Turner." This one was going to be different because he wasn't reviewing a book, rather he was questioning the very source of books.

He had been greatly distressed over his experience in trying to download books onto his LEAP e-book. Time and again he tried. Most times he got the dreaded NOT AVAIL-ABLE message. If he did get one to download it had missing passages or lost characters or even altered meaning.

What troubled him most was his unshakable feeling that this was being done on purpose to actually eliminate a certain message or point of view. Specifically, he noted that the books he could not access were those that expressed the ideas of individuality, free enterprise, and restraints on government. Could that be possible? Was he just being par-anoid? Or was someone, or some unknown power, trying to enforce a kind of censorship over free thought? But who? Was it organized? Could it be someone in the government? That seemed crazy. But e-books were taking over the pub-lishing industry. That was a powerful force to be in control over what people read. Why would they want to do that?

His fingers now flew over the keyboard as he told the story of his search for books. Rather than give his usual opinions to guide the reader in a search for a good book, this time Brad's post asked the questions that were flooding his mind. Were other readers experiencing the disappointment of not finding their favorite books to download? Was he simply inept at using the technology? Was he being too critical? Where are my favorite books? His frustration grew with each typed word.

Finally he added his title, "What's Wrong With e-books." And he hit send to distribute the blog to all of his usual outlets.

Three people quickly took notice as it landed in their inboxes, John Lloyd, Peter Arter, and Edgar Thornton.

• • • •

Jimmy Armond stood in the middle of his wheat field. He couldn't hold back the tears. There simply was no crop because there was no water. The seeds didn't even open. They were lying in their rows looking like tiny rotted prunes.

What was he to do? How were he and his family to survive? By what right did this government have to destroy his livelihood? His father and grandfather had worked this same land for almost a hundred years. They didn't hurt the environment. If anything, they helped the land be stronger and more fertile. They had to take care of the land or they would have been out of business long ago.

Jimmy was a mild mannered, peaceful man. He had never initiated force against anyone. His friends called him a gentle giant. His big hands had gently cradled his children when they were babies. And the same hands had gently and lovingly held the soil of his farm as he proudly walked over his fields. Then they were lush with growth and abundance. Now they were brown and dead.

Agents of the government told him he could no longer work the land. They treated him like a criminal. They said he and the other farmers endangered wildlife along the river. They said his use of the water was dangerous and selfish. They blocked legal appeals. They used their power as government to control the judges whom they had appointed. They simply left the farmers with no way to argue their case.

And so now they left his family with nothing. Who were the real criminals here? That thought ran through his mind over and over. Inside, this man who had never broken the law, suddenly felt an emotion unfamiliar to him. He felt nothing short of a murderous rage. His fists clenched. And his jaw tightened.

As he stood there looking over the devastation of his little farm, he knew what he had to do. Fight back. What did he have to lose? But how? What would be the most effective tactic against such a huge government power? Was there one? He couldn't do it alone.

# Chapter 13

There were more than two thousand on the hillside that spring day, just outside Kansas City, Episcopalians all, for an event sponsored by the Episcopal Diocese. Such events were being sponsored across the nation by every denomination as the nation's religions were coming together in one great spiritual awakening. It appeared that a new spirituality was taking over the population. There had been mass rallies with hundreds of thousands of people in Washington, D.C., New York City, and Los Angles. Now the movement had come to Kansas City.

There was excitement in the air. A tension. Something major was about to happen. And so they came and they waited expectantly.

In a now familiar ceremony, as the congregation sat on the blankets they had spread across the hillside, a black robed, self-proclaimed high priest stood ready to receive the procession of animals. Up to the makeshift altar they came. People brought their dogs on leashes. There were cats and birds in elaborate cages. Behind them came the farm animals of pigs and cows and goats, all to receive the Earth blessing. Next came members of the congregation carrying bowls of dirt and stalks of corn and wheat. To the sounds of drumbeats, came acrobats and jugglers. It all had become commonplace at these events, a celebration of the Earth spirit.

Suddenly, from the makeshift pulpit at the top of the hill, the head of the Diocese called them to attention. "Good afternoon, as we begin please join me in a new Earth Pledge celebrating the global village we call Planet Earth." Everyone had been handed a paper with the Earth Pledge printed on it so as he began, all joined in, "*I pledge allegiance to Planet Earth, Mother of all Nations; and to the infinite universe in which she stands; our Planet, among millions, expressing truth and unlimited possibilities for all.*" As the last words rang out the crowd cheered.

Then came a familiar voice over the loud speaker. Standing in front of the congregation was the President of the United States, Eric Gravell, who was recognized as a virtual guru in the new religious spirit growing across the nation. His message was what they had come to hear. Said Gravell, "God is not separate from the Earth."

He held his hands up to the sun overhead and he said a prayer to the grandfather spirit. And then he said a prayer to the Four Directions as he slowly turned, first to the North, then to the West, then to the South, then to the East. And the crowd stood, turning with his every turn, hands raised, eyes closed, chanting, "Thank you Mother for each new day you give us."

He prayed to the sprits to bless the Earth and oversee this vital gathering of the new faithful. And then he moved forward and blessed each animal arrayed before him.

Again the President turned to the gathering and raised his hands, offering an Earth prayer, claiming the Earth was speaking through him as he said, "On this Earth Day let us say an Earth prayer and make an Earth pledge. In the Bible 'Ruah' means both wind and spirit, so let us take time to breathe with the universe, connect with the Earth, and remember what we need to know and do." And the crowd chanted, "Ruah. Ruah."

Gravell continued his prayer saying, "Celebrate that ancient spirits are born again in us, spirits of eagle vision, of coyote craft, of bear stewardship. Of buffalo wisdom, of ancient goddesses, of druids, of native people, of Thoreau and Sitting Bull – born again and over again in John Muir and Rachel Carson and David Brower and Alice Walker. These," said the President, "were the new saints of the New Earth society. The grand ones who had the vision to save the Earth against the evil poisons brought on by greed and so many disconnected selfish humans."

Most in the gathering worshipped these new saints for their selfless determination to save Mother Earth. And most now carried the sacred written word of their new patron saint, President Eric Gravell. It was a small, pocket-sized green book they each carried with them, ready to read passages of his wisdom whenever they felt challenged.

And now, before his presence they vowed to carry his written words into official deeds. To carry out policies that promised to save the Earth, to wipe out the evils of selfish capitalism and so-called private property where greedy individuals sought to exclude the children of the Earth.

As the President finished his Earth prayers, another figure came to the pulpit. He was a famous Earth musician, Evan Spring. He explained to the crowd that he had gone into the Superior Forest and began to play his saxophone. "It wasn't long," he said, "until he heard in the distance a response to his sounds. It was the distinct howl of the wolf. It was then," he said, "that he had turned on his recorder and captured the exchanges of howls between his saxophone and the wolf."

Now, Spring played a recording of the wolf howling and then made the same sound on his saxophone. The crowd cheered. He then asked the congregation to join him in a "Howl-le-lu-ia Chorus." He made a wolf sound on the saxophone and 2,000 Episcopalians from Kansas howled back, expressing their oneness with the wolf.

Finally a third figure came to the top of the hill to address the crowd. This was the great spiritual leader and teacher, Poncho Delegrade, the leader of PAN and New Age Transformation. He was the man who had the vision for the coming together of all the great religions of the Earth, to merge together into the great spiritual awakening that was transforming the nation and the world.

He began to speak in a slow, soft voice as he presented the gathering with a new idea. "Close your eyes," he said, "and open your hearts and minds to new ideas. See the Earth as a living, spiritual being that can feel pain." He then asked the gathering to tune into the crystal matrix frequency – what he called, "Mother Earth's Heartbeat." He told them to relax. Many lay flat on the ground totally concentrating, feeling the Earth's pain, hearing the heartbeat. And many went into trance-like states.

As people felt they were being filled with the Earth's energy, like a drug that affected every one of their senses, they became vocal, making guttural sounds that were rising and falling rhythmically. Some swayed and some fell down on the ground and began writhing. Moans, shouts, and sing-song type chants filled the evening air.

Then Poncho stood before them and brought them to silence.

He told the group to concentrate on a cloud floating overhead, just drifting, and then told them to invite the cloud in to fill the empty spirit, the empty soul. He then paused and, in an almost hypnotic voice, said, "invite PAN in. Accept PAN as the leader and the guide for your lives." And he raised his hands for complete silence. Still speaking in that hypnotic voice he said, "PAN was the first son of Mother Earth and used to live close to his mother in the primeval forest with his brothers and sisters. PAN's brothers and sisters were the ones who went out and founded the temple-building societies. These were the Aztecs and the Egyptians and others."

Then Poncho Delegrade, settling into his message, began to speak louder, with flashes of anger as he said, "But when PAN refused to join his siblings in the cities, they called him evil and SATAN! The siblings," Poncho shouted, "invented their own selfish religion – Christianity! It must be removed from the face of the Earth because it teaches that there is a higher authority than our beloved Earth Mother. Christianity has nothing but disdain for the Earth Mother," he shouted. "Christianity says humans have dominion over the Earth Mother. Christianity teaches an individual selfishness that will only lead to the total destruction of Mother Earth."

The Kansas audience of Episcopalians began to stir. Angry looks on their faces. Some shouted "Shame! Shame!"

Poncho smiled knowingly, putting up his hand to again silence the crowd. And again, in a low, hypnotic voice, almost as a private prayer, said, "Right now, Mother Earth is bringing PAN back to save us and lead us into the New Age. You, each and every one of you, can help her by surrendering to PAN. Turn to the Crystal Matrix frequencies and carry out the directions you receive." Poncho stopped and looked up and down the crowd then said, almost in a whisper, "This might include the removal of Christians, because they are the biggest obstacle to our transformation to the New Age of Mother Earth."

The crowd began to cheer and chant, "Mother Earth" and "PAN." As Poncho Delegrade backed into the shadows, Evan Spring took center stage again with more sounds of the Wolf as the crowd again chanted the Howl-al-lu-ia Chorus. President Gravell and Poncho Delegrade joined hands and the crowd cheered. Kansas City was now fully ready to join the new direction of human society all to be one with the Earth Mother.

It was then that President Gravell returned to the pulpit for a special announcement. He held up his hands to hush the crowd. "Now we are ready to take the next step. The step God and our Earth Mother are demanding of us. Today, we must all take the pledge to protect the incredible creation that God has entrusted to us."

As the crowd anxiously anticipated his words, Gravell continued. "He has given us so many chances. It started in the garden, but Adam and Eve couldn't keep the promise, so he threw them out. Later, he tried again with Noah as God cleansed the Earth of all of man's wickedness and started over again. Yet, here we are again, with the Earth once more on the verge of destruction from man's wickedness and total disregard for the creatures of the Earth, and for the rivers and oceans, and for the air we need to breath.

"Christianity has been the power behind the idea of man's ego, teaching that man is the center of God's universe. Insisting that man decides what should live and what should die. That, is going to stop. Today you have joined with the creatures of the Earth to understand that man is a cancer on the Earth. That man IS slowly killing the Earth Mother. As God proved with Noah, he wants us to save all the creatures, every slug and every salamander. It is time for us to truly allow God to decide which creatures live and which die. It is not for man to decide. It is our job to help God, when he decides which creatures live or die. If creatures become extinct on the account of man's greed or neglect, then we are playing God and that is blasphemy. And that is a sin.

"And so," continued Gravell, moving now to his point, "let all of the religions combine into one voice, one force for one specific mission – to protect Mother Earth, even if it means the destruction of man. Man's population is growing while those of other species die. That must be reversed and the human populations must be reduced if the Earth is going to live. We must reduce human childbirth. We must control the spread of human habitat. If our dams, roads, and buildings are destroying species' habitat then we will tear them down. We will confine man to his own territory – his own habitat -- and leave the rest of the world alone," he said with great passion as the crowd cheered.

"My friends, today I want to announce that we are going to fix a great wrong. For almost 2000 years, ever since the

Roman Emperor Constantine put together a false Bible, Christianity has been operating against the real teachings of God. So today, to correct that wrong, I am announcing the publication of a new Bible based on the teachings of the God of the Garden and the great cleansing of Noah. From this day forward, we will begin the task of replacing the dangerous bible of the Romans with a new Earth Bible. This new Green Bible will teach us all how to learn of God's teachings through a Green lens. We will learn that the true coming of Jesus is through the planting of a tree. From this day forward our churches will become the place where we will all learn to become a Deep Green Family, learning to live on less, to sacrifice and live as one with Mother Earth."

As Gravell finished, nearly shouting the final words, the crowd was whipped into a near frenzy, cheering as they held up their arms toward the sun and, almost spontaneously, another round of the Howl-le-lu-ia Chorus broke out as they began to disperse. As they headed to the parking lots all were handed their own copy of a LEAP e-Book containing the new, *St. Gaia's Version of the Green Bible, a Universal Standard for Every Denomination.*

Pastor Dave Delray stood in the shadows, filled with fear and despair over the scene he had just witnessed. They're growing stronger, he thought. Who would have believed so many Christians could be so easily duped into rejecting their faith and blindly follow these lies, believing they are doing God's work? I have to stop this. But how do I counter these lies? Pastor Dave then looked up into the heavens and said his own prayer.

· · · ·

The sound of his ringing phone jerked John Lloyd out of deep concentration as he was reading yet another discouraging report on his falling book sales. It was Peter Arter calling. "John," he said, sounding in high spirits, "I've got an idea!"

"Spill it, I could use some good news right now."

"Well, I think I have the solution to our problem. Think about this. What's our biggest roadblock to selling your books?" Before Lloyd could attempt an answer, Arter rushed ahead and answered himself, "Stores," he shouted into the phone. "Your whole problem is that book stores are disappearing and you have no outlet for your books. Am I right?"

Lloyd just listened, wondering where Peter Arter was going with this. Arter rushed on. "We tried to compete with LEAP on its terms. We failed miserably. So, what if we build our own stores that feature your catalog of books plus thousands more out there that we can get access to? The only difference from our original plan is that we will be able to do what we do best, publish real books, and put them in our own stores!" He sounded absolutely jubilant.

"Peter," Lloyd said in a tired voice, "don't you remember, the problem is that book stores are going out of business. How can we compete if other established stores can't?"

"That's incorrect. The other stores are going out of business because LEAP is buying them up and putting them out of business."

Suddenly Lloyd perked up. Maybe Arter hadn't lost his mind after all. "Tell me more. How would it work?"

"Look, you and I have decades of experience picking the right books and selling them. In addition to your ability to pick the best authors, I have created a system of online bookselling that is based on customer ratings, pre-orders, sales, and popularity. I have all of that data."

"So, how does that help us sell books in stores?"

"Think of it, John. We can take that knowledge and put the very best selling books in the stores. They are already pre-screened for popularity. Most have been rated four stars and a great many are award winners. In short, we will have knowledge from my main online business that no one else has ever had before. We can create bookstores that are packed with the very best sellers."

"What about LEAP?" The company still controls the growing e-book market. People want to use them."

"Well, first, we can stock the e-books that we developed in the store as well as sell them on line. So we aren't giving up on that effort. But, there is one more secrete weapon I think we can fire at LEAP."

"What's that?"

"Did you see that blog called "The Page Turner?" The guy who writes it is a school teacher, I think."

"Yes, I think I did see it."

"Well didn't it make you jump out of your chair when you read it? Is sure did me."

"I don't understand what you mean."

"John, he made our case for us! Here is a guy who was just trying to download a book on his e-book and he couldn't find anything he wanted. And when he did find one, he found that it had been changed. Just like you told me in our first meeting. John, that's huge! We can destroy LEAP with that information. We can use it in our advertising. Maybe we can file a lawsuit against LEAP. And I can get it into Congressman Morris' hands and demand an investigation. This guy has given us everything we need to go after LEAP, destroy their reputation, and build our own product.

Suddenly Lloyd became as animated as Peter Arter. "Peter, you're a genius. No wonder you've been so successful. What's the next step?'

"I've already laid out a basic idea for the layout of the stores. I think we could open the first one in about six months. I've got my people looking for locations right now."

"OK, you keep working on that. Meanwhile, I'm going to get hold of this Brad Jackson and see what else he might want to share with us about his e-book experience."

"Will do, John. I really think we're on to something big here. This is the break we were looking for."

"You may be right, Peter. I'll talk to you in a few days," Lloyd said as he broke off the call. Then he called out to his secretary. "Peggy, see if you can find some contact information for a blogger named Brad Jackson."

# Chapter 14

It wasn't reported as the lead story of the day. In fact, it was sandwiched between an item on a delicious new recipe for a broccoli and soy casserole and tomorrow's weather. "Yum," said the anchor in the usual happy talk with his co-anchor about the new recipe. "In other news, the federal government announced plans for the destruction and removal of a series of dams across the nation. According to Jim Sears of the Army Corp of Engineers, this is being done in the name of 'naturalization' in order to restore vital fish and other wildlife habitat along the nation's rivers."

The report then showed a video of Jim Sears making the announcement and answering reporters' questions. Said Sears, "All this dam construction is the most obvious human intervention leading to the loss of wetland habitats. The dams are built to support growing human development and industrialization, but are causing deforestation and damage to riverbanks. As called for in his recent Executive Orders, the President has determined that the best way to stop this destruction is to begin a comprehensive program to destroy key dams across the country in order to control where new development may occur."

Several reporters raised their hands to ask questions. "John," said Sears to a reporter, "I believe you had your hand up first."

"Yes, Mr. Sears, how many dams do you intend to remove?"

"Well, there are 65,000 dams in the United States and some 22,000 have been targeted for removal."

There was a low rumble of voices in the room, someone let out a whistle. More hands shot up.

"Mr. Sears, what will happen to the much needed power these dams provide?"

And another shouted out, "How about the industries that depend on the dams?"

Still another reporter asked, "Won't this damage property downstream of the dams?"

Sears took the questions in stride. "We have already begun to cut back on power usage and so are lowering the nation's power needs. The nightly power curfews are doing a great job toward this goal. We're going to be able to do without this power as we build more and more wind and solar plants. Hydro-electric power is a left-over from a primitive age. As for industry, it's vital that they find new ways to produce their products without damaging the environment. And the people downstream of the dams are living on land that should have been under water anyway. They are in a flood plain and we intend to move everyone off of those areas. Living there is not natural."

As the reporter switched back to the studio, the smiling news anchor added that finally the government was taking bold steps to assure human populations had respect for the natural habitat. "After all," he said to his co-anchor, "the rivers and the wildlife were here first. We are just visitors."

With a big grin his co-anchor said, "And you know, there is another great unexpected benefit in taking down those dams and turning the lights off at night. We can now see the stars at night, right here in the cities, because we are eliminating dangerous light pollution!"

"That's great," said the lead anchor. "It's wonderful that our government is restoring these vital natural wonders for us all to see. It's great for the kids."

"Now, for the weather… Brrr, it's cold out there for late spring. What happened to those predictions of major warming?"

•  •  •  •

Brad Jackson opened his apartment door to greet John Lloyd. "Mr. Jackson, thank you for seeing me."

"My pleasure sir. I've long admired your company's collection of authors," said Brad. As they moved into Brad's study, John Lloyd couldn't help looking over the rows and rows of Brad's collection.

"As one book lover to another, I must say I'm impressed.

You have the classics, like Shakespeare, O'Henry and Poe. And my gosh, look at all of these history books."

"I'm a history teacher, so I'm just kind of drawn to them. But look over here at this beauty." Brad took a very old book from the shelf and presented it to Lloyd. "This is an antique. An original copy of Ulysses S. Grant's memoirs."

"Oh, man," said Lloyd, holding the copy with great care. "This is the book he wrote while deathly ill and was rushing to finish it just before he died."

"Yes, he desperately needed the money for his family. He died within weeks of finishing it."

The two book lovers spent several more minutes talking about Brad's impressive collection; Lloyd noted that several of the books had been published by his own company. Then Brad invited Lloyd to take a seat in one of his comfortable old leather chairs.

"How may I help you, Mr. Lloyd?"

"I was very interested in your blog that reported on the difficulty you had in finding something to download into your e-book. You said that most of the volumes you searched for weren't available and some of those you did find were changed."

"Yes, it was a very frustrating experience."

"Can you give me the details?"

Brad told him of the several kinds of books he had tried to download, but were unavailable. And then he related his findings of such books as *Huck Finn* and the *Mayflower Compact.*

"Very interesting." Can you show me just what you did and what you found?"

"Sure," answered Brad, and he turned to his computer. As he duplicated the search he had conducted on that frustrating day, Brad began to share his suspicions about the possibility that someone was deliberately eliminating or even changing the books that contained a certain philosophy.

"I'm certainly not a conspiracy theorist," Brad assured Lloyd, "but look at these changes in the books I've shown you. *The Mayflower Compact* was a significant event in man's history. The Pilgrims learned that individuals acting on their own were more productive than when acting through a collective. History has taught us that lesson over an over. But that whole part of Bradford's account has been eliminated from the e-book version."

"Yes, I see it is"

"And, look at the books not available at all. Nearly every one of them carries a message of individuality, free enterprise, and limitations on the power of government, and free enterprise. They are simply not available. But, look what is available," he said as he went through the list of available books. "Look at all of these very radical, anti-individual, anti-freedom messages. Does that seem strange to you?"

Lloyd sat there looking at the computer screen, deep in thought. This teacher, he thought, has discovered what I have suspected all along. But it's much more extensive than I had thought. Lloyd had known there were changes in some of the books, but he had never put together the idea that it was done to stifle an entire philosophical point of view. This issue seemed to be much larger than he expected.

As Lloyd came out of his thoughts, Brad was saying, "As a history teacher, this looks to me like a deliberate attempt to erase actual history. In fact, it could be much more dangerous than that. They are erasing ideas," Brad almost shouted in his frustration. He actually felt sick, thinking about the enormity of it. "That can't be true, can it Mr. Lloyd? That would be diabolical," he said, not even wanting to believe his own words.

Lloyd rubbed his chin thoughtfully, trying to come up with a suitable reply to this teacher. Finally, he began to speak slowly, saying, "Mr. Jackson, I don't have an answer for you. My own publishing business is feeling a great pressure from these e-books and their manufacturer, that company called LEAP. It has been my belief that they are up to no good. But I haven't been able to prove it or to even put my hand on what is really wrong. Just a feeling. You have given me a great deal more to think about."

As John Lloyd rose to leave he said to Brad, "My associate, Peter Arter, and I are working to build a case against LEAP in an attempt to fix the very problems you have discovered. It may even result in a lawsuit. Your blog could be a valuable tool for us. Do I have your permission to quote from it?"

"I'm happy to help anyway I can," replied Brad.

"Thank you. That will be very helpful to our efforts. Let me know if you find anything else about the books," said Lloyd as he shook Brad's hand to leave. "I'll be in touch."

# Chapter 15

Pastor Dave was resplendent in his white suit, red tie and ever-present blue pocket scarf. It was his traditional uniform for the camera as the coordinating colors gave him an air of command, someone to be listened to. And today Pastor Dave was determined to be heard.

His cathedral, where his weekly national television program was aired to twenty million viewers, held an audience of three thousand. Every seat was filled today. There was anticipation along with a bit of anxiety for what their preacher was about to say. Pastor Dave was not known to mince words.

As the gospel choir sang their last stanza, the music stopped and Pastor Dave walked to his pulpit. For several seconds he stood, head bowed in silent prayer. Then he looked up into the camera and began to speak.

"My friends, my religious family, my faithful, you know

me. You know I love the Lord above all else. You know I have devoted my life to sharing His word. Our religion, our faith, has been challenged many times over the years. But I want to tell you today that none of us have ever before faced the challenge that is about to confront us. It is a challenge so powerful that it will go right to the very core of our deepest beliefs in the Lord. And, my friends, if we fail to meet that challenge, I tell you now, everything you and I hold dear, every ounce of faith we have professed in the Lord, will be destroyed." There was an audible gasp in the crowd.

Pastor Dave paused for a moment to let those words sink in then he began again. "Over the past few months I have observed firsthand a movement that is sold as a means to bringing all religions together under one umbrella. I must admit that, at first, I thought it could be a wonderful new beginning for a rebirth of God's rule over our land. I thought it could be the end of strife and petty differences as the great spiritual leaders came together to lead the people back to God. We have lost so much over the past several years. We have seen many of our churches reduced to small-er and smaller groups of worshippers each Sunday as more and more people turn away from God. We have watched in disbelief as God has been virtually eliminated from the great religious holidays sacred to our teachings. And we have seen God kicked out of our children's classrooms, leav-ing them with no moral guidance in the schools."

Then, heading into the crux of his sermon, Pastor Dave's passion grew stronger; his voice cracked a bit with emotion. "I thought this new movement, which was billed as a spir-itual rebirth, was a new beginning. It is even being led by our nation's President. I've seen Americans turn out by the thousands to sing and pray and rejoice. What an exciting time to stand with the Lord, I thought."

Then Pastor Dave stopped. He stood there for a few seconds as his lower lip began to quiver. And then slowly, in a nearly inaudible voice, he said, "But, I was wrong. This new spiritual revival isn't to praise our Lord God and His Holy Word. It is a lie designed to get you to actually denounce God and worship a new, false god -- the one they call Mother Earth or Gaia. I tell you that they are worshipping a false idol that in reality intends to diminish God to an earthly level.

"This new religion tells us that man is equal only to the lowest life forms on Earth and that we must sacrifice our society to live in equality with rats. They preach that man is nothing more than a destroyer and that the only hope for the Earth is that man is withdrawn from huge portions of it, instead herded into specific living spaces, leaving the rest of the world to wilderness." He could feel his audience starting to stir as he plunged forward.

"They demand an end to private property ownership because they charge that such ownership enslaves the land. They actually insist that pet ownership is slavery. And they declare that Capitalism is destroying the earth. They tell us that we have no right to the natural fruits of the world. Food, drink, and housing are to be severely limited to the barest of necessities. Sacrifice in the name of a false earth god is the mantra they preach."

He heard a few people involuntarily utter a soft, "No."

Pastor Dave now spoke a bit softer as he discussed the details of the new religion. "This new Earth-bound religion teaches that we are entering into a new 'earth consciousness' and that the world is being called to a new post-denominational, post-Christian belief system that sees the earth as a living being."

He paused for a moment, then, in a loud voice, he charged, "My friends, they attack Christianity and have targeted it to be eliminated because the Gospel of Jesus Christ teaches the exact opposite to their pagan ideas of Earth worship. The God I know and worship did not preach that man's lot was to suffer in government-inflicted poverty. He talked of plenty and that it was available to all. He did not condemn man to be equal to a slug. He gave man dominion over the Earth to produce and to use the resources He has provided."

"Amen," shouted many in the crowd.

Now he was into his element, preaching the truths of his belief, the reasons he had devoted his life to teaching the Gospel. "Christianity is the root of the idea of private property rights. Owning private property is the path out of poverty. Christianity promotes the ideals of the individual. God made each one of us different for a reason. Each one of us is to make our own path by making our own decisions. We can choose to follow God or ignore Him and go our own way. It's called free will.

"And Christianity is the driving force behind the creation of free enterprise. Again, it means each of us finding our own way. Christianity is why we have democracy, allowing for all to participate in deciding our direction. Why? Through these tools man has the capacity to achieve His promise of happiness." As he spoke, he held his hands in the air, and then to make a point, he pounded his fist on the pulpit, making a loud boom. No one was dozing now.

Now he spoke even faster. "The opposite of God's path is a powerful central control in which one force dictates how we shall all live. That is not the teachings of God. Would it shock you to know that such ideas of a powerful central authority making your life decisions is the philosophy of one of the greatest tools of Satan the world has ever know? That tool was Adolph Hitler. His philosophy that he used to create the greatest misery in world history said, "There must be no majority decisions…. But the decisions will be made by one man."

Pastor Dave slowed his speech. It was almost hypnotic. He paused. And then he began again in a hushed tone. "The result of such powerful control over our individual lives has always been pain and misery and darkness over man's progress. Death, destruction, and failure are always the result.

"My fellow Christians, we are witnessing an all out attack on truth and freedom of thought. And that is quickly leading us back to the tyranny of the darkest ages of human history."

"Let me take you on a quick trip through history. The last time the human race was faced with such an attack on reason and free thought was during the Inquisition in the thirteenth century. Then, most of Europe lived under the tyranny of one small self-appointed gang that had used fear to grab power. They alone made decisions about what people were allowed to think or believe. Anyone who disagreed with the gang was charged with heresy and called a lunatic. Most were automatically found guilty and were either ruined, tortured, or killed. People lived in terror. Human progress ground to a halt."

Again he stopped. He looked around at the entire congregation, and then again into the television camera. There was a bit of a cry in his voice as he said, "And now, here again, this tyranny is back. This time, instead of trying to openly repulse religion, they seek to pretend to embrace it, to help them solidify their power over you WITH your help. They are openly seeking you out. They have expressed their policies using language that sounds like the Word and the works of God. They twist words to pretend that protecting species is akin to Noah's Ark. Let me remind you, Noah's Ark was not about protecting species but to destroy the earth because of man's wickedness. A good part of that wickedness which God wanted destroyed was man's effort to control the lives of other people."

Then he held up the new *Saint Gaia's Version of the Green Bible* which the President had just introduced. He slowly moved it from one side to the other so that everyone in the congregation could see it as he said, "They have now created a new bible that is openly anti-Christian. It calls for the massive reduction of human life on Earth. It demands that we accept the guilt that we humans are nothing more than a cancer on nature that must be controlled or eliminated. Think my friends. How will those ideas be used against you and your family? How will this affect your future?"

As he placed the Green bible on the pulpit, he paused for only a moment. "Let me share a story, something that happened just the other day. I was visiting a classroom in a large Christian school here in town. During a break in the classes I sat down to talk with one of the teachers. I asked her about the curriculum being used in the school. She took out her LEAP e-book which had the entire curriculum set up by class subject. She taught biology. She showed me a lesson called 'hug a tree.' It was a game, really, for the kids to play out in the schoolyard. The curriculum called it a Nature Study."

As he told the story, he slowly acted out the parts he was describing. "The students were told to gather around a group of trees. A blindfold was to be put on one child. Then the child was turned around several times. Then, another student was to lead the blindfolded student to a tree. The blindfolded student was then instructed to give the tree a hug and then feel it very carefully and try to learn everything they could about the tree without looking at it. After everyone in the class had done this, they were asked if they could then locate their tree. Then the entire class was instructed to sit on the grass and discuss the experience. During that discussion the teacher was guided to mention that by planting a tree they are actually experiencing the resurrection of Jesus."

Now Pastor Dave shouted in a near rage. "That is not biology. It is not science. It is pagan earth worship. Yet it's in a Christian school curriculum. It's really nothing more than behavior modification. We used to call it brainwashing."

Growing angrier still, the passion and disgust pouring out of his every word, he said, "I asked the teacher if she uses the Bible in her class teachings. She showed me the bible she was using. It was this new Green Bible, not the Bible of our Lord. 'Why this bible?' I asked. She told me that Christian Bibles are no longer available for her e-book." With that, Pastor Dave dramatically threw the Green bible across the stage.

Again he paused and grew quieter as he slowly said, "Now YOU have been targeted to be their next prey. The forces behind this new religion are openly seeking to recruit you into it because they know they can never succeed in ruling the earth unless you join them. They fully believe that, because you blindly worship a God who they consider to be a myth, you are gullible. And they believe that, if they use enough Christian-sounding words and emotions, you will be tricked into following them."

With all the indignation he could muster, Pastor Dave said directly into the camera, "This new religion is not of God. Those who promote it are not believers. They are an evil force that seeks to use you to destroy your own beliefs." Then he said very solemnly, "But we, as Christians, do not worship the creation – we worship the Creator. You must understand this simple truth: The Bible doesn't need to be re-written, it needs to be re-read!

"My friends, Christianity teaches that God created the Earth and that no part of His creation was by mistake or without intent. He created the Earth to benefit humans. We appreciate nature, and certainly believe we must not abuse or damage it. We value the Earth and the bounty it provides. Yes, man has made mistakes in the past as we created new technologies. And it is man who has fixed such mistakes. No other species on Earth works to protect nature. No other species on Earth cares more for the creatures. We learn. We fix our mistakes. That is not evil and it is not sin."

Now, he moved toward his conclusion. "My question to you, my fellow Christians, as you are confronted with the pressure to denounce your faith for this false idol, will you stand with Jesus as the Apostle John did, ready to sacrifice everything for truth? Or will you sell your soul like Judas?"

Again he held his arms over his head, bringing each listener into his embrace. "The future of Christianity is surely at stake. Moreover, the future of our civilized human society is in the balance. Which will you choose? Misery, sacrifice, and false idols?

Or the promise of God Almighty? You alone must choose your path."

Finally, speaking directly into the microphone so that each word echoed around the cathedral he said slowly, "And as you choose, just remember this wisdom from His Holy Word; In Ephesians 6:12, God tells us, *For our struggle is not against flesh and blood, but against the rulers, against the authorities, against the powers of this dark world and against the spiritual forces of evil in the heavenly realms.* Onward my Christian soldiers."

As Pastor Dave walked away from the stage and off his viewers' television sets, there was enthusiastic applause by many, but others weren't so sure about the message they had just heard. Many were asking themselves how so many respected religious leaders could see things so differently from the bombastic Pastor Dave. Did he really mean that the Earth Mother was a false idol? It was all so confusing to understand God's true purpose.

• • • •

The local Grange Hall was packed with farmers and neighbors from the entire county. Jimmy Armond had called a meeting to appeal to them to stand up and take action against the government's shutdown of their irrigation ditches. There was great fear and concern from most; some were even so scared they didn't show up to the meeting. After all, they weren't political activists. Nothing like this had been done before by any of them. How would they possibly know what to do?

"What do we have to lose?" Jimmy cried out to them.

"We are already losing everything we have. Our farms are in ruins. Our families are suffering. Our babies are hungry!

"You know me," he continued. I obey the law. I don't take this lightly. But either we take action now, or we will have to leave our farms and be forced into living in the city. What other choice have they left us? Aren't our farms worth fighting for?"

There was great discussion. Some were obviously scared to defy the government. "We will be arrested," warned Dave Sanders. His family had farmed his property for three generations.

Jimmy put his arm around his long time friend and quietly said, "Dave, we are not the criminals here. We have done nothing wrong. It is a load of crap to suggest we are doing anything to hurt the environment. That's a lie to move us off our land. But I'll tell you this, if we do get arrested then we will finally get our day in court. We sure haven't been able to do that so far." Others began to nod their heads in agreement.

Don Wilson said, "Yes, I know all that is true, but we could be killed. My family needs me."

Another farmer, Eric Sands answered Don. "They're not going to start killing farmers. Not in America."

That's when Danny Spence laughed and said, "What's the matter Don, do you want to live forever?"

That comment made the whole crowd laugh. But Don, without smiling, responded, "Well, we never thought they would cut off our water, but they did. How do we know how far they will go?"

Jimmy Armond again spoke to the gathering. "I believe that if we take this action and take our case to the people of this nation they will be behind us. They are facing empty shelves in their stores. They are facing hunger. We are the ones who provide their food." Others began to agree. Jimmy could tell he was beginning to turn them to his point of view. So he pressed the real issue they had come to decide. "How many of you will join me?"

Dave Sanders asked the question on all of their minds. "What do we do?"

"We pick up our shovels and go straight to the riverbank where the Army Corps of Engineers built the blockage to our irrigation ditches. We dig it out and let the water flow back into our fields."

Don Wilson suggested, "OK. Let's call the news media and tell them what we are going to do so they have their cameras there to report it. That might keep the government boys from taking any dangerous action."

"Is that the best we've got?" asked Bill Jeffers. "Do you really think that's enough to make our case?"

"Well," asked Jimmy of Bill, "What would you do?"

Jeffers looked down at his feet and thought for a moment. "Nope, I've got nothing better."

With that Jimmy said, "Then it's settled. We reopen those ditches." There was enthusiastic response. Somehow it did make them all feel a bit safer.

"OK," said Jimmy. "Tomorrow morning we all meet at

the main channel. Bring your shovels and we'll open it. Eric Sands said he would bring his backhoe" They all cheered and agreed to meet the next morning at 7:00 a.m.

With the news cameras rolling and federal agents watching from a distance, the farmers opened the ditch and water flowed toward their fields. The government took no action. That night, more farmers along the Mississippi saw the news and realized they, too, needed to take action. Within days the movement spread as more and more farmers joined forces to open the irrigation channels to save their crops. The Mississippi Shovel Brigade was born.

• • • •

News Item: As the Gray Bridge Dam in Michigan was removed, fifty homes downriver were flooded and destroyed, forcing the residents to move into government subsidized apartments in the city.

News item: Crime is growing in cities. Vast population growth is overpowering the system and the infrastructure.

News item: Food riots broke out in San Francisco as hungry shoppers became enraged by empty supermarket shelves.

# Chapter 16

There would be no classes today. It was State Teachers' Meeting Day. Brad never really cared much for these days when it seemed all learning stopped and he was forced to sit through the mind-numbing ramblings of education bureaucrats telling him the latest teaching techniques and fads he was supposed to use. So far he had been able to get around them without too much difficulty.

He was snapped out of such boring thoughts by the crackle of the loud-speaker in the classroom. It was Principal Andrews. "Attention all teachers. Please head to the parking lot. The buses are here."

It was starting. Like a condemned prisoner on death row, he slowly, reluctantly, got up and headed out the door toward the buses which would take them all to the huge arena to be joined by more than 10,000 teachers from across the state.

In the parking lot were two big chartered buses waiting, their engines running, pouring out diesel fumes as he and his fellow teachers began to climb aboard. Just getting on was Bill Conrad, who had been teaching economics for over twenty years. Talk about mind-numbing. Just sitting in one of his lectures was a cure for insomnia. How could any human being speak in such a droning voice, thought Brad.

As Brad stepped on the bus, he noted that sitting in the front row, just behind the driver, was Kate Little, the cute young health instructor, fresh out of teacher's college. Brad sometimes talked with her in the teacher's lounge. His impression was that she knew less than her students. Her entire class seemed to focus on the government's new mandated list of tasteless foods being touted as the 'be all and end all' for healthy meals. Tasteless foods and condoms seemed to be Kate's entire curriculum. When did health class stop teaching how the human body worked?

Uh oh, there was an empty seat next to Frank Peterson, the school's excuse for a teacher of literature. The most negative human being Brad had ever met. He always dressed in a tweed jacket and baggy pants and his shirt usually looked like it needed to be washed. That was probably because he appeared to wear the same one every day.

"Brad," said Peterson, "what do you think they're going to throw on us today? They'd better tell us about that raise we were promised. If they want us to spend all day with these brats they need to pay us for the trouble!"

Brad gave a quick, shallow smile and found a seat several rows back.

After an hour-long drive, their two buses arrived in front of the arena where the meeting was to be held. They saw many more buses unloading teachers and school staff members from across the state. The meeting had been announced and promoted for weeks as a major event.

There was great concern across the nation as test scores continued to plummet. Worse, when compared to those in other countries, American kids just weren't cutting it anymore. American students rated 27th in the world in math skills, 15th in reading comprehension, and a dismal 45th in science. The only category where American students excelled was in self-esteem. Apparently, Brad thought cynically, they were proud of being stupid.

There was now a national outcry to do something about this terrible decline. For years the mantra from politicians was "smaller class rooms, more money for schools, and higher pay for teachers." You heard it in every election, at every PTA meeting, in every teachers' meeting. It had become undisputed, acceptable truth – the children aren't learning because they are lost in oversized classes and don't get enough individual attention.

But, Brad noted, while there was a rush to implement these so-called solutions, the resulting test scores showed no improvement. Nothing had changed. There must be some other reason for the failure to learn.

So, over the past year there had been much heavy-duty activity at the top levels of government to come up with a workable solution. All this culminated in President Gravell signing an Executive Order dictating that the education system must be transformed from the bottom up. This, declared the President, "was to be the Decade of Educational Excellence!"

And today, in mass meetings across the nation, teachers

were going to learn firsthand how that excellence was to be achieved. No wonder Brad's headache had returned.

As they took their seats in the giant arena there was a nervous tension in the air. Good or bad, everyone seemed to feel that something major was about to happen. They were all a bit on edge with a feeling of uncertainty, perhaps even dread, which they couldn't explain. Something in the atmosphere of the huge hall felt different from the teachers' meetings they had attended so often.

The stage looked tiny from Brad's seat located high up toward the rafters. To help those in the far seats see all that was going on, located behind the stage were two massive video screens.

The program suddenly began with loud, dramatic music. On the huge screens images appeared of happy children. Some were in classrooms, engaged and involved in science experiments. Others suggested children taking part in the community, cleaning riverbanks and helping the elderly and underprivileged. Still more depicted doctors and firemen standing before large crowds, all with happy faces. Each of these images was pieced together in a giant collage moving forward rapidly as the dynamic music built to a crescendo.

As the music receded, along with the final image of children holding hands across the globe, the round, smiling face of the Federal Secretary of Education appeared, large and imposing. He had taken the stage and stood at the podium.

Now, his voice boomed over the loud speakers, "My fellow teachers, welcome! Today begins a new era in our honored profession. Teachers have always been the conduit to open the doors of the unknown, to lead the children to answers, to secure our future as a society. And we salute you today."

Then his voice went lower and the smile was gone as he said, "But times change. And new challenges arise. And we have to find new ways to meet them, new ways to lead our profession to greater heights." Brad felt his uneasiness grow.

"My fellow teachers," he continued, "I am so excited to share with you today a new era in education. The information we are going to present to you represents nothing short of a new beginning for our society. This is a new way of thinking to assure that the futures of our children are secure -- full of hope, opportunity, and peace.

"We are rapidly moving into a new world that demands international understanding and global awareness with a knowledge and working use of the information explosion. And we need to make sure we have the right tools in our classrooms. We're sometimes far too inclined to cling to the past, the old, comfortable, but out-molded ways. As of today, we move out of the past and into the education system of the future," the Secretary proclaimed with a flourish, receiving strong applause from the gathered teachers. Brad felt a bit stunned by the enthusiastic response. Where was this going?

As the applause died down, the Secretary said, "I want to introduce someone who is going to tell you about the great new direction of our national education system. Then he paused, saying "No – in fact, that's too small a vision for what you are about to hear – this is going to be a global education system," shouted the Education Secretary.

"I'm proud to introduce to you the woman who has been a key leader in developing the dynamic new system that will now guide your classrooms, she is the Director of the Center for Education and Global Interdependence. Please welcome Dr. Beverly Twetcher."

As Dr. Twetcher moved to the podium, her face now filled the massive screen. She was a physically large woman. Frankly, Brad thought, her face reminded him of a nasty bulldog. Her eyes squinted through thick glasses and her thin, graying hair was pulled back in a tight bun. As she began to speak, her voice sounded like fingernails across a blackboard. She looked down at the crowd with a mixed expression of arrogance and disdain, as if she really wanted to be anywhere but here talking to yet another group of lowly high-school teachers.

"Fellow teachers," she began slowly, in an almost disinterested voice, "our education system is failing and we are going to change it. Here's how. We are going to take our bored, unmotivated children and grab hold of them by making education relevant to their modern lives." Brad looked around the room to the faces of his fellow teachers to see if any of them seemed bothered by what they were hearing. He saw no such reaction.

Dr. Twetcher continued, "Here's a modern fact. Our children don't care about what happened in the past. They want to know what we are going to do for them today. They are concerned about their futures. They want to know they will have jobs. And they are looking to us to make sure they are ready for those jobs. That is our duty. That is our mission."

As she said those words, the big screen flashed the

words EMPLOYMENT IS FULFILLMENT! And Dr.
Twetcher shouted out to everyone to say it with her. "EM-
PLOYMENT IS FULFILLMENT." Say it again, she shouted.
"EMPLOYMENT IS FULFILLMENT." Again and again the
teachers shouted the phrase as everyone in the huge hall
picked up the chant. Now Dr. Twetcher seemed to pick up
energy from the crowd.

There was applause in the audience and smiles on
teachers' faces. Yes, they were saying to each other, we have
a mission!

As the room quieted down, she continued, with the
teachers now listening intently. "How do we fulfill that
mission? How do we know who is qualified for which jobs?
Who will be the bakers, the mechanics, and the electricians?
Who will be the scientists, the political leaders and the
teachers to keep us progressing? How do we answer those
questions for them?" she shouted.

Then on the large screen behind her appeared the words
"ANALYZE," "EVALUATE," "SCRUTINIZE." "Yes," said
Dr. Twetcher. "First, we are going to analyze, evaluate, and
scrutinize every single student to find what makes each of
them tick inside. We're going to test and test again to find
the ideas that fill their heads. We need to fully understand
the effect of outside influences on the children so we know
how to deal with it inside our classrooms. Unless we know
how they think we can't reach them with new teaching techniques. Now, with these new teaching tools we are going to
finally focus on changing or eliminating those damaging
ideas that hold them back. That's the first step."

Dr. Twetcher hesitated and took a deep breath as she
prepared for her next words. Finally she said, "Yes, com-

puter technology and testing will, of course, help us in that vital evaluation. But we need to do more. As you well know, the children spend most of their day in our schools. It's becoming the most important influence on their lives. The children need to learn they can trust you, perhaps even more than their parents. After all, you live and work in the same atmosphere as they do. Their parents live in a different world from them. It's up to you to become their most trusted friends so they will feel comfortable sharing their secrets, fears, and dreams. How else can we be an effective force in their lives?"

She continued, "One of the great failings in our education system is our insistence that we dwell on the past." Now Brad felt his chest tighten. Where was she going with this? Twetcher's next words provided the horrible answer.

"For hundreds of years education has focused on one thing, academics," she proclaimed with distain in her voice. "We have wasted the children's time learning events and dates from a distant past that mean nothing to them. How can they be expected to relate to times that had no electricity, modern transportation, or even cell phones? And of what good is it to drill into their heads poetry and literature that use words and ideas irrelevant to their lives?"

Now Dr. Twetcher was fully involved in the part of the presentation that interested her most, "You know if students are interested in learning those things there is nothing to keep them from exploring. The information is readily available to them on the Internet. They can spend their own time learning anything they want." But," she said in a near whisper, "it's a crime to waste their time in our classrooms filling their heads with pointless information for which they will probably never have a use."

Then on the great screen blasted the words, DWELL-
ING ON THE PAST HOLDS US BACK! "Say it with me,"
she shouted. "DWELLING ON THE PAST HOLDS US
BACK!" Again, the chant took over the great arena.

As the chant fell away, Dr. Twetcher slowly intoned, "We
intend to throw out all of the old ways and start over. We
will diligently track the attitudes, values, and beliefs of the
children to make sure they are all learning together. They
will learn to accept each other as equals. They will learn
that there is no room for destructive, selfish individuality.
Instead, they will come to understand that everyone working as a team is how we will move forward as a people. Their
minds will be kept uncluttered and open to our leadership
so they will readily accept our new instructions and become
more efficient and more trainable for the jobs our society
needs them to perform. And, as a result, peace, hope, and
opportunity will be there for every student."

Again, Brad looked around the room, desperate to see
if anyone was reacting to this as he was. Why weren't these
other teachers sharing his disbelief? What they were hearing was the utter destruction of the entire education system,
a system that had been developed over centuries. This was
not education, he thought to himself. This was psychology
designed to manipulate the minds of the students.

Now Dr. Twetcher came to her final words. "You are
being given a huge responsibility. From this day forward,
the future of our human society depends on how well
you accept your new mission. My fellow teachers, in your
classrooms you will build a new citizen -- a global citizen.
To achieve that goal, we are moving from the old academic
education to a new, revolutionary, values education."

As the teachers again began to applaud, onto the mas-

sive screen came the bold letters MEETING THE CHAL-
LENGE! CULTURE, CONTINUITY, CHANGE! "My
fellow teachers," said Twetcher in a booming, triumphant
voice, "say it with me. MEETING THE CHALLENGE!
CULTURE, CONTINUITY, CHANGE!"

"That," she said, "is your mission!" She left the stage
with the teachers still chanting, applauding and cheering.
All, except one. Brad Jackson couldn't move. He could only
sit there, stunned.

On the bus ride home most were upbeat and excited
from the meeting. But Brad spoke to no one. His mind was
racing, thinking about all that he had just heard and wanting to disbelieve that it had even been said.

Then he thought back to the conversation at Christmas
with his brother Mike. Brad knew that Mike was part of a
radical political movement that found conspiracies in every
change of society. Brad usually dismissed what he said, but
there was no denying that what the teachers had just been
told was nearly identical to Mike's fears.

Suddenly, in his mind he heard another distant voice,
"They let you say such things in the classroom…you won't
be allowed to do it much longer. Teaching basic academics
to enable children to think and grow on their own is a danger to the Order. Changes are coming. You won't be permitted to teach such things much longer. Academics are being
replaced with social engineering…you'll soon learn that
your academic skills are about to become irrelevant."

It was the homeless man in the park. What was his
name, thought Brad. Harold, yes that was it. Again Brad
thought, how did he know this? Who is he? Why was he

talking to the kids that day? Why were they listening to him? It now became a matter of urgency for Brad to find him and learn what he knew.

As he rode home in the dark bus, he also thought about his meeting with John Lloyd and the unshakable suspicion that a whole idea of individuality was being removed from books. That's almost exactly what was said today. Plus Dr. Twetcher had basically said academics were no longer to be part of the curriculum. That, thought Brad, was the death of knowledge, just as his brother Mike had warned. He had thought both of them were way off-base. Now he realized he was the one who had been out of touch.

The bus ride home felt intolerably long. Brad now had his own mission. Find that homeless man. Find out what was happening in his school, in his own classroom to his students. Above all, figure out what could he do to stop this.

As he entered the door of their apartment, Kate sensed a change in Brad. He said nothing as he stormed by her and closed the door to his small office where he sat for hours, just thinking. Finally he crawled into bed where sleep eluded him.

• • • •

A large crowd had gathered in Times Square along with an impressive representation of the news media. On the sidewalk in front of a store, a small stage had been erected that was brightly decorated in red ribbons and bunting billowing in the breeze. A microphone was placed in the middle of the stage. Across the top of the storefront was a tarp that hid what was underneath. Across the front door was a wide red ribbon tied with a large bow.

At exactly twelve noon, John Lloyd and Peter Arter

stepped up on the stage and greeted the crowd. "Today," began Peter, "marks a new era in the publishing industry. From this day forward you can enter a supermarket of books, make your selection and then you can decide what format you want. You can download it in our new e-book as you have been doing online, or you can choose to have it in printed book form, which we will produce for you, instantly, right here in the store."

Then John Lloyd took the microphone and said, "There are three more, very different offerings -- dare I say revolutionary offerings -- from this new store that have not existed until now. First, we are now working around the clock to make sure that very soon every book ever written and published will be available for your e-books. No more frustration from the dreaded message, NOT AVAILABLE. Second, each book will come with a guarantee that the downloaded book is accurate and unchanged from the original published version, just as the author wrote it. And third, each of our e-books comes with special software to prevent any possible changes without the author's permission."

As the crowd applauded enthusiastically, Lloyd indicated he had one more thing to add. "To the representatives of the news media who have gathered, I want to announce a couple more developments. First, my company and Peter's are filing a joint lawsuit against LEAP claiming damages from their inaccurate publishing of books. And second, we are calling on Congressman Albert Morris, Chairman of the House Committee on Intellectual Property to begin immediate Congressional hearings to investigate possible LEAP racketeering practices designed to destroy the publishing industry. We intend to once again create a publishing industry that readers can trust to provide them with unlimited and accurate access to ideas from across the ages!"

With that announcement, Peter Arter again took the

mic and said, "It's time to introduce to you the very first of the stores that will soon be spreading to communities and shopping malls across the nation. Ladies and gentlemen, I present the Buy Right Book Supermarket!" With that, Lloyd pulled the rope to remove the tarp to reveal the *Buy Right* logo across the front of the store. Then Peter Arter took the large ceremonial scissors and cut the ribbon as the front doors swung open and the crowd flooded in.

Unlike their first news conference, this time the news media couldn't wait to start throwing questions at them, especially about the charges against LEAP. To prove his charge that LEAP was changing the books, Lloyd was only too happy to present Brad Jackson's blog as evidence.

As Peter watched, the crowd enthusiastically began to order books and the cash registers started ringing. He began to plan to open ten more stores as fast as he could get them underway. The war with LEAP was finally underway.

# Chapter 17

As the demolition of dams accelerated across the country, the communities in the most rural areas were the first to feel the greatest consequences. It started with the flooding of homes, forcing the residents to move out. Next, came cuts in jobs, first in the recreational industry as boating and fishing were stopped. Then the local power plants began layoffs of workers. Eventually some of the plants themselves were forced to close, leaving many areas without power, again causing residents to flee, usually to the cities, which were the only destinations left to them. A drive through many back roads was becoming a depressing tour of ghost towns.

But as most headed to the cities, a small number of courageous residents headed to the banks of the Mississippi to join the protesting farmers of Jimmy Armond's Shovel Brigade. The Shovel Brigade had been able to open a few of the irrigation channels to allow water to flow into those fields. New sprouts of wheat were beginning to poke through the ground giving expectation of a much-needed harvest. However, with each new government action the pressure was building within the ranks of the protesters to take stronger action to fight back. Still, Jimmy and his fellow Shovel Brigade leaders held out hope that such strong action wouldn't be necessary. But, their hope was beginning to dim as the BLM troops facing the farmers continued to grow in number.

Meanwhile there was a growing protest among citizens across the country who supported the farmers. Surprisingly, with each new government action, the apathy of so many of the people who had allowed the government to gain such power, was giving way to a visible opposition. Why, they kept asking, would the government take such drastic measures to destroy their homes, their communities, and their livelihoods? Why destroy the infrastructure of the nation? Why cause food shortages? Who was benefiting, they wanted to know. What was the end game?

Thousands had now taken to Facebook, Twitter, and other social media to express their outrage. There was now a large email campaign to gather petitions to apply pressure on Congress and demand that it come to the aid of the embattled farmers, and to reopen all the irrigation channels and stop the destruction of dams. So strong were the growing ranks of the protesters that even the news media was forced to report their actions on the nightly news.

To help encourage locally elected officials to take direct action, Voice of Adams leader, Mack Richards, began to travel to affected communities up and down the Mississippi. He met with city councilmen, mayors, and county commissioners; many of whom were nervous and afraid to stand up against the federal rules.

Richards told them, "You don't have to sit there and cower in a corner, afraid to act. Stand up and protect your communities and your people as you were elected to do. This is how tyranny wins," he warned again and again. His anger was hard to control as he witnessed their immobilizing fear of action.

In one community he scolded the officials for their inaction saying, "One doesn't take the freest society on earth and turn it into a sniveling pile of paralyzing fear without firing a shot, as this government has done. For that to happen they need the sanction of the victims. They need you to voluntarily give up your property, your wealth, and your liberty. And that is exactly what you are doing as you sit there afraid to stand up to them."

In another community he was confronted by a belligerent county commissioner who attempted to lecture Richards on the morality of the policies that were changing the nation in order to protect the environment. Richards stared at him for a moment, clinching his fist behind his back as he gathered his thoughts.

Finally, in a controlled voice, he said, "Our cities, once vibrant and alive with men who understood that man's progress was his greatest achievement, are now slipping into silent decay. Vital services we all need in order to survive are beginning to break down. Vast amounts of our land are being locked away and our great factories are in rusting ruins as our economy is on the verge of collapse. And you tell me this is moral?"

Stepping in front of the Commissioner, getting right into his face, Richards went on, "And what is this morality you are selling? That it's OK for a beaver to build a dam, but not for man? That it's OK for a wolf to hunt, but not for man? That it's OK for a lion to eat meat, but not for man? You, sir, are perpetrating hysteria and fear, using the environment as the excuse for one purpose and one purpose only – the subjugation of the people for the sake of power. Look at what you've done as a result of your own arrogance in believing that you know more of how people should live than they do themselves. You've only achieved misery, taxes, and death for your own people. One thing is true about the natural environment -- other animals don't turn against their own species to force its destruction."

As Richards finished, several of the gathered Commissioners simply stood there with their mouths open. No one had ever addressed their destructive policies before in quite that way.

Meanwhile, Interior Secretary Phyllis Jasper continued to appear in front of news cameras calling for calm, and delivering the government's party line that all was well, even as she became more and more aware of the coming disaster that was growing on the shores of the Mississippi. In one interview her own fear and frustration showed as she pleaded with the protesters to disperse and not challenge the government. "I fear the consequences for you," she said. Silently she also was beginning to fear as much for herself, feeling trapped inside the belly of the beast called Eric Gravell's Administration.

• • • •

It was Brad's first day back in the classroom after the teacher's meeting. As if he weren't agitated enough from that experience, the first thing he now saw as he sat at his desk was his teacher's copy of the new LEAP e-textbooks that all of the students were to receive.

With a bit of trepidation, considering what the teachers had been told at the meeting about the new curriculum, he began to look through the contents. He happened to open to the section on civics education, and specifically to the area dealing with the Bill of Rights.

As he looked over the part discussing the First Amendment in dealing with freedom of speech, he read, "Freedom of expression is no more sacred than freedom from intolerance or bigotry." It went on to say that expressing 'dangerous' ideas was a threat to the peace and security of the nation. Brad's feeling of dread began to return.

He looked to see what it had to say about the Second Amendment and the right to keep and bear arms. It wasn't there. The Second Amendment to the Constitution of the United States was simply not mentioned in the new curriculum for teaching American civics.

Now in a near panic, he flipped through the section to find the Declaration of Independence. There was only one mention of that historic founding document. It said simply that the Declaration of Independence was nothing more than a political statement and, indeed, just a petition to the King of England. The actual document was not provided. Instead, there was a copy of the United Nation's Universal Declaration of Human Rights.

"What have they done?" he shouted aloud. Gone were the two most important documents in American History. Gone was the groundwork for the nation's philosophy of government. Gone was the document which specifically laid out the system to organize that philosophy into a government.

Brad sat there in the still of the room, just staring into empty space. After some time had passed he came out of his thoughts enough to look down at the e-book and noticed something wet on the screen. It was then he realized he was crying. Almost as a reflex, he stood and violently threw the LEAP e-textbook to the floor and it shattered. "How dare they?" he shouted.

He sat down at his desk, troubled by his thoughts. "What do I do? I can't teach such outrageous ideas. I cannot and I will not," he said to himself in growing frustration and defiance.

Then, in his mind, he heard it again. The voice of the homeless man in the park, "You'll soon learn that your academic skills are about to become irrelevant."

"Who is he?" Brad said again to himself. "I've got to find him."

At lunch that same day he returned to the park to see if the man was there. He wasn't. So Brad wrote a note that said, "I need to talk to you. Please contact me." He included his phone number. He then taped the note to the park bench.

Several days passed and Brad heard nothing from the man. Many more attempts to leave a note produced nothing. Finally Brad got a crazy idea. With little hope of success, he placed a classified ad in the local paper, "Imperative I talk with you. Please reply. The teacher you met in the park."

Again, several days passed. Then, returning to the park one more time, he noticed a newspaper on the bench. Brad walked over, picked up the newspaper, and unfolded it. He was surprised to see that the paper opened right to the page containing his ad. There, written in red maker over his ad was an address and a time of day, and it was simply signed "H."

• • • •

The reaction to Pastor Dave's sermon had been mixed. He had hoped that it would help unite the Christian leaders behind his cause and bring an organized effort against those forces he saw as a threat to Christianity. It didn't happen. While many of his congregation and TV viewers were moved and did begin to speak out, many others were clearly afraid to act or just confused. Pastor Dave was now constantly and viciously condemned on the twenty-four-hour news networks. Recognized leaders of the church were interviewed, each calling him a radical and "out of touch" with their mission to bring "peace and sanity" to the world. His phone rang with angry callers and his mailbox was full of nasty letters accusing him of advocating the evil destruction of the Earth Goddess.

The strongest voice against him was Shawn Trent, the head of the Religious Partnership for Justice that had sponsored the New York gathering. During one particular interview that was being repeatedly broadcast on CNS News, Trent's normally serene look had changed to that of one who professed to be deeply offended and hurt. In his deep voice, sounding like it was on the verge of cracking from emotion, he said, "We have created a new understanding among our great religions. That is historic. They've fought among themselves for centuries, sometimes violently. And now, for the first time, they are all working together for the good of the Earth. But this TV preacher is determined to destroy that historic peace and goodwill. Well, I assure you our alliance is strong and we will stop Pastor Dave Delray by any means possible."

But the verbal attacks didn't stop Pastor Dave. He was just as determined to expose what he knew was a great threat to the very foundation of God's teaching. Week after week, from his television pulpit he pounded on what he called the lies and pagan teachings of the Religious Partnership for Justice. He began digging into its sources of funding, showing a spider web of financial connections from some very suspicious resources with no previous religious interests. "Why do these forces want to control the Word of God?" he challenged in one of his weekly broadcasts. "What's the end game?"

Though the attacks against him increased as more and more members of the Partnership took up the fight, Pastor Dave took great delight in learning that he was starting to make progress. The latest reports showed that his television audience for his weekly broadcasts was clearly beginning to grow. Someone was listening, he thought.

His next action was to organize protests and boycotts of Christian bookstores that were found to be selling the new *St. Gaia Version of the Green Bible*. He would announce a location for a protest, and as large crowds gathered, Pastor Dave would show up in front of the store, bullhorn in hand, demanding that the store stop selling such blasphemy under the name of Christianity. He was now affecting sales.

That didn't go unnoticed inside the Gravell Administration. Discussions had already begun about finding an expedient ways of removing him from the airways for distributing hate speech.

• • • •

There was a new blast of graffiti. This time it was written right over the front doors of the Federal Department of Education. Glowing in the familiar fluorescent red paint it read: **"America's future vanishes with America's past."**

# Chapter 18

As usual, Steven Daniels just walked into Secretary Jasper's office as she was meeting with her senior staff to discuss the growing violence springing up around the nation over the restrictive farming regulations and food shortages.

As Jasper was talking, Daniels pushed his way to her desk and plopped down a stack of papers. "These just came over from the White House," said Daniels with a sneer.

It took courage for Jasper to respond. "You're interrupting my meeting," she said with undisguised irritation. "You're going to have to either make an appointment or at least start knocking. I'm not going to have you just walk in to my office anytime you please. Do you understand, Mr. Daniels?"

Daniels simply smirked and basically ignored her. "These are from the White House. These are your latest action orders. Do you want me to tell the President that you're too busy to be bothered by his orders?" sneered Daniels.

Jasper picked up the papers and began to read.  As she looked over the paper, she almost fell back into her seat in complete disbelief of what she was reading. The Order addressed to Secretary Jasper stated, "The Department of Interior will take immediate action through the Bureau of Land Management, the Army Corp of Engineers, the Forest Service, and the Fish and Wildlife Service, to implement plans to begin the removal of people now living in rural areas, including those who lack basic water and food supplies, rely on septic systems rather than central plumbing, or lack communication services such as cell and cable services. These people living in such backward rural areas are taxing the government's ability to feed and service them. In these troubled times, they have become a burden on the taxpayers of this nation. Many are now posing possible threats of violence. Therefore, they will be removed from their lands and resettled in major cities across the country for their own safety and for the good of the nation. Please organize a plan for such action within the next two weeks and have the details delivered to my office for approval." It was signed by President Gravell.

An intense anger began to grow in Phyllis Jasper. She looked at the others from her staff now gathered around her desk. A look of concern was on each of their faces as they watched her reaction to the document Daniels had basically thrown at her.

"Ladies and gentlemen," Jasper said in a voice that quivered on the verge of losing control, "please excuse me. I have to go the White House right now."

As she got up from her desk, Daniels stood in her way. "You can't do that," he said, putting up his hand like a traffic cop. Jasper looked at his hand and then at Daniels and said, "You mealy-mouthed little toady, get out of my way or prepare to lose that hand."

Daniels' mouth fell open and in an almost involuntary reaction he stepped back as Jasper rushed out of the room.

•  •  •  •

Brad searched for the address written in the newspaper and was now standing in front of a run down building in a rather unpleasant area of town. As he stood, trying to decide if he should try the door now or simply walk away, he smelled something like gas and then everything instantly went black.

He awoke unable to see or move his arms. He was lying on his side and the surface was hard and rocking him back and forth. He felt the vibration of movement and then heard what sounded like a running motor. Then a car horn honked. "I'm in a vehicle," he thought. Then he smelled the gas again and blacked out.

When he woke again, he found himself sitting upright in a chair. He could hear activity around him. He felt a chill and sounds echoed, as in a large warehouse. He tried to move, but his arms were bound and he realized his sight was blocked because of a blindfold.

Now he became aware of someone standing close to him and then heard a voice saying, "I'm sorry for the cloak and dagger stuff but I've got to be very careful." It was Harold, the homeless man. "I had to be sure we didn't reveal where we are."

Brad said almost in a cry, "Why have you done this to me?"

Harold answered with his own question. "Why did you want to see me?"

"That day in the park when we talked, you said some things to me that I didn't believe, but now many have come to pass. I need to know how you knew that would happen. I need to know who you are. That's why I wanted to see you."

Harold smiled a bit as he heard the frustration and tinge of fear in Brad's voice. That's what happens, he thought, when your world is suddenly shattered and you don't understand why. Harold Riggers knew that feeling well.

After a few moments, he said to Brad, "What happened to open your eyes?"

"Please," said Brad, "can't you remove this blindfold and untie my hands? Why have you done this to me?"

"It's necessary for your safety and mine," replied Harold. "Both of our lives are in danger by your being here. Did you tell anyone you were looking for me?"

"No," answered Brad. "I told nobody. I just need to know..."

"OK," said Harold, "I'll remove the blindfold and we can talk. But you must understand that you're responsible for you're own safety. And you must keep what you see to yourself."

"Agreed," said Brad. "I promise you can trust me."

With that Harold untied his hands and Brad pulled off the blindfold. Squinting from the sudden rush of light into his eyes, he looked around his surroundings and was shocked by what he saw.

He hadn't expected it. He was sitting in the middle of an old rundown warehouse. Bright lights were shining from bare bulbs in the ceiling. The real surprise came from realizing that they were not alone. There were several young people working at benches. And he recognized that they were some of the students he had seen talking to Riggers in the park that day. They were busy working with large pieces of cardboard. They looked like they were making signs. No, thought Brad, not signs, those are stencils!

"What in the world is going on?" he said as he continued to look around the huge room. Then he saw a sight that really stunned him. Stacked against the walls were a series of used stencils stained with a familiar color of florescent red paint. One said, "Check Your Premise." Another said, "The Power of One."

Brad slowly turned to look at Harold with his mouth wide open. "You…you're the graffiti bandit."

"Yes," said Harold hesitantly. "That's what the news has been calling me."

"Why? Why do you do that? What is this all about? What are you doing with these kids? WHO ARE YOU?" Brad demanded to know.

"It's a long story," said Harold in a weary voice. "Before I can answer your questions, please answer mine. Why did you want to see me? What happened?"

"OK," answered Brad. And he proceeded to tell of the teacher's meeting and the new anti-academics curriculum. And then he told him about the new LEAP e-textbook and the missing history.

"You told me that day in the park that I wouldn't be able to teach my history lessons much longer. You said I would become irrelevant. How did you know that? I need to know. I need to understand what is happening," said Brad almost pleading.

Harold began slowly. "I think you are an honorable man, Brad Jackson. So, I'm going to tell you my story, but after we part today you will never see me again, for your safety and mine. I'm going to reveal information to you that hardly anyone else in this world knows and most of whom have known or learned of it are now dead. In fact, the last person that I shared some of this information with was found murdered in Utah not long ago."

Now Harold stopped, and studied Brad's face, then asked, "Do you want me to continue, or do you want me to send you home to remain ignorant and innocent of this information?"

"I have to know," answered Brad.

"Well, there is one more demand that I must make of you," said Harold. "It is also a matter of life and death that you will not reveal the involvement of any of these students. Frankly, I've endangered them letting you come here and see them. But I think I have judged you well enough to know you have great respect for their wellbeing. If certain people find out they are here with me, it will destroy their lives. You and they will face a sure death sentence. Do you understand?"

Brad took a deep breath and could only nod acceptance.

With that, Harold began to tell his story. He seemed relieved and even a bit anxious to share it. His was a lonely and hidden existence, void of friends and family, except for the students who were here now.

"My full name is Harold Riggers. For a number of years I worked for the federal government. I started with the FBI. I did my job well. I followed the rules. Eventually I moved into counter-espionage, digging out potential spies who sought to steal the secrets of our nation. Over the course of time, I began to see in some of the stolen secrets very troubling information.

"This included details about some who have plans to destroy our nation from within. According to the information I received they intend to change our entire system of government and give themselves the power to dictate how the rest of us would live. They would control the economy, the money supply, commerce, food supplies, even where and how we live. It was a massive plan. Frankly, to just tell it to someone it simply sounds like lunacy. Who would believe me?

"But in time, I came to know the plans along with the names of many of the perpetrators. These were high-up officials, trusted and respected in the nation. And there were specific connections with forces outside the government who seemed to be even more powerful. They controlled the money, and in many cases they controlled the government officials.

"I didn't know what to do. Who could I turn to? Who could I trust to even discuss it? I knew I certainly couldn't trust my supervisors. If they were holding positions in this government, there was a strong possibility that they were in on it. That's the way it works, you see. No one and no decision is left to chance by these people.

Over time, I learned that one of my colleagues was gathering the same information and was as concerned as I. Slowly we began to trust each other and share information. We started to research everything for ourselves and to confirm that the information we had acquired from the spy documents was, in fact, true." Harold paused for a few seconds, as though reliving some of those discussions in his mind.

"After many sleepless nights, my colleague, Eugene Trent, came to me. He was very agitated and I could see his fear. He said that we had to get this information into the hands of someone in Congress who could take action. It had to be someone who was very independent and a strong opponent to this administration. Eugene was such a great patriot. He loved this country and didn't want to see it destroyed by these people.

"So, I agreed to help him. We decided the best way was to write a detailed report, leaving out nothing. We needed to provide every detail, give dates and locations of the meetings, just like the spies had reported to their own governments. And above all we had to supply the names of everyone involved.

"Then we planned to deliver the report to several Members of Congress with whom we had some dealings. People we trusted, people who would believe and trust us.

"We outlined the entire plan to change the nation, at

least as much as we knew. We exposed some very powerful people. It took us several months to prepare it. We researched every single detail to assure its accuracy. We knew that if these evil people were ever able to lie their way out of our accusations because of questionable evidence, then our entire effort would be destroyed. They are good at destroying people, to this very day. They do it regularly. They won't hesitate to take whatever action is necessary to keep their secret and their hold on power."

Harold paused, as if thinking of details not considered for a long time.

"How long ago was this?" asked Brad.

"Over two years ago," answered Harold.

"Well, then, what happened to your report?"

Harold sighed, and then began to speak slowly, in a quiet tone. "Somehow they found out about us. I still don't know how. We were so careful. But just as we were ready to deliver the report, they struck. They killed Eugene. I knew they were coming for me, so I got out of there as fast as I could."

"But, what happened to your report?" asked Brad. "Do you still have a copy?"

"No," said Harold. I hid it on the Internet under a code name. I named it ERASE. Then I left town, leaving behind all of my possessions and anything they could use to trace me. I went completely off the grid. My FBI training had taught me how to hide. That's why I don't have a home, a phone, or a computer. I ceased to exist."

"Then what is all of this about?" asked Brad, waving his arm around the warehouse.

Harold answered, "The only way I had to communicate and try to issue a warning and create some opposition to what is happening was to paint messages on walls. It has gotten attention. The government is getting nervous about it. That's why I've stepped it up, putting the messages directly on government walls. It forces them to look over their shoulders. I guess you could call it psychological warfare. It works well on a guilty conscience, I'm told," Harold said with a chuckle. "That's all I could hope for."

"But what do the messages mean?" asked Brad. "Such as The Power of One or Check Your Premise? How does that reveal anything of their plot?"

"Well, you see, Brad," said Harold, almost sounding like the teacher himself, "one of their main targets is changing the way we think."

"How?" asked Brad.

"That's where you come into the story. They intend to change the way people think by eliminating knowledge. The best way to do that is to control the curriculum in schools by replacing academics with social engineering. It only takes one generation to completely erase a nation's history. Once you do that the nation forgets who it is or who it was.

"And you just learned in your teacher's meeting how it will be implemented. They are slowly eliminating individuality and personal creativity, the most valuable and unique qualities of the United States of America. Gone! The result is our young people are slowly being turned into perfect

Global Village Idiots, void of individual thought, completely pliable, and indoctrinated to the point of accepting any
voice of authority without questioning it. That's the point of
my graffiti – to keep those ideas of individuality alive until
someone can take action to stop this evil."

Brad just sat there taking it all in. Under any other
circumstances he would have argued that it simply wasn't
possible to enforce such an outrageous plot on his country.
This was a nation of free thinkers and proud of it. But after
attending the teachers' meeting and seeing the new e-text
book, he now had to believe it. After all, here was a man
who had seen his entire life destroyed trying to stop it.

Then Brad asked the question that kept churning in his
mind. "How do they think they can stop knowledge? It's
there, no matter what."

Harold thought for a moment, and then said, "They stop
knowledge by banning it."

There was silence for a few seconds. Brad didn't even
know how to respond to that. Then Harold continued. "The
powers in charge of this drive to control understand that
the ideas of educated individuals are their greatest threat.
They have concluded that there is simply too much knowledge and it must be stopped for them to succeed. So they
have created a system of thought control they call, 'Globally
Acceptable Truth.' This dictates the things we are allowed
to believe. This assures that bad thoughts are controlled or
obliterated. For it to work, the rest of us must be convinced
or forced to stop thinking or using our own life experienc-
es, along with academic and scientific absolutes. That way
we can no longer be able to draw our own conclusions. In
other words, we no longer have the ability to question their
authority."

Again Harold paused. Then he said, "Once such control of thinking is established, it's just a short journey to rejecting morality and losing the ability to know right from wrong. Then they set themselves up as the answer."

Brad's mind was in turmoil. It was just too crazy to even be able to fathom such evil minds that could create such a plan. Then a thought occurred to him and he asked earnestly, "Why are they trying to destroy their own food supplies and destroy the farmers that provide what we all need, including them? What do they gain from that?"

Harold smiled and said simply, "It makes people more desperate as they look for answers. They become more dependent and consequently more pliable. Government becomes the answer to every question. That is the root of their power. Fear and need."

Then Brad's attention was drawn back to the students who were now hard at work on the stencils. "What about them?" he asked. "Where do they fit in to all of this? Why are they here with you?"

Harold looked over at the students and got a tear in his eye. "Don't you understand? It's their future that's being destroyed. They are here because they want to stop it so they can choose their own."

Then he added, "Brad, you know history. Do you know about the White Rose?"

Brad thought for a moment. "Do you mean the students who fought Hitler?"

"Yes, they distributed anti-Nazi literature and painted

anti-Hitler graffiti on walls to defy him and to give the German people a message of defiance to the dictatorship."

"Yes," said Brad. "Yes, they were a true voice of freedom during that black time."

"Well, said Harold, waving his arm toward the students, "these are our White Rose. I couldn't do this without them. They are the reason I can cover so much territory in one night. And that really puts the fear of the unknown into the enemy."

Brad had just one more question. "Who is that enemy, Harold?"

"The enemy is vast, but you are well aware of one of the leading forces involved. You hear of them every day in the news and now you are dealing with them directly in your classroom."

"Who?" pleaded Brad.

"It's no secret, said Harold. "It's called LEAP."

Brad just blinked and shook his head. "LEAP? Well, just who are they? I thought they were just book publishers. What do they want?"

Harold looked at him with a devilish twinkle in his eye as he said, "Don't you know? LEAP stands for League to Eliminate America's Past."

# Chapter 19

Phyllis Jasper took the White House by storm. At least that's the way it seemed to the Marine guard at the side entrance. There were certainly storm clouds covering the look on her face. As she rushed toward him he simply stood to the side and opened the door for her with a smart salute. She was, after all, the Secretary of the Interior.

As she rushed up to the receptionist outside the Oval Office she simply said, "Is he in?"

The receptionist said, "Yes he is, but you can't…" that was all she got out as Jasper rushed past her and threw open the door to the most famous and most powerful office in the world. This time its assumed power appeared to be no match for her fury.

President Gravell had been sitting at his desk, with his back to the door, talking on the phone. As the door flew open he spun to face her. One look at her fury and he said into the phone, "I'll call you back," and hung up.

"Phyllis, what's wrong, asked the President with his own look of alarm.

"Mr. President," she nearly shouted, "with all due respect, are you out of your mind?"

"What...?" was all he could get out before she started a verbal assault rarely heard by a sitting president.

"You want me to use the power of my agency to initiate force against a bunch of farmers? And you want me to move them all into the city? I repeat, are you out of your mind?"

Gravell, now growing upset himself said, "Those people are dangerous. They may break into violence at any time. I've got to defuse the situation. It's for the good of the country."

"Mr. President," hissed Jasper, "what did you expect when you issued Executive Orders to destroy their livelihood, their private property, and their economy? I warned you this would happen. Now you're tearing down dams, destroying their homes, and cutting off their electricity. How do you expect them to live?"

Now Gravell stood and walked around to the front of his desk, getting very close to Jasper, saying, "I don't expect them to live there. As I told you in my memo, I expect you to move them off that land, defuse the situation, and bring them to live in the cities where they will have the food and electricity they need, and where we can keep a watchful eye on them. And I expect you to carry out my orders, Madam Secretary." Gravell was now openly angry at her challenge.

"Again, Mr. President, I ask you, if you destroy the farmers and force them into the cities, where do you think that food is going to come from? Did you miss Economics 101 in college? Farmers grow the food that people in the cities eat. That food doesn't magically appear in the backroom of a Safeway grocery," she said with a sneer.

"Phyllis," Gravell said, now with almost a whine in his voice, "we are making big changes in the way this nation operates. For the safety of the people and the planet, we need to make sure everyone is living inside our system. We can't have renegades making their own rules or living independent of our systems. That causes chaos and anarchy. Under my new system, we will live more efficiently, using less energy and less open space. Government will run more efficiently as people are brought together for their common needs. And every community will be responsible for providing all of their own necessities, right inside the city limits, including food and energy. So, of course we'll need those experienced farmers in the cities." Gravell stopped and looked as Jasper, daring her to respond.

Phyllis just looked at him, her mouth open, unable to say anything. Finally she said, "Are you telling me that you plan to reduce this nation to nothing more than a bunch of cities, like feudal states?"

"No," not exactly," said Gravell. "We will have local councils that directly oversee it all and they will answer directly to the central government. But don't you see, we've got to control the population and protect the environment or we will not be able to survive on this planet. I'm just doing what needs to be done," he said, now almost pleading for her understanding.

"Mr. President, you are talking about a revolution to change our system of government and destroy our way of life. At this very moment, because of your policies, we have food riots taking place in your precious cities, the infra-structure – especially water, sewer and electricity are shut-ting down -- and people on the verge of revolt. People are going to die, Mr. President."

"Well, of course, there will be some turmoil. It's neces-sary because there are those who just won't listen to reason and will refuse to help us help them to a better life. It's un-fortunate, but necessary if we are going to succeed."

Jasper stood there for a moment, thinking about her next move, because she knew it was going to be dangerous. Finally she said, "Mr. President, you appointed me Secre-tary of the Interior, not secretary of cities. I intend to do my job. I will not help you destroy lives and property. I will not use the firepower of the departments under me to kill Americans who are just trying to protect their rights and their property. I believe there is a higher law, Mr. President. One that you swore to uphold and protect! You might want to read it sometime. It's sitting just down the street at the National Archives."

Gravell sat down on the edge of his desk. No one had ever talked to him this way, certainly not in the Oval Office. Slowly he began to respond, using all of the force of his of-fice. "You will follow my orders or I will fire you as Secretary of the Interior."

As he said those words, Gravell looked straight at Jasper, expecting to see either fear or regret on her face. Instead he saw even greater defiance as Jasper said, "Go ahead. But you have already lost one Secretary of the Interior in the past few months. How will it look to lose the second one so soon? And I promise you this, if you put me on the street

I will go to the news media and tell them exactly why you fired me! No, Mr. President, I'm not going anywhere. I'm going to serve the people of this nation as I swore I would do."

Gravell just stood there, unsure how to reply. As Jasper began to leave, she turned and said, "Oh yes, one more thing, you will get your puppet Daniels out of my office and you will deal directly with me from now on." With that, Jasper turned and left the Oval Office.

As the door closed, Gravell made a fast phone call to the Department of the Interior. "Daniels," he said, "order the BLM to take direct action on those Mississippi rabble-rousers and get rid of them now. And say nothing to Jasper." Then he dialed another number. When the party answered, Eric Gravell said, "I've got some serious trouble. I think it's urgent that we meet."

• • • •

Brad rushed home from his meeting with Harold Riggers. Of course, the students had blindfolded him again and driven him around town to hide their location before dropping him off in front of the school. At least this time he didn't have to be bound or knocked out.

His mind was racing, thinking about all that Harold had revealed to him. It was such a fantastic tale. Could any of it be true? But so much of it made sense considering all that he had seen and heard in the past few weeks. It certainly helped to connect the dots to the new education policies. It's just nuts, he thought. But now he had to get to the bottom of it and find out the truth. Was there such a secret report that had all of the answers? If so, he needed to find it, but how?

And what about the things Harold had told him about LEAP. Then he thought of his meeting with John Lloyd. He had said LEAP was bad news. It was then that Brad knew what his first step needed to be. Call John Lloyd and tell him what he had learned. Maybe he would know what to do with the information.

The second call he made was to his brother Mike, remembering what he said at Christmas. Mike, too, had warned him about the education system. Both Lloyd and Mike agreed to meet him in two nights at his apartment.

However, neither of them showed up alone. John Lloyd arrived with Peter Arter, the head of *Buy Right*. And Mike arrived with a tall imposing man he learned was Mack Richards, the head of that group, Voice of Adams. Richards had also brought with him a young man named RJ Stevens. They all crowded into his living room. Kate and Tracie brought in extra chairs and provided some refreshments. And Brad noticed a quick glance from Tracie to RJ and a bit of a smile between them.

They all listened intently as Brad told of his meeting with Harold Riggers, and he was surprised by their reaction. No one scoffed or had a look of disbelief. Instead there were several knowing glances exchanged around the room. There was a look of satisfaction on the face of the young RJ. As if he had just found the answer to a difficult riddle.

Mack Richards leaned forward and asked, "Did this Harold fellow give you any information on where he hid this report?"

"No," answered Brad, "He just said he hid it under a code name on the Internet. He was in a big hurry to get out of there, I guess, so he didn't take a lot of time trying to hide it."

Peter Arter asked, "What was the code he said he used?"

"Erase," said Brad.

"Hmm," said Lloyd, "I wonder what that stands for. Why would he call it that?"

"Maybe it has to do with LEAP."

"What do you mean?" asked Lloyd.

"Well, he told me that LEAP stands for League to Eliminate America's Past."

Peter Arter quickly glanced over at John Lloyd, and Lloyd looked straight at him. A huge question had just been answered. "John," said an excited Arter, "that's why they are changing the books, to erase our past, our culture."

Then he grabbed Brad by the arm, saying, "Isn't that just what you wrote in your blog? That you wondered if someone was trying to eliminate the ideas of individuality and such?"

"Yes," I did write that," said Brad excitedly, suddenly beginning to understand.

Mack Richards said, "Gentlemen, I think we are onto something. If any of this story of Harold's is true, and if this Erase report actually exists then we've got to find it. All of us have faced ridicule and have been ignored when we've tried to stand up to stop what is happening in our nation. If this report does name names and reveals hidden facts, it can be a very powerful tool in our hands."

"But," Brad jumped in, "Harold said it's very dangerous. He said several people who have read it have been killed. And don't forget, he's had to live in hiding for almost two years after his own partner was killed. So our very lives are obviously at risk."

"You're right," said Lloyd. "If this report is anything like it's been described, then we've got to be very careful."

Then Brad's brother spoke, "I think the biggest challenge we face is to actually find it. We have no idea where to start."

"I think I do," said Arter. My whole company is based on Internet use. My staff and I know pretty much where all the bodies are buried on the web, so to speak," he joked.

Then RJ spoke up. "I do too. Research on the Internet is my job."

Mack Richards agreed, "If anyone can find it, RJ can. And my staff is there to help and protect him. We've uncovered lots of hidden dirt in our day."

Then Peter Arter suggested, "Why don't RJ and I work together, putting two heads on it. That should help us move faster."

As they all agreed to that strategy, Mack Richards suggested how the rest of them should prepare to proceed once it was found. "Harold Riggers said his plan was to get this report into the hands of some congressmen, right? Then let's begin there. Let's hand pick the people we know would listen and take immediate and serious action if they had this proof in their hands." With that the meeting was over.

• • • •

The farmers of the Mississippi Shovel Brigade had continued to open more irrigation channels and plant their crops. Meanwhile, their loose organization of volunteers had gotten stronger as farmers all along the Mississippi merged together and united their forces. It reminded some of the way the farmers in early America had organized into the Minute Men to face the British in the Revolution.

There was still a strong presence of news media that reported every shovelful of dirt and every planted seed. Letters and emails were pouring in to express support and thanks to Jimmy Armond and his fellow farmers for giving them hope that the food crisis would soon be over.

Then, without warning, military trucks began to arrive, full of heavily-armed swat teams of the Bureau of Land Management, BLM shock troops. The government had arrived in full force, determined to disperse these farmers and again close the channels. Their first target was Jimmy Armond and his farm. The BLM set up a line of force right on his property boundary. More troops were pouring in daily.

As the news media reported from the scene, Americans from around a nervous nation grew angry and many wanted to stand with the Shovel Brigade against an oppressive government action. So, in groups of ten and twenty, they began to arrive on Jimmy's farm and set up their own line of defense, as they called it. Ordinary citizens were joined by city councilmen, county commissioners and sheriffs, and state legislators from across the country. American flags began to fly. More than 2,000 had gathered and the stand-off began. There was a definite feeling of dread among many that perhaps the second American Civil War was about to explode right on this spot.

# Chapter 20

The moment Brad Jackson walked out the front door of his apartment building into the still dark, early morning air, the first sight he saw was startling. On nearly every light pole, signpost, and mailbox glowing in the dark, in familiar red fluorescent paint was a single letter, "I". As far as the eye could see, all the way down the main street, glowing red "I's" were seen.

People were starting to gather to look at the impressive, yet somehow unsettling sight. There was a murmur as people questioned and discussed what it meant. Someone shouted out, "It's that graffiti bandit they're looking for. He's done this."

"But why?" asked another. "What does it mean?"

Down the street a TV crew was filming the scene. Apparently the stream of "I's" ran all the way into Washington. Brad knew it would be a sensation on tonight's evening news.

As he hurried to the train station on his way to school, Brad could only chuckle as he thought to himself, "I am, I think, I will, I know. The Power of One! And, yes, Harold, there is an "I" in Liberty!"

• • • •

Peter Arter and RJ Stevens put their heads together to try to figure out how to find where ERASE was hidden on the Internet. Peter had an incredible staff of talented programmers who fully understood the World Wide Web and how it operated. It was the root of his very successful business.

However, he refused to involve his staff. After all, several people had already died looking for this. He couldn't risk their lives too. So the progress was slow and frustrating. RJ had suggested some ideas, but so far they hadn't made any headway.

Tonight, his staff was gone and Peter was working alone in his office on the thirtieth floor of the Rachel Carson Building. Sitting at his computer he put in several combinations of a code using ERASE as the center. He tried various numbers to go with it.

Harold had said it had been two years since he wrote the report. Perhaps a date would match. He tried several. Nothing. He said it was written for congressmen. Perhaps a name. He entered several names. Nothing.

"Think, Peter," he said, holding his head. "What is it?" Then he got an idea and downloaded special software designed just for searching. It was kind of a hacker's tool. Using a TOR browser he went into what was called the Dark

Net where drug deals, money laundering, and other illegal transactions were made, undetected in a hidden Internet world. It was a place where the innocent dare not tread.

Now, inside that dark world, Peter again entered ERASE, adding the various number combinations and possible dates he had tried before. Suddenly there was a click and up it popped. ERASE.

Peter nearly fell off his chair. There it was! All seventy-five pages of it. He could hardly wait to tell everybody that he had found it. He grabbed the phone and called John Lloyd. He got his voice mail. "John," he shouted into the phone, leaving a message, "I got it! I found the report. Come see me tomorrow and we'll get it to everyone." With that, he saved it on his computer. As an afterthought he then took out his personal flash drive and downloaded the file saving it again. He didn't want to take a chance of losing it.

He was just about to forward it to RJ Stevens when suddenly the power went off and the lights went out. Peter was sitting in the dark. "Oh crap," said Peter in great anguish. "The energy curfew." He had lost track of the time. Sure enough it was 11:00 pm. The power would be off until 6:00 am. So there was nothing to do but go home and sleep.

Armed with just a flashlight, Peter headed for the stairwell and prepared to walk down thirty flights of steps in the dark. How he hated this energy curfew. It had destroyed night shifts for industry. It hurt productivity. And as far as he could see, it did absolutely nothing to protect the environment as it was sold to do. It had just put a lot of good oil industry employees out of work, not to mention other companies that couldn't operate at night. "When will government and its misguided ideas just get out of the way and let us do our jobs?"

He was still grumbling as he made his way down the cold, dark stairway, with each footstep making its own echo in the quiet of the building. He must be the only one there, he thought.

He went down ten floors. Then five more. Now, approaching the fifteenth floor, he thought, "Good, halfway." He went cautiously with each metal step because they were steep and slippery. And as they wound around in that circular motion toward the first floor, there was always the danger of falling through and nothing to catch you until you hit bottom.

Vito Mangreen had the same thought as he waited in the dark on the landing of the fifteenth floor, listening to Peter's approaching footsteps. As Peter reached the landing, Vito stepped out, picked Peter up over his head and simply threw him over the railing. He had been taken by such surprise Peter didn't have time to resist. He didn't even scream as he plunged into the darkness. But Vito could hear him hit bottom.

Vito climbed the fifteen floors to Peter's private office and, broke in the door. Once there he disconnected the hard drive of his computer and took it. No one saw him as he quickly descended the full thirty floors and stepped over Peter's body at the bottom on his way out.

• • • •

As more supporters from across the nation continued to arrive and fill the ranks of the Mississippi Shovel Brigade, so too did the numbers of the BLM force grow. Along with more troops they brought in more equipment, including high-powered telescopes, heavy-duty trucks, sophisticated listening devices and a lot of firepower. However, the worst weapon they had employed was a massive speaker system that was now playing non-stop music at a deafening level twenty-four-hours a day. No one in the Shovel Brigade was getting any sleep. The news media and other observers had pulled back to get relief.

In the middle of this tense standoff, four young men arrived. The leader sought out Jimmy Armond. "Sir," he said after finding him, "My name is Josh Logan. My friends and I are former special forces trained by the government in guerilla warfare, specifically to be snipers."

Instantly Jimmy was alarmed. The last thing he needed was someone starting violence from his side. He asked why they were there. Said the young man, "I saw on the news how the BLM troops are deployed in a classic offensive arrangement. Sir, there are BLM snipers hidden to the left and to the right of your position here. And they are also up on that hill. I'm quite sure that they intend to create a situation that will push you into action and then blame you for instigating it, certainly killing you and many more."

As he pointed to the BLM line, Jimmy squinted into the sun to see what he was pointing at. Sure enough he could now see the sniper positions. He was shocked. "We're just American citizens protesting a political action. We aren't dangerous. We aren't an army." Lack of sleep was playing heavily on his emotional state and he was near the end of his rope from the stress. Now he was learning that the government apparently intended to kill him and his friends.

"What do I do?" asked Jimmy. "What can you do?" he said to the young man.

"Sir," he said, "we are trained to deal with this kind of action. With your permission, I want to deploy my friends into positions there and there, just this side of your lines. That way we will have their snipers in our sights to prevent them from taking such action against you. Most important-ly we can supply you with an early warning for any actions they begin to take and that can save lives. I promise that we won't do anything unless provoked. We will keep you safe, sir."

# Chapter 21

John Lloyd was devastated to learn of the death of Peter Arter. He had just listened to the excited voice mail Peter had left him the night before to let him know that he had found the document.

Then the phone rang and it was a reporter wanting his thoughts on the death of his business associate. "Do you think it was an accident?" asked the reporter.

All Lloyd could say was, "No comment."

Immediately he called Mack Richards to see if he knew anything. That's when he learned that Peter's office had been broken into and hard drive taken from his computer. Richard's agreed with him that there could be no doubt that the ERASE curse had gotten Peter Arter.

Later that day a police detective asked him to come down to headquarters to answer some questions. He wanted to know if he knew of any enemies Peter had. Lloyd kept quiet, denying any possible threats.

Then the cop really surprised him when he said Peter had no living relatives. Lloyd had not known that. He had never thought to ask. "He wasn't married and had no siblings so," the cop said, "I have his personal items but no one to give them to." Lloyd, still in disbelief that his friend was dead, agreed to accept the bag of Peter's belongings.

Back in his office, he sat, unable to move or think. Yesterday it seemed they were on their way to a solution. Peter had been so excited to search for that report. And his voice on the phone message had been near euphoric. What had happened in the time between his leaving that message and his discovery at the bottom of the stairwell? How did this murderer, whoever he was, find everyone who simply downloaded that report? Why was the report such a dangerous secret?

Absentmindedly, Lloyd picked up the plastic bag that contained the things the police found on him. These were basically the contents of his pockets, his wallet, keys, his rings, and his watch. Not much here, he thought. But attached to his key ring was an interesting item. There were three or four keys on the ring. But there was also a computer flash drive permanently attached to the key ring as well.

That's interesting, thought Lloyd. He had never seen a key ring made that way. Leave it to Peter, he thought. Everything he had, even his key ring, seemed to be connected to computers in some way.

Out of curiosity Lloyd took the key ring and inserted the flash driver into his computer. The file directory popped up and listed a number of documents that had been saved on it. There were several personal items for his accountant, and Peter's detailed plans for more *Buy Right* book stores. And then Lloyd stopped at one file. It was dated from the day before and labeled simply "E."

He hesitated for a minute. If this could possibly be the secret file was he too in danger for having it? He decided to be careful. As long as he didn't open it then it couldn't be downloaded into his computer and trigger any kind of alarm, whatever that might be.

Instead, he called Mack Richard's office in Washington. Richards wasn't there so he asked for RJ Stevens. When RJ answered Lloyd described what he had found.

RJ said, "How fast can you get here?"

Lloyd was on the first air shuttle from LaGuardia to Reagan National airport. Two hours later he was picked up by a Voice of Adams employee and driven to the national headquarters where RJ was waiting for him.

About that time Mack Richards also entered the office from his meetings on Capitol Hill, surprised to see John Lloyd standing at RJ's desk. When Lloyd explained his find, Richards called in all of the staff and ordered the office to be put on lock down. "No one leaves and no one comes in, do you all understand," he ordered the staff. "This could be a matter of life and death. And I want all of you safe. "

Immediately the doors were locked and several stood guard at every possible entrance, including watching the windows. Several more stood outside RJ's office door, alert and ready. No one was sure what to expect. They didn't know how it happened, but they knew too many had died when this file was opened.

Lloyd and Richards gathered around RJ's computer as he inserted the flash drive. Up came the file directory and Lloyd pointed out the E document. RJ clicked on it and there it suddenly was. ERASE.

Listed as its authors were Harold Riggers and Eugene Trent. Both were agents in the Department of Justice's Counter Intelligence Division. According to the report, these agents had been detailing evidence captured from known spies which was then being passed on to foreign governments.

By simply doing their job, Riggers and Trent began to piece together the work of these foreign agents and investigated the details of the information that had been stolen. At first, said the report, it all seemed too fantastic to be true. But as they investigated further, they were shocked to find it was all factual. That's when they came to the conclusion that it was their duty to report their findings to Congress. Because, said their report, what they had found was nothing short of treason from inside the government.

First, they discovered a shadow government operating inside the President's Administration, detailing that Cabinet Members didn't actually seem to control their Departments. Instead, each Cabinet Secretary was forced to follow instructions given to them through unofficial surrogates that were placed in all of their offices. The Cabinet members were simply puppets used to pass the Congressional approval process in order to make it appear that the government was functioning properly. Worse, their research showed that the instructions did not actually originate with the

President, though he was the one who passed on the orders. Obviously, concluded the report, he too was being directed.

As Richards and Lloyd read the ERASE report, they kept looking at each other in disbelief. There was a list of thirty-seven members of Congress and two Supreme Court Justices who were also being used by this force to help impose what amounted to nothing less than a hidden coup of the government. "You know," said Richards, "this report is over two years old. I suspect there are a lot more than thirty-seven involved now." Lloyd nodded in agreement.

The details of that coup involved plans to change the system of government away from the elected representative system into appointed councils, which would gradually eliminate the U.S. Congress. It, according to the report, was to be replaced by an "Assembly of the People," made up of appointed delegates from private political organizations.

Erase went on and on, detailing plans to control all aspects of American life and specific details on how to control and eliminate opposition to the plans. Both Lloyd and Richards recognized many of the tactics as they had already been on the receiving end of many of them.

"Who is behind this?" demanded Richards, as he continued reading. He yelled at the computer screen in his frustration, "Tell me!"

The most important evidence in the report was presented via a detailed transcript, written by one of the participants of a secret meeting that had taken place almost six years earlier. The FBI had intercepted a foreign agent, who had somehow discovered the notes, as he was in transit, planning to hand them over to a government leader overseas. That transcript reported the remarks made by one specific person as he detailed how they would take control:

"The key target is the middle class. They are the ones who foster opposition. The poor can be controlled by making them dependent on the government. The rich can be controlled by providing them with incentives to support us; make them richer if they play along.

"But the middle class will recognize the danger. They are the ones constantly talking about opportunity to improve and succeed. They will become discontented in our new society. They will rebel. So they must be the first destroyed and forced to live under our dictates."

Then the transcript continued, detailing how that would be done:

"First we destroy their ability to live outside of our control. No water, no energy, no food, no jobs outside the boundaries of the cities that we control. If they live in the rural areas, they are harder to watch."

"When someone in the meeting asked how such a mass exodus into the cities could be achieved, the speaker answered: They will do it voluntarily because we will make it impossible for them to survive in the rural areas. We will cut off the water and their ability to obtain energy for their homes, cars, and trucks. We will enforce rules that will make it impossible to develop land or farm it. We'll just use that excuse about protecting the environment. Fear works in our favor."

Apparently, according to the transcript, there was laughter around the room as that was stated. Then the question was asked, "Where will our food come from if we shut down the farms?"

"Every city will be assigned a quota for producing food on our controlled land. Ultimately, we'll have all of those farmers living in the city. We'll make it their duty to feed us."

Again laughter filled the room. And, again a question. "How do we avoid a rebellion? After all, there are a lot of people who believe they have a right to live where they choose and a right to stand up to the government. What about the guns in private hands? What about the Constitution?"

"Eventually, when the time is right, we will declare Martial Law and confiscate the guns. Meanwhile, before we are ready to take that drastic step, we are running education programs in the cities and the schools suggesting that guns are dangerous and for their own safety they should voluntarily turn them in."

"As for their need to cling to their so-called rights, we're going to make them forget all of those things. That Constitution has been in our way from the beginning. It has made our job harder. Eventually we will emasculate it and make it irrelevant."

"The key element of our plan is the need to control how people think. Our control of the education system will eliminate their concept of Freedom. The new generations will grow up having never heard such words or concepts. It will become forbidden to even talk about individualism and Freedom. Their concept of freedom will be to accept their dependence on us.

"All goods and services will be provided and they will learn that to question or object will assure they lose those services. We will control jobs, housing, food, and energy. By moving them into the cities we will have the means to monitor their activities, even in what they think of as the privacy of their own homes. Above all, we will have complete control of their personal bank accounts and can cut off anyone who tries to rebel. Very soon we will have no opposition."

"Just as importantly, we will need to eliminate the message of Christianity because its teachings are the very root of those radical concepts. While it's recognized that people still have the need to pray to give them comfort as people have always had that need, we will give them new reasons and a new god to pray to. Tell them their Mother Earth is hurting and desperately needs them. They will eat it up."

"We already control most, if not all, of the mainstream news media, so we can control the information outlets. Our goal now is to control every avenue of the flow of ideas and knowledge. Technology will allow us to control that flow of information. The people will be totally unaware that it's even happening.

"All dangerous concepts must be wiped off the face of the earth. Freedom is the root of strife and violence worldwide. And once we get rid of such ideas, no one will protest our control.

"In short, gentlemen, we are going to erase all memory of these radical ideas. And the nation will very quickly lose its identity as one promoting free enterprise and limited government.

"The most important thing for you all to remember as we move forward with these plans is that the people will become dependent on us and actually fight anyone who suggests such ideas of freedom and independence. Such concepts will scare them to death. Who will take care of them in such a freedom, they will ask. The answer must always be WE WILL. Voluntarily, rebellion will be eliminated forever, without even having to fire a shot.

"In short, we are going to erase America's past!"

Richards and Lloyd each finished reading the transcript and then the real shock set in as they read the bottom line. It was the first time they were about to make the connection. And yet, they should have known. All the signs had been there for them. But it was just too diabolical to think such a thing was possible.

The name of the speaker and the leader of this diabolical coup was Edgar Thornton.

# Chapter 22

Edgar Thornton put down the phone in undisguised irritation. It was rare that he showed his emotions, even to himself. But that sniveling idiot was starting to get to him. Well, he knew what had to be done, but now it was obvious things had to be accelerated or that crybaby might just crack. OK, I'll fix it. Just like everything else, he thought.

He was a meticulous, orderly man. In Edgar Thornton's world everything was in its place. His desk never had a paper on it. Every chair was perfectly positioned around his huge mahogany desk.

His personal appearance was just as controlled. His shoes were always polished to a blinding shine and he always wore lifts to make himself taller than his 5'6" frame. His suits were always of the highest quality, pressed with a sharp crease in the leg and they were always of a dark color and accessorized with a bow tie. Every hair on his head was in place. Yet, it was thinning on top and he wasn't happy about that. It seemed that was one of the very few things he couldn't control.

When he spoke it was always in quiet, even precise sentences. Every word was used to its best effect and well thought out before being uttered. The calendar of his daily activities, meetings, and meals was always full, every movement designed with a purpose. There was not a wasted moment in his day.

Of course, he hadn't always been in such control. As a student in high school he was just a nerdy, awkward loner. He was sullen, quiet, never in command of a room. In fact, in those early days he rarely walked into the middle of a room. Instead he preferred to just creep around the outside walls, trying not to be noticed. He kept to himself.

In that hidden world that only he occupied, Edgar quietly studied the other kids, watching their every move. He noticed everything, even their facial expression. In that way he learned to read people, to understand the motives for their actions. He could usually tell what they were thinking. One thing he learned from this ability was that he didn't like those other kids. He was suspicious of any who tried to talk to him, always wondering what they wanted from him.

Edgar especially disliked the silly, wasteful games the other kids played. Instead he spent his time reading, educating himself, driven to understand why people took certain actions in directing their lives. So much of it was an utter waste of life. But they never seemed to learn. He did.

He had never married. Saw no point in it. Instead he decided that relationships were just wasting time on sentimental foolishness. He had long ago rejected such notions of family. In fact, as soon as he could break out on his own he had shut himself off from his immediate family.

His father was no more than ordinary. He didn't count for anything. To Edgar his dad was just a common laborer with no ambition. How he loathed him for keeping the family poor with his lack of ambition. The loser was content to go to work each day and be told what to do. Edgar's impression was that his dad thought the whole world revolved around earning a mediocre paycheck to get by. He resented his father. And he resented the shabby clothes he was forced to endure.

That was why the other kids had picked on him in school. And that was why he did everything he could to hide so that he didn't stand out as a target for their attacks. But his attempts to hide had backfired on him. Some soon began to notice the strange, quiet kid who would slink around the room, talking to no one. They started to call him "Mousey" -- a nickname that stuck and drove him crazy when he heard it. Daily his hatred grew.

Had he been born in a later era he might have been one of those kids who suddenly lost control, let his anger rise to the top and suddenly finds himself roaming the halls of the school shooting anything that moved. They thought that was revenge. How stupid, thought Thornton, as he read such accounts today. What did they gain? DEATH. That wasn't for him. He would stay cool, quiet, always in control. Listening. Waiting. Preparing for the moment when he would make them all pay. Someday, he vowed, he would get his revenge. Someday HE would control THEIR world! They would be forced to answer to him! It was a silent warning that went off in his head. Control. Stay in control. He heard it over and over again. It was his driving force in life.

Eventually he gained full control of his life. He put himself through college, then he discovered Wall Street. Here was his world. Here his habits of study and control allowed him to excel. Manipulation was the center of every decision. Being able to read what others were thinking, sensing their fears, looking for loopholes, it was all here and he quickly began to build a financial fortune.

Financial wealth, however, was not real power and Edgar Thornton had plans. He wanted control. Ever since those terrible days in school when the so-called 'in crowd' had made fun of him and laughed, he craved the ability to stop them, to assure no one would ever again hold any kind of power over him. Over the years, as he worked in various companies building what would become massive wealth, he experienced, yet again, the same kind of ridicule. His money alone hadn't stopped it. Power! That was the only way to truly control his world. He determined that he would create the world to suit himself, rather than trying to live in theirs.

Politics, of course, is the answer to power. But Thornton had no intention of running for office. How messy. Kissing babies and trying to win over people for their votes was just not his style. Pulling the strings from behind the scenes is where the real power lies.

To that end, Thornton became an expert string puller. First, using his wealth as seed money, he established a private foundation. Through the foundation he dispensed money to finance organizations that would in turn drive movements designed to achieve the ends he wanted. Most importantly, the foundation was creating mass sums of money that filled his private coffers.

With his newly gotten gains he began investing in major industries including energy and transportation. His goal was to compel communities to use his services. If they were reluctant to do so, he put his money to effective use. First, he would target established, respected organizations in the community that had influence over policy makers, such as the Chamber of Commerce, private service clubs, and the local news media. All he had to do was shove a little money in front of them and soon they were promoting his vision of the "need" for a light rail train system or the "independence" of locally-produced energy supplies. It was, of course, all for the good of the community.

If there was still resistance to his plans, then Thornton got really creative. He sought out local leaders of established, but radical organizations that operated in the ghettos. For a small sum of money they could be counted on to organize "peaceful" demonstrations in support of the "community needs." With a timely rock thrown here or a bottle tossed there, violence would break out. Scared local officials could be counted on to break into a panic and Thornton's projects would be approved rapidly,  and filling his pockets, for the "good of the community."

Over time, through his foundation he established an extensive and complicated web of organizations in every state and nearly every community, all funded by his money. They became his private army. Whatever his need, the answer was just a check away.

Then, after perfecting the power of pulling strings from the shadows, politicians became his next prey. Gaining control of them was too easy. They were so stupid and greedy. They stood for nothing. They didn't care about philosophy or history or economics. What a dangerous combination.

Thornton simply guided them in the direction he wanted just by dangling in front of them pockets full of money or promises of power. He took control of one fool at a time. They came and went as they were useful. His wealth and power grew. And with every move forward, with every bought-and-paid-for politician doing his bidding, Edgar Thornton laughed.

He owned local officials on city councils and state legislators across the land. He had some judges; eventually even a couple of Supreme Court Justices were procured. It was usually money that did the trick. They all wanted something. He provided it. Power was another enticement.

He remembered the case of the Forest Service official who was taking bribes from businessmen and developers so they could evade strict rules about destroying designated wetland areas, allowing them to build their developments. The official was getting pretty wealthy from his little scheme when Edgar Thornton found out about it. Thornton then ran a blackmail scheme of his own against one of the developers, threatening him with what he knew. In exchange for keeping it all a secret, Thornton forced the businessman to set up a trap for the official. Wire taps and video showing them discussing yet another deal did the trick. Thornton then went to the official and showed him the proof of what he knew. Now Thornton owned both the businessman and the official to do his bidding. This environmental scam, thought Thornton, had created so much government corruption that the pickings were just too easy.

In a more unsavory situation, a congressman was being blackmailed for a sexual video that threatened to destroy his career. Thornton made sure the tape and the blackmailer disappeared forever. So now he owned another politician for whenever he needed leverage. Such officials were useful when he needed to block some opposition that tried to use the rule of law against him.

Then, six years ago, he added a President. That's when Thornton was able to move his plans forward and he could see them unfolding just as he had envisioned. The great thing about President Gravell was his incredible zealotry over that environmental hoopla. He was amazed to watch how Gravell was able to manipulate others simply by using the fear of environmental armageddon to get them to do whatever he wanted. It was magical, thought Thornton. Out of fear of the threat of a collapsing planet, Thornton watched people actually voluntarily sacrificing their futures. And it was an incredible fact that the more the people gave up, the more powerful the government became. If people were going to be that easy to dupe, then Edgar Thornton intended to be the one in control of that power.

So he set out to charm Gravell and bring him under his thumb. First Thornton supplied Gravell with all the tools and influence he needed to win the party nomination for President. He helped raise the money. He provided the campaign team. He used his people from the news media so that every story led with Gravell's name. It was a cinch and Gravell won the election.

Now, with him in place, Thornton began to think about how to use that power. How does one really control people? It takes vision. It takes dedication. It takes creativity. It takes ruthlessness. He had all of these.

As he saw it, the worst danger to the authority of the state was the renegade individual who questioned authority. He believed that you must build the power of the state by eliminating the influence of single individuals. Everyone must adhere to the dictates of the state and work for the 'common good'. Individuals are pathetic. They just want to whine about their own selfish wants and needs. What a waste of time, he thought.

Thornton had come to recognize that there was a small but vocal minority that was resisting the change that he, through Gravell's Administration, was working toward. They were what he called the "Freedom Freaks," made up of the older generation that had been raised on the old idea that individuals were somehow given rights at their birth to do exactly as they wanted. Really? Granted by whom? Thornton had really learned to hate them for their dogged interference in his plans. They would learn not to question him!

However, as long as those old ideas remained and new generations were taught that this was the path to some promised freedom and prosperity, it was going to muck up his plans; those nobodies could actually make it impossible for him to succeed. But how do I stop them?

Then one day the idea hit him like a rocket. It was so clear. It wasn't even an original idea. Thornton's study of history showed that when this idea had been fully employed in one nation, it had become one of the great success stories in human history.

Of course, as usual, he noted that when this particular plan was first introduced, its leader was vilified and called a monster. All great ideas are met with resistance. But this leader succeeded and today his achievement stood in the world as one of the great economic and social achievements in human history. His vision showed the power and benevolence of the state. It brought one of the poorest and most backward nations in the world to the very forefront of economic and social power.

Thornton's model for his plan was the People's Republic of China which became a monument to state power and guidance. And it was all accomplished through the unwavering vision of one man -- Mao Zedong. How did he do it? His plan was called the "Great Leap Forward."

As Thornton saw it, Mao took a nation drowning in ancient cultures, and turned it inside out. Old ways were banned. Old religion was shut down. Population was tightly controlled. The State rose up as the ultimate authority. The court system was changed. The old ruling class was eliminated. In short, Mao erased China's past and replaced it with a new vision.

Of course there was anger and fear and opposition. But Mao stuck to his vision and forced it onto the people until they were able to see his magnificent wisdom. And the result was that today, China stood as the economic miracle of the world. Its factories became the busiest in the world. Its goods flooded the market place. And its economy led the world. "It is the model for us all," Thornton proclaimed.

"Yet," he lamented, "there is the United States and its antiquated ideas of the individual standing in my way to such power. What do I do? America needs its own Great Leap Forward. It needs to be completely reorganized and those old ideas of individuality and limited government need to be eliminated from the national memory. "What I'm going to do," Thornton declared to his face in the mirror, "is erase America's past and start over. And these power-hungry political hacks are going to help me do it!"

He began to move forward, starting with legislation to slowly begin the process of changing the American system of government, using environmental protection as the means -- the surefire scare tactic. Then Thornton began to think ahead. I have to control how people actually think so they will accept this new plan.

The idea of American uniqueness and individual freedom was completely ingrained in each and every citizen. The nation even has a statue dedicated to Liberty. Every school-child was being instilled with the ideas and the "virtues" of the power of the individual right in the public school classrooms. Thornton knew if he was to succeed, those ideas had to be eliminated. To do it, there had to be a way to literally eliminate the very words that promoted the philosophy, including words like "individual," "I," "freedom," "ego," and "patriot" from the vocabulary.

But the nation was full of books with those ideas. There were more books on individuality in America than there were guns in private homes, Thornton observed. The books had to be eliminated. But how? Personal and public libraries were full of these books. Bookstores sold them.

Old fashioned book burnings in the public square would cause too much attention and would only serve to rile up the people. If America was going to be changed, then it had to be done quietly, behind the scenes, at least until it was too late to stop the plan.

Throughout history, others had tried using propaganda by controlling the media and what was permitted to be reported. Sometimes it worked for a while, but it always collapsed as pockets of resistance inevitably would rise up. What he needed was a way to control what was read and taught to completely wipe out those opposing ideas. Erase them so they didn't even exist. Somehow, he thought, if we could, right from birth, control the attitudes, values, and belicfs of an entire generation, they would never even know there was another way of thinking.

The answer came in the form of America's driving force -- its technology. The creation and popularity of electronic books -- the e-book. They were just computers. They could be edited anytime from anywhere. Whole books could be deleted without a trace – without even a public stir.

Thornton was ecstatic as he realized the potential of the e-books. He realized that if he could take over the e-book industry he could control exactly what was published.

Then he found out that the manufacturers of the e-books, in their greed, had actually developed software that allowed them to, in fact, monitor what people were reading – right at the very moment they were doing it. It was created so that publishers could find what the readers enjoyed so they could create similar books to sell more that the public wanted.

Now here was technology that, if corralled under one force, would provide the ultimate tool to effectively control the written word for an entire society.

That's when Thornton organized LEAP -- the League to Eliminate America's Past, he called it with a grand laugh. Now, with gusto, he began to use all of the expertise he had acquired on Wall Street. This was his world of ruthless ma-nipulation, betrayal, and outright theft. He loved the term used by Wall Street, mergers and acquisitions! What a great name for outright theft.

First he targeted all of the producers of e-book prod-ucts. He bought some of the companies. Still others he ran out of business. Of course, a few stubborn fools had to be dealt with in … other ways. Now he had the ultimate tool to control ideas, knowledge, and thought.

As LEAP was editing certain popular books that contained dangerous and offensive "freedom" messages, it was also slowly eliminating the existence of certain books all together.

The second phase of the plan was to eliminate the availability of printed books that couldn't be changed once produced. It was dangerous to have them available. That meant LEAP had to find a way to make them unavailable. If there were no bookstores to sell them, the publishers would stop printing books. How to do that? Make sure everyone had an e-book and therefore had no use for printed books. After all, with an e-book they could carry their entire library with them wherever they went.

That's when Thornton came up with the idea for LEAP to donate e-books to every single school student. He sold it to the public as a wonderful benevolent gesture to the nation's over-strapped public education system. Schools could now eliminate the massive cost of textbooks. They just needed to download them into the e-books. And of course, LEAP also supplied the curricula. "People are so easily manipulated," he said laughing.

Then, after talking to one of his state legislators, he discovered another major way to insert e-books into everyday life. He began a plan to convinced legislative leadership across the nation to begin using e-books as their primary means of communication among their members. Of course it was sold to them simply as a way to make their lives easier. They could send leadership memos, hearing calendars,

and other vital information through the e-pads, again supplied for free by LEAP. Only now, LEAP would effectively
control communications thorough every government entity,
permitting legislators to see only information Edgar Thornton wanted them to see. Now he had a way to control every
legislature in the nation. And they were excited to let him
do it. Edgar Thornton was having entirely too much fun, he
often thought to himself.

With such tools at his disposal, Thornton had found the
way to bring about a revolution to the entire American system without causing a stir. People just went about their daily
lives, unaware that everything was steadily changing.

Thus began American's Great Leap Forward. And now
nearly everyone in the nation thought exactly as Edgar
Thornton wanted them to think. They knew only what he
wanted them to know. They were like children, unable to
question authority because they were unaware there was
even a question.

Edgar Thornton had managed to accomplish it all by
staying out of the middle of the room, still hugging the
walls, unnoticed and unthreatening. But now he controlled
nearly every thought and action in the nation. No one called
him Mousey now. Today, the United States of America, the
world's model of free thought and independence, was firmly
in his hands and ready for the final solution that he planned
for it.

But first he had to deal with the immediate problem of a
very weak politician.

• • • •

So, as the bothersome President had requested, Thornton called a meeting of several of his most trusted inner circle, including Beverly Twetcher, Poncho Delegrade, and Steven Daniels. There were also a couple of judges, some leaders of reliable non-governmental organizations like the Religious Partnership for Justice, and Dave Perry, speaker of the Ohio House, among others. They had all been instrumental in bringing the necessary policies to their respective areas, including religion, education, and public policy.

All were now sitting around Thornton's expansive conference table, securely locked away from prying eyes and eavesdroppers inside his near fortress he like to simply call his Washington, D.C., office. Far from just an office it was staffed with experts trained in surveillance, research, and security. There were rooms full of computers, secured two-way conference screens and even connections to the most secret government surveillance satellites. Very little happened in the nation without this office knowing about it. Access was only possible through a sophisticated biometric scanning system. It was the most secure place in the nation's capital.

Perhaps the most impressive secret was that the President of the United States was able to come and go completely undetected, due mainly to the fact that only Thornton's hand-picked security people now served on Gravell's Secret Service detail. And there he was this morning, sitting at the opposite end of the table from Thornton, fidgeting and looking nervous and extremely uncomfortable in his chair.

Thornton opened the meeting saying, "OK, Eric, you wanted this meeting. What's the problem?"

Gravell began by describing his confrontation with Jasper. "She refuses to carry out the orders I gave her. She said it will destroy the economy. I threatened to fire her and she said she would go to the news media if I did and tell them everything," whined Gravell.

"Is that all," asked Thornton in a bored voice.

"No," said Gravell. "We've got cracks showing up everywhere. We've got those Voice of Adams radicals stirring up Congress. That nut preacher has gotten the attention of people all over the country with his TV sermons. He's even attacked our new Bible. And then there are those farmers on the Mississippi, not to mention food shortages and even food riots breaking out."

"So what?" asked Thornton with all the sarcasm he could muster in his voice.

"Well, people are starting to ask questions. What if Congress starts some inquiries? What do I tell them? What if Jasper goes to the media? That could destroy everything." Gravell was obviously near panic in his fear. "We've got a revolt brewing on our hands. Perhaps we've gone too far too fast," he continued. "I think we've got to pull back. At least we need to pull back a bit from the farmers. People need to eat," he said with a pout in his voice. "You got me into this, help me get out," he pleaded with Thornton.

The others around the table remained silent as the President spoke, but now they began to turn to Thornton to see how he would react to this questioning of his decisions. No one had ever done that before.

Thornton had been growing increasingly weary of this whining President. While he was usually quiet and controlled, he had finally had enough as he suddenly stood up and slammed his open hand down on the table. "Get hold of yourself you sniveling cry baby," he shouted. Everyone at the table suddenly jumped almost out of their chairs. President Gravell was visibly shaken.

But Thornton continued in a near rage as he came around to Gravell's end of the table and got right into his face. "You've been worrying from day one, always afraid of your own shadow. For god's sake, what more do you need. We now control most of the industry in this nation. We decide what legislation will be passed. We control the courts. We control the schools, industry, and the news media." Thornton stopped to let that sink in.

Then he slapped his hand down again as he shouted to the President, "Do you understand that we actually control what everyone thinks in this nation? No one but a few outdated and outnumbered radicals even think to question us. Do you get that, Mr. President? And yet, here you sit, actually worried about Congress. Have they ever once stood in your way? Have they ever made a single move to block any of the policies we have demanded?"

Gravell sat there, looking down like a scared little boy. Finally he gave a weak, "No."

"Then what are you so afraid of?" Thornton shouted. "There is simply no way they can stop us."

"But, what if Jasper goes to the media?" Gravell asked.

Again Thornton snapped back, "They are our media – don't you get it? No one is going to print a word she says."

Gravell tried again, "But those farmers have the attention of the nation – the news media are there reporting on it."

In a tired, exasperated voice Thornton replied, "By the end of next week that problem will be gone. Daniels has seen to that, right Daniels?"

Finally a different voice was heard as Steven Daniels explained how he had sent orders to the BLM to take immediate and forceful action to disperse the farmers and eliminate the leaders.

"There," said Thornton. "That protest will be over before Jasper can react. And, by the way, that pesky preacher will be off the air before he can give another sermon. Trust me."

"So," he said, "I repeat, Eric, what's your problem?"

Gravell said nothing. Things got quiet for a few minutes as everyone began to catch their breath.

It took a few minutes for Thornton to regain his self-control and return to his usual quiet, precise voice. Then he looked around the table at each person and said, "I want to know if any of you now have any doubts about what we're doing or where we're headed?"

No one spoke. Some shook their heads indicating they had no doubts.

Satisfied, Thornton continued. "OK, since our esteemed President is so worried about the possibility that our enemies are growing stronger, I think it's time we take some really bold action. Let's finish this now. What do you say?"

Dr. Beverly Twetcher had been enjoying this verbal assault on the President. She had always seen him as the weak link in their plans. He was necessary, but a real pain. Twetcher was probably Thornton's most loyal follower. She had taken on her task of completely rebuilding the education structure with real gusto. She had fired anyone in the Department who stood in her way. She had even learned to use the media to plant stories and destroy careers of the few Members of Congress who had tried to oppose her. She was ruthless and she was feared. She was just the kind of acolyte on which Thornton relied.

Her voice was now the first to be heard. "Whatcha got in mind, Boss?"

Thornton smiled. "I think it's time for us to accelerate our timetable a bit. Here's what you're going to do, Mr. President. You're going to deliver a national address to the nation next Thursday morning. You'll alert the news media that you are going to announce significant emergency policy actions by your Administration."

All eyes were on him as Thornton passed around folders containing a set of papers. To Gravell, he said, "Here is a list of four new Executive Orders you will issue on that day." He paused to let all of them read the documents.

A look of surprise covered Gravell's face as he read over the list. But most of the others around the table broke into broad grins. One even let out a long slow whistle. Thornton noted their surprise at his bold move, taking a quiet satisfaction in it. He had gotten the reaction he had hoped for. He knew he was about to make history.

Yet again, Gravell hesitated, worried about how it would

all be received. But he accepted his responsibility. Then a smiling Thornton said, "Believe me, you're not going to get any resistance. I've got an idea about how we can add some dramatic flair to this broadcast that will grab their full attention while we simply rush these Executive Orders into place. And I assure you this little stunt will help remove any obstacles in our way forever!"

Standing and walking around the room, he looked at each one seated around the table as he passed.  Daniels glanced back for a moment and then quickly looked down again, almost afraid to lock eyes with Thornton. Most of the others had the same type of reaction. This man controlled them. He held their futures in his hands. Make a wrong impression, make him feel you couldn't be trusted and, as they knew, it was over. They had all seen it happen many times before to now-departed colleagues. The only exception was Beverly Twetcher. She held his stare and a cruel smile crossed her face. "Two of a kind," thought Poncho Delegrade as he noticed the exchange.

In parting, Thornton said, "And when that is over and these orders are fully implemented, we will never have to worry again about this pathetic so-called freedom movement. The power will be ours. We are unstoppable. Now, all of you, go and prepare each of your respective areas so that everything is ready by next Thursday."

As they all rose to leave the room, Thornton had one more thing to add. "By the way, Eric, I'm even going to take care of that pesky graffiti bandit for you. He has tweaked us long enough. I've grown tired of it." As he watched them leave Thornton thought to himself, "And soon I won't need any of you either. The control will be all mine."

# Chapter 23

Vito knew that carrying out the instructions ordering him to find this graffiti bandit, as everyone called him, wasn't going to be easy. This time there was no address and no one had ever seen him actually doing the painting. It just appeared. The only clues Vito had were that the bandit operated at night and that his messages were mostly found in the Capitol City and surrounding areas. Not much to go on. But the boss said it was an important assignment and he had promised a very large bonus for this one.

So, night after night, Vito prowled the streets. He searched in all the places where graffiti had appeared before. He searched around government buildings, and in train and bus stations. As he searched, there had been new messages left around the city. This graffiti bandit was a busy man, Vito realized. But so far he hadn't been in the right place to catch him.

Then, Vito just happened to enter that train station in

Gaithersburg late one night on his way home after another fruitless search. It was completely quiet. No one was there. Then he saw him. A lone man, standing next to the wall, one hand held a large piece of cardboard against the wall and the other hand aimed a spray can over it.

Just as the man started to spray the paint onto the stencil, he looked over his shoulder and saw Vito racing toward him. He dropped the stencil and threw the can at him. It bounced off Vito's shoulder as he closed in on the small-framed, but wiry man. He was quicker than Vito had anticipated, and so was able to avoid his grasp. Vito gave chase and managed to corner him near the escalator, blocking his escape.

Just then he heard a train approaching the station. Quickly Vito grabbed the man by his hair and plunged a knife into his back and dropped him. Before anyone could see what he had done, Vito got on the now departing train and disappeared.

The next morning the news media carried the story that the Graffiti Bandit had been stopped in the middle of painting another message.

As Brad entered the station on his way to school, police were still at the crime scene. Brad stood on the edge of the crowd that had gathered. He saw the partial message on the wall that said, "If there is no fix…" Still on the ground was a pool of blood and the stencil which revealed the full message Harold had been trying to leave: **"If there is no fixed concept of justice, how shall men know it is violated?"**

• • • •

After reading ERASE, Mack Richards and John Lloyd felt as if they had witnessed the great mountain opening up to reveal all the secrets that had eluded them. Now they had the full blueprint to guide them to what was really happening, where it was headed, and, most importantly, who was behind it. While up till now they surely had suspicions of who it could be, now they had proof. Still it was a surprise to learn that they both knew the tormentor behind so many of their struggles. Now it all began to make sense. Above all, it should have been obvious that it was the work of one man.

It was Edgar Thornton and LEAP behind the near collapse of John Lloyd's publishing empire. And with great pain, Mack Richards now understood that it was Edgar

Thornton who had surely ordered the murder of Terri Miller along with Scott Jacobs and Peter Arter. He must be stopped, Mack vowed. So, there in the offices of the Voice of Adams, they worked on a plan to do just that.

"OK," asked Richards, "what can we do? We have this damning information about the most powerful people in the nation. We have few friends and fewer assets to help us."

Then Lloyd spoke up. "Harold Riggers wrote this report for Congress, but never got the chance to deliver it to them. He must have known that there were people there he could count on to do something."

"But," replied Richards, "we don't know who he had in mind. I know a few people on the Hill. Peter believed that Congressman Morris could be trusted. In fact, the Congressman had told Peter that if we could supply proof he would do something. Now we have it."

Richards responded, "My experience in working with people up there is that they are all scared of their own shadows. They are terrified to step out and take risks. So, to get them to do anything requires a huge amount of pressure that usually threatens their cushy jobs. But I have an idea. Let's attack from several positions. Let's make copies of this report for every single Member of Congress. That way we will reach the ones Riggers was counting on. It will also send a shot across the bows of those Members who are in cahoots with Thornton. That should cause them to panic and they may run for the tall grass to hide."

Then Lloyd jumped in with a suggestion. "Let's also send a copy to every single media outlet. Even though they are usually clueless or only report one side, I have some close allies there who will report this. If some outlets start to report on this others will jump in, afraid of letting the competition get ahead of them. At least we will start a firestorm."

"OK, sounds like a good start," said Richards. "My staff is equipped to handle the load. RJ, can we send copies out to all of our supporters and members across the country and instruct them to make more copies and send them to everyone they know, including local media and local officials?"

"Sure," said RJ. "I can reach over a million through email in the next hour. And we can reach more on social media. It could go viral in a matter of minutes."

Replied Richards, "Let's not have this trickle out in a piecemeal fashion. It won't have near the effect we want. Instead, let's plan to put everything out at exactly the same time. We'll hit Congress, the news media, and all of our activists in one big sweep. It will be like storming Normandy!" There were excited looks all around the room.

He continued, "We need more. We need to reach out to certain people in authority who we know will take some action."

"Who do you have in mind, Mack?" asked Lloyd.

"John, you follow through with a personal visit to Congressman Morris. Take him a copy of the report and show him all the details. Make sure he reads it while you're there. Urge him to then issue Congressional subpoenas for hearings to those named in the report.

"I am going to take a copy to General Hugo Hollingsworth, the Chairman of the Joint Chiefs of Staff. This report reveals treason against our country by the highest levels in government, and that is of interest to the military. I intend to destroy Edgar Thornton and his scheme and leave nothing to chance. We need to flush every one of these traitors out of their holes and make sure they suffer for their actions." Mack Richards was a leader on fire as he began to direct the staff on their assigned tasks.

"OK, said RJ. "When do you want me to be ready to launch?"

"How about three days from now. That will be Thursday morning," said Richards.

# Chapter 24

Edgar Thornton was sitting on his couch in the living room of his lavish home. Very few people knew he even had such a place and that it sat squarely in the center of a private island in the Chesapeake Bay. This was where he came for quiet time. Few ever came here, and then only by his invitation. Tonight, since he had an aversion to bright lights, he sat in the dim glow of a single lamp, waiting for one expected guest. Sitting on his couch as he read over a document received earlier by special currier from the White House, he became aware of movement in the shadows at the doorway behind him.

"Ah, Vito, there you are. Come here. I have one final assignment for you and then our work together will be at an end."

But the face that emerged from the dark was not that of Vito Mangreen. Rather it was the hard, impassioned, look of a rising storm -- the face of Mack Richards. There he was,

standing just in front of Thornton, pistol in hand, aimed at
the chest of the LEAP founder.

Following his meeting with General Hollingsworth,
Richards had felt that there might be great danger if their
plans failed and Thornton was left in power. He decided
instead to find Thornton and deal with him. He never revealed his plans to anyone, but then, as he wondered how he
was going to get inside Thornton's office fortress, he opened
a package the General had given him. To his amazement,
it revealed the location of Thornton's secret lair along with
details on how to get in without detection.

Hollingsworth had apparently been watching Thornton
for some time and even had some of his men operating
inside Thornton's operation, and so had gathered this secret,
detailed information. Apparently Hollingsworth, acting like
a Marine, was thinking ahead that Mack Richards might
just feel the need to take some action against Thornton.
Without a word, he simply handed Richards the information he would need to do it.

As Richards stepped out of the shadows, Thornton,
for a quick second looked startled. He was obviously a bit
shocked at the breakdown in his security. But the surprise
registered on his face for just a second, then his practiced
self-control took over again and the arrogant tone returned
to his voice.

"Oh, Mr. Richards, we meet at last. I've got to tell you,
I'm impressed. What a merry chase you've given me. But if
you've broken into my home thinking you're going to stop
me, I'm happy to tell you that you're too late. By tomorrow
morning there will be no possible way to stop what I've
started, even if you had any chance of exiting this house

alive, which you don't. Walking in my door spelled your demise. I'm sure the alarm has already sounded."

But Richards didn't flinch. He held the gun steady, alert for any interruptions. He wasn't sure exactly why he felt such a need to come here and confront this monster who had caused so much damage and pain. Perhaps it was a foolish thing to do. But now he had him in his sights and he meant to stop him any way he could. How, he still wasn't sure.

Even as Richards moved further into the center of the room, Thornton continued to taunt him, confident that help was on the way. He wasn't worried about Mack Richards. "You and your fanatical friends are pathetic, Mr. Richards. You never had a chance to stop me. You never had the means to do it because you had no idea what you were up against." Thornton was again enjoying that familiar look of frustration these crusaders always seemed to get on their faces when they understood they were defeated. Richards was trying to be defiant, but he knew he was finished, Thornton had no doubt.

"LEAP," Thornton continued almost in a whisper, "Is now the most powerful force in the nation. Not only do we control the entire publishing industry, government, religion, and education, but we control the very thoughts of the nation. Can anyone really comprehend how complete my control is? There is hardly a citizen who even dares to question our actions. They simply accept everything we do," he said as a smile began to cross his cruel lips.

"The only agitators we have to deal with now are you and your ragtag band of so-called freedom fighters," Thornton continued in a mocking tone. "And that will end by

tomorrow." Now his hatred came bubbling up as he continued to verbally degrade Richards, the man he most wanted
to destroy. "You're a sorry lot. Always sticking your nose
in where it doesn't fit. Thinking you understand what is
happening around you. You don't. You can't possibly grasp
the magnitude of the changes we are about to make. The
precious America that you hold so dear no longer exists!"
Thornton declared with obvious joy. "I've erased it!

"Of course we have had some challenges along the way.
Your Voice of Adams' zealots have given us a run. But the
greatest danger came from those two idiot government
workers who wrote that report and tried to get it to Congress to expose us. That would have been most unfortunate
and untimely had they succeeded. They came so close when,
just before we disposed of them, they tried to hide it on the
Internet," continued Thornton, a near laugh in his voice.

Mack Richards listened in nearly unwilling fascination.
He had wanted to hear these things revealed for a long time.
He had been laughed at and called a conspiracy theorist
many times when he tried to issue warnings that the government was becoming a danger. And now, here he was, in
the belly of the beast, having all the hidden details revealed
to him personally by that very beast.

Thornton continued, obviously enjoying this chance to
finally tell someone the secrets he had hidden for so long.
"And that title code he gave to that report, ERASE, clever.
But did he think we were so stupid that we couldn't find it?
After we did, we figured that anyone who actually made the
effort to search it out to read would, in fact, be someone
who was a real danger to us. So we parked it on a special
DARKNET site where it could be found with a bit of difficulty. That way, anyone who took the time to search for it

would think they were very clever and actually outsmarting us."

Now a broad, evil smile took over Thornton's face. "We embedded a tracer chip in the file. That way, when anyone actually found the ERASE report we were notified immediately. The tracer even provided their name and address. It was that easy. We simply eliminated everyone who read that report. No whistleblowers. No exposure. The report that was designed to capture us became a trap for our would-be captors. Problem solved.  It was brilliant," he said with a flourish of his hand. "No one has ever read it and lived! So now it's our weapon, not yours."

Thornton hesitated, looking straight at Richards. Then he continued slowly, quietly, "And imagine our excitement when your precious Terri Miller found ERASE. Along with you, she had become a real thorn in our side.  Eliminating her solved many problems. And now here is the one and only Mack Richards, coming right into my door, saving me the time and expense of looking for you," concluded Thornton with obvious satisfaction.

The mere mention of Terri brought a stab of pain to Mack. Her face, with the fire in her eyes, flashed in his mind. How he missed her energy. Then it was Richard's turn to land a verbal punch on his tormentor.  He felt certain that his next words were going to ruin Thornton's self-satisfaction. Richards leaned in close and said, "I have news for you Thornton. It's not entirely true that anyone who has read the report is dead. You see, when your hired assassin killed Peter Arter he did take his computer hard drive, and that should have kept the report hidden. But Peter had also downloaded it onto a flash drive and your boy missed it. So now I have read every word of that report."

Thornton was visibly shaken by that unexpected news. Then again he quickly recovered his renowned self-control. "Well, Richards, I'm glad you got to read it. Now you know my entire plan and how it's being enforced in every corner of this nation. Now you know that it can't be stopped and that all of your efforts to the contrary have been an utter waste of your life. Good. I can't describe to you how much satisfaction that gives me. Because you see, Richards, it doesn't matter that you know it all, the plain truth is that you are never going to leave here alive to tell anyone. So it will remain our little secret, won't it, Mack!"

"Well Thornton, sorry to burst your bubble. By tomorrow morning every single Member of Congress and the entire news media will be receiving a full copy. By dinnertime the entire nation will know every single detail of your monstrous plot to manipulate them and to destroy their country and their lives. You are going to go down in history as one of the most evil, but pathetically failed villains in American history. You'll be arrested and tried in front of the entire nation. And none of your pocket of judges or powerful pawns can save you because we have their names too!"

Just as Thornton was about to respond, his eyes darted to something behind Richards, whose reflexes automatically forced him to jump to the side. He turned just in time to see Vito Mangreen rush toward him. Mack's sudden movement threw Vito off balance, but he still managed to grab Richards by the leg, knocking him to the floor. Richards quickly aimed his gun at the assassin and fired. It managed to hit Vito in the shoulder, but it wasn't enough to stop the powerful man. Vito was now on his feet. He stomped Richards in the head almost causing him to lose consciousness. But Mack shook it off. Vito charged him again, ready to strike another blow. But Mack Richards was not a small man himself and he had been professionally trained for such hand to hand combat, first as a Marine and then as a law man. He deflected another blow by Vito that had again targeted his head. This time, able to control his balance, Mack took careful aim and fired a single bullet that hit between Vito Mangreen's cruel eyes. He slumped to the floor and did not move.

Still in combat mode, Richards immediately turned back to Thornton who was staring at Vito's lifeless body. Now, Richards observed, Thornton was not looking so smug and self-assured. The security he had been quietly counting on suddenly lay dead on the floor. In fact, Richards saw a look of terror register instantly in Thornton's eyes as he realized he was actually alone with his most dangerous enemy.

The thought raced across Mack's mind that Thornton really was just a trapped rat full of fear like everybody else when confronted with his own mortality. There was certainly nothing special about him. In fact, Mack was startled to watch this once arrogant, invincible manipulator of so many powerful forces as he seemed to physically shrink before his eyes.

As he looked down on this pathetic creature Mack thought about how much pain and misery Thornton had caused. He thought about his victims, like the farmers who, even now, were having their lives and property destroyed. All of them could be facing death by morning. And then there were the children, a full generation -- the nation's future -- now damaged, perhaps forever, as a result of his social engineering of their young minds. How many elderly and sick had actually died when the power in their homes was cut off under the excuse of environmental protection? And he thought about the good people like Scott Jacobs and

Peter Arter who were just trying to save their country.

Pain and misery were all Thornton had brought to everyone in his path. And for what, Mack thought? It wasn't for a personal belief or philosophy. It was simply for his own personal, tortured satisfaction and need to control. What fueled this monster's demons?

Mack saw the fear in Thornton's eyes which were darting back and forth in desperation. He was completely alone and he knew it. And he knew that by tomorrow he could be ruined unless he could get back into control of this situation. Thornton slowly searched for a way to appeal to Mack. Perhaps they could reach an agreement, he was saying. "You can have power like you've never known," said Thornton, almost pleading, but starting to gain back some of his composure.

As he stood over him, trying to decide his next move, a new thought brought Mack a stab of pain that was almost unbearable. He thought of tender moments he had shared and the future he had planned for his own life. A life he desperately wanted and would never have. All because of this man.

At that moment Richards felt numb. The painful thoughts simply ceased as he quickly, without hesitation, approached Thornton. He reached out and grabbed both sides of Edgar Thornton's head, feeling him begin to shake from fear. It didn't matter now if Thornton begged for his life or started to cry for help. It didn't matter if, in the eyes of the law, it was wrong. Now, Richards moved one hand behind Thornton's head. With the other he pinched Thornton's nostrils closed and covered his mouth so he couldn't take in any air. The great manipulator of the powerful now struggled for a few minutes, but Richards wouldn't release his grip. He watched the fear grow in Thornton's eyes. And he watched it turn to desperation. And then Richards felt the life go out of him.

"That's for Terri," he whispered, as he disappeared back into the shadows and left Thornton there to rot in his own self imposed exile, not to be discovered until long after anyone cared that he had even existed.

# Chapter 25

"Today," said President Eric Gravell to Steven Daniels, "I want that mess on the Mississippi over. When I'm through addressing the nation we will have a whole new situation and I don't want any of the old dirty laundry hanging around. Do you understand?"

Daniels simply nodded in agreement and headed back to his office to issue the order for the BLM to prepare for action.

In Missouri, the standoff on Jimmy Armond's farm had reached a critical situation. The news media had been ordered out of the area. Supplies had been cut off to the farmers and friends gathered. And things were getting desperate. Still more people arrived from around the country to join the band of protestors. They were blocked by heavily armed federal agents from entering the area. But they refused to leave and so were jamming roads.

Jimmy and his fellow farmers had done everything possible to reach a peaceful solution. The last thing he wanted was violence. He had a family and they were still in the farmhouse, now unable to leave because of those federal roadblocks.

Just yesterday the Mississippi Shovel Brigade had issued an appeal to the government asking for return of their water. It read, "*We the Farmers of the great Mississippi River declare the blockage of our rightful use of these waters to be invalid and unlawful, depriving us of our historic use of our land. We unanimously appeal to the U.S. Government to remove the blockade and let it be known on this day that common sense was restored and we agree to work together for such a solution.*"

The petition was delivered under an old fashioned white flag. Those gathered across the farm had high hopes that this appeal would provide an opportunity to begin peaceful talks and end the standoff. They were shocked to watch the head of the BLM simply rip the document into pieces and immediately arrest the volunteer who had delivered the appeal. There was to be no honorable settlement.

Meanwhile, in Washington, D.C., just before he was to address the nation, President Gravell was signing four new Executive Orders that Edgar Thornton had provided. The first was now in place and ready to be carried out. Across the nation, military bases were ordered to be on high alert and to begin deploying troops and equipment into the cities to enforce a "Protective Martial Law," effectively controlling the movement and communications of the American people to "assure order and safety."

The order was to begin in coordination with the President's scheduled national address. Set for 10:00 that morning.

On Jimmy Armond's farm the members of the Mississippi Shovel Brigade, after witnessing the government's response to their petition, now knew their efforts for a peaceful settlement were hopeless. They also knew that there was little chance that any of them would be allowed to leave the area alive. After a brief and emotional meeting of their leadership, a decision was made for the Shovel Brigade's next and final move.

At the White House, a large, heavily wrapped package arrived in an armored truck, guarded by a strong security force. It had been sent from the National Archives and was now delivered to the Oval Office where the President was preparing to make his address to the people. The package was unwrapped and the object inside, encased in glass, was placed on a table next to the Presidential podium along with some other equipment. The cameras and hot lights were all now ready for the 10:00 a.m. start.

The President, grim faced and seeming nervous, entered the Oval Office promptly at ten as an announcer was heard to say, "Ladies and Gentlemen, the President of the United States."

On the field in Missouri, finally the moment had come for the protestors to take action. Jimmy's friends, fellow farmers and supporters were essentially trapped. They knew the BLM wasn't going to let them leave on their own. And they couldn't just stay there until their dwindling supplies ran out. So they saw no way to move except right through the BLM line.

The time for negotiating and waiting had passed. Now this moment, in which their own actions would determine their personal fate, was all they had left. To stay meant certain death. To surrender, meant imprisonment and ruin for their families. Perhaps, they hoped, this act of sacrifice would have some meaning around the nation to encourage others, just as desperate as those in the Mississippi Shovel Brigade, to take a stand. And maybe they would finally find a way to overcome this tyranny and be able to once again live on their own land. What else could they do?

So they lined up, grim-faced and ready. American flags were flowing in the breeze. The front line consisted of Jimmy and his fellow farmers, followed by a contingent of city councilmen, county commissioners, county sheriffs and state legislators from across the country. Behind them were simple citizens who believed the farmers were suffering an injustice by a tyrannical government. All had come here to take a stand, come what may. If a civil war was the only way, then let it begin here, today.

The line stood there for several minutes, looking across the field at the heavily armed BLM force facing them. The government agents were prepared in military combat fatigues and bullet-proof vests with helmets to protect them from toxic gasses, backed by heavy equipment. And on the hill Jimmy could see the BLM snipers with their rifles aimed at him.

Finally, hesitantly, Jimmy just said in a low voice, "Let's go."

The line of citizens, farmers and local officials began to step forward. At the ready, Josh and his fellow veterans moved their fingers to their triggers, the BLM snipers clearly in their sights.

Suddenly, a government issued Black SUV appeared on the field and raced toward the center between the two lines. As it reached the very middle ground of the opposing forces, the vehicle stopped. The passenger door flew open as Interior Secretary Phyllis Jasper jumped out and rushed toward the BLM line. The Shovel Brigade stopped its advance as they heard her shout to the BLM leaders, "I am the Secretary of Interior of the United States and as your superior, I order you to stand down immediately. You will disperse and leave this area now!"

• • • •

"Good morning, my fellow Americans," said President Gravell. "I speak to you from the historic Oval Office in the White House where so many monumental decisions have been made for our great country. This morning I want to announce to you perhaps the most significant changes the nation has experienced since its founding."

As Gravell's image filled nearly every television set in the nation -- in homes, airports, bars, and on the jumbo screen in New York's Times Square -- another scene was mutually taking place in cities across the nation. Military vehicles carrying armed troops were moving out of bases and National Guard Armories to set up road blocks and patrol neighborhoods.

In Washington, D.C., an impressive sight was noted by some watching from the sidewalks. Coming out of the Navy Yard was a Marine Combat Assault Battalion, consisting of a command car and two personnel carriers which transported a full platoon, and they were accompanied by five tanks. It was headed to the heart of the city. Other units were already taking up their appointed positions in neighborhoods around the nation's capitol.

In the Oval Office Gravell continued to address the nation. "As you are well aware, we have been facing great challenges in meeting the needs of the people as we endeavor to improve your lives. My only concern is for your prosperity, safety, and happiness.

"I want to explain to you why we are making these changes. For too long people have been allowed to make their own decisions that have led to massive, unfair imbalances. These imbalances come in many ways, from income inequality, to housing, where a few get to live like kings while others are forced to live in overcrowded ghettos. Imbalance is found in education, where some are able to excel, while others struggle, often failing. This leaves many devastated, without hope. And, of course, there is the fact that many of our private industries operate without regard for our precious environment.

"Why has this been allowed to happen? Why are so many suffering, you may rightfully ask. The answer is selfishness and a system that allows it to exist. Specifically the source includes ownership of private property, which is a social injustice because we can't all own and profit from it. And it comes from this so-called free enterprise system through which a very few are able to control the lives of so many. They dictate who has a job and who doesn't. Then they decide what your wages will be if they even grant you a job. They decide what products will be produced and made available to you. And, as I said, they have no concern whatsoever about protecting the environment they force you to live in.

"There is another reason for much of your misery. You may find this odd of me to say, but the fact is there is simply too much knowledge in our world. You are forced to make so many decisions that it causes you stress. You have to try to figure who is right and who is wrong. Who is telling you the truth? Whom do you trust? There is so much technology thrown at you, forcing changes to take place every day in your lives, that you simply are not prepared for. It simply isn't fair.

"Egotism and greed cannot be corrected. It must be destroyed. That forces us to understand that we must go beyond minor controls and corrections. We need to create something that strives toward a whole new system of social co-existence. That's why I'm addressing you today to let you know that my Administration is taking steps to change that imbalance. These changes will start today!

"From this day forward we are going to begin to measure our successes and our knowledge in a completely different way. We will no longer measure your success by how much money you make or by how many things you own. That causes an anxiety that forces you to compete and collect things you don't need and probably don't want. It's pushed on you by greedy companies that want you to buy their goods. From now on, the nation will no longer measure our success based on the Gross National Product, which simply measures how rich a few have gotten. From this day forward we will measure the health of the country through Gross National Happiness. We will spread the wealth of the nation equally among all of you and that will remove the unwanted competition and guarantee to each of you a longer and happier life.

"Second, we are going to eliminate the stress over making all those decisions you are faced with every day. From this day forward, knowledge, as promoted in our schools, our churches, and on our jobs will be controlled through a measure we call Globally Acceptable Truth. This is knowledge you can count on. Knowledge you won't have to question, because it will come from your government and from your teachers. No more doubts. We as a nation will be free to move forward.

"To begin to put this new order of our society in place, I am today announcing four new Executive Orders that are being implemented as I speak.

"The first two orders deal with our system of government and how we are organized. I know most of you feel left out and distant from your government. We are going to change that.

"To that end, I have issued an Executive Order to instruct every agency in my government to begin the process of reorganizing away from the unworkable existence of fifty different and sometimes opposing States. Instead we will reorganize the nation into nine Super Regions. Each of these regions will be governed from the largest city inside it. We call it Urban Corridors. Inside those cities, the Super Regions will be run by selected and proven leaders from the area. They will control development in the cities, providing housing for all. All food, energy, and water will be supplied directly from the region.

"The second Executive Order deals with our U.S Congress. It has proven to be an ineffective and unworkable burden on the nation. Here is where those big corporations get their power to prey on you with their high-priced products. Members of Congress are simply too susceptible to bribes, and as a result they have become a roadblock in our efforts to bring equality and balance to you. We will now begin to replace Congress with an Assembly of the People. The bur-

den of electing Congressmen will be replaced with representatives of non-governmental groups. They represent our
civil society and will be appointed by the heads of the Super
Regions so they represent equally all regions of the nation.

"The third Executive Order deals with those selfish
forces I have been talking about. Starting today, all private
property ownership will be banned and all property will
be controlled by government to assure its proper use and
to assure protection of our environment. Concurrently, all
industry will be nationalized and run by your government.

"Now, as we move to make these very necessary changes
for your brighter future, we must remove every roadblock.
First, as we all know, there are forces in the nation which
will stop at nothing to block every move we have made
for you. They preach the selfishness of individualism and
property ownership at the expense of those who can't own
or fend for themselves. They reject our vision of equality for
all.

"I know that they will not quietly accept these changes.
And so, to assure your safety and the stability of this nation,
I have, this day, issued a fourth Executive Order calling out
our military to impose a Protective Martial Law so that your
government can assure these disruptive forces are prevent-
ed from causing unrest in the nation as we reorganize our
governing system.

"I ask you, my fellow Americans, to please bear with us
for the temporary inconvenience to your daily routines. It
will only last as long as necessary to assure our success over
these negative entities in our midst."

As Gravell continued to speak, across the nation, more

and more military vehicles were moving through the cities. Roadblocks were being established and command centers were set up to monitor all citizen activity.

In Washington, D.C., the Marine Combat Assault Battalion turned onto Pennsylvania Avenue.

Now Gravell paused and seemed to take a deep breath. Then he began again.

"Finally, and perhaps most importantly for the secure future of our newly organized government, we need to remove once and for all the single biggest roadblock we have faced in our attempts to make these changes."

At that, Gravell turned to the table next to his podium. There was the large glass enclosed item that had been delivered from the archives. Gravell now began again, "This, ladies and gentlemen, is the actual Constitution of the United States. I had it delivered here today from National Archives, and for a very special purpose. Let me explain.

"As you know, this document was written over two hundred years ago to govern our nation. Then, it was praised as a revolutionary model for government. But it has a major flaw. You see, there is no way its authors could have ever foreseen the challenges our modern, technological world would face.

"Even more damning is the fact that this has become a very oppressive document because it was actually created to prevent your government from having the necessary tools it needs to help you. That's because, far from being revolutionary for the sake of the people, it was actually written by rich, slave-owning white men who wanted to assure government

could never stand in their way. They had no care or understanding of the problems faced every day by the common
man. This document was written to allow them to plunder
you. And that is exactly what has been happening for two
hundred years.

"It is for these reasons this Constitution has been a
roadblock every step of the way in our efforts to create a
more humane, caring government to provide for your every
need. Today, I intend to remove this roadblock once and for
all."

With that, two aides moved into the camera shot to take
the document out of its protective glass case and hold it up
to for the President. Gravell then continued, "This day will
be looked on by future generations as the most significant
day in our history. It is the day when we finally throw off
our shackles of this oppressive document." The nation now
watched as the President moved toward the table to reveal a
large shredder.

The Marine Combat Battalion had now arrived at the
gates of the White House. As White House security guards
and Secret Service rushed to the gate in an attempt to block
them from entrance, the lead tank smashed through the
gate and was followed by the command vehicle along with
one of the personnel carriers and a second tank. The other
three tanks moved into position around the fence surrounding the White House. At the gate a squad of marines from
the second personnel carrier deployed and held their rifles
on the White House security. No one moved.

The command car stopped at the front portico. Three
officers got out. Several more Marines exited the personnel carrier. The group rushed up the steps and entered the

building, pushing more security out of the way. They headed straight for the Oval Office.

The second tank and the remaining Marines in the personnel carrier entered the grounds and headed around to the back of the house, stopping in the Rose Garden just outside the Oval Office. The remaining Marines exited the personnel carrier and rushed onto the porch just outside the Oval Office, guns trained on the door.

Yet unaware of the commotion outside, Gravell moved to stand behind the shredder indicating to the two aides who were now holding the Constitution over the shredder as he said, "Now my fellow Americans we are going to finally free ourselves of these chains by removing this oppressive document forever. It's time for our new order to begin." With that he flipped the switch to turn on the shredder and the television audience could hear it buzz.

At that moment the Oval Office doors flew open with a mighty crash. Two armed Marines rushed through taking positions on each side of the door. A third came straight at Gravell. In their shock, Gravell's two aides dropped the Constitution to the floor as General Hugo Hollingsworth, followed by two other men, rushed in and straight to Gravell who was still standing at the table in front of the television cameras in view of the entire nation.

Gravell got a look of sheer panic on his face and looked for a way to run. But one of the men with Hollingsworth grabbed and held him as Hollingsworth indicated to the third man with him to come to his side. Then Hollingsworth said in a commanding voice, heard by the entire nation, "Eric Gravell, with me is Major General Cecil Davis. He is the U.S. Army Provost Marshall General. He has a warrant for your arrest. As Chairman of the Joint Chiefs of Staff, I hereby enforce that warrant and, on behalf of the People of the United States, place you under arrest for treason to your country."

The entire nation, now glued to their television sets, watched in absolute shock as Gravell was placed in hand cuffs and was about to be led from the Oval Office. At that moment the live television feed was cut and televisions across the nation went black.

# Epilogue

For several minutes stunned Americans just sat there looking at their blank television screens. Not a sound was heard in Times Square as the huge crowd stood in stunned silence looking at the giant blank screen. Finally the networks switched to some very startled reporters who looked back at their cameras like deer caught in the headlights, struggling to say something beyond a stutter.

It would take some time to undo the damage to the nation and its systems caused by Edgar Thornton and Eric Gravell. Americans were shocked to learn all the details outlining the betrayal revealed in the secret report called ERASE. For months new details were uncovered disclosing the incredible control of the nation and its economy by Edgar Thornton. The former President and Thornton were now the two most despised men in the nation.

Thornton's body was found by U.S. Marshals who had
been sent by Congressman Morris to serve a warrant for
his arrest. His body was placed in an unmarked grave over
which he had no control. He was soon forgotten. No one
ever bothered to investigate his death. Vito Mangreen was
suspected but no conclusion was ever reached.

A new popular movement sprang up across the nation
as radio disc jockeys called on people to bring their LEAP
e-books to large public gatherings to throw them on a bon-
fire for melting. There was irony in that fact since Thornton
had worked so hard to use e-books to avoid the specter
of book burnings. LEAP books were banned from every
school district and state house. Within a matter of months,
LEAP simply ceased to exist.

More than fifty members of the Gravell Administration
including the President and Vice President, several Members of Congress, and more than twenty federal judges including the two Supreme Court Justices, were charged with
treason. Fifteen of them had fled to escape arrest, including
Dr. Beverly Twetcher. She and nine others were eventually
caught hiding in secret compounds concealed in locked
away wilderness in rural Wyoming. All were eventually
found guilty and sentenced to prison. The remaining five
continued to be the focus of a world-wide manhunt.

And so, once again, the nation was riveted to its televisions as it watched the public trial of the President of the
United States. Several times during his trial Eric Gravell
stood, declaring his innocence. These outbursts were fol-

lowed by disconnected diatribes in which he insisted that the Earth had only days to live and that it was futile to continue with the trial because none of his accusers would survive to carry out his sentence. He was eventually found guilty of high treason and sentenced to life in hard labor. As he was escorted out of the courtroom, he shouted that it had been necessary to lie in order to scare people into sacrificing their lives for the planet.

In an interview, General Hugo Hollingsworth declared that the show trials were necessary in order to assure that such corruption of the Americans system would never be allowed again by an alert citizenry.

So many in the government had been involved in the plot that the public demanded a special election to bring in new leadership. Congressman Albert Morris, who had led the effort to bring them all to trial, was elected President and Phyllis Jasper was chosen as Vice President. There was still a smile on her face from the incredible joy felt when she had personally locked the handcuffs on Steven Daniels as the Federal Marshals led him off to jail. He had cried all the way to the awaiting police car. His trial would start soon.

Regaining access to food, especially being allowed to eat meat again, took nearly two years before the farming industry could be fully restored. Ranchers and farmers were again back in business. The locked away seeds were distributed to farmers across the nation as fields once again sprouted new crops and the grocery shelves began to fill.

Jimmy Armond and his Mississippi Shovel Brigade were honored at the White House by President Morris who promised them new legislation to assure they would never again face interference by their government.

Brad and Kate had a good laugh the night she finally brought home some steaks and watched as little Jeremy got his first taste. He kept taking it out of his mouth and then tasted it again as he chewed with great care. He seemed to be savoring every bite. This year Brad was very much looking forward to a Thanksgiving feast with real turkey. He just got word that RJ and Tracie would be joining them for the feast.

Elsewhere across the nation, dams once again harnessed the energy of the mighty rivers; power plants served millions at greatly reduced cost; and the real estate industry thrived as people rushed to get out of the stifling cities to once again look out over their own yards and watch their kids play.

Operating on a tip, Pastor Dave found a huge warehouse filled with King James Bibles. He sent truck-loads of them across the country to help restock Christian book stores. To date, he has never missed a Sunday sermon on the public airways.

John Lloyd fulfilled on Peter Arter's dream of *Buy Right* bookstores in every shopping mall as he opened the 400th unit. LEAP was no longer a threat. The publishing and printing industry flourished again with great new books, some with leather bindings and rich paper pages that were brimming with new ideas for a new generation. Of course, even as the LEAP e-books were destroyed, the concept was still popular for book readers, especially now that all books were available and could be trusted to carry the full intent of the authors. Whether through e-books or traditional printed copies, either way, John Lloyd was the publishing industry's king once again.

The Voice of Adams was now recognized as one of the main think tanks in Washington. It helped to write policy papers as well as serving as the premier watchdog to assure the nation stayed on course to preserve and protect its founding principles. Specifically the principles demanded that liberty is indivisible and that political freedom cannot long exist without economic freedom. That position was used as the measuring stick for every policy advocated by the Voice of Adams.

Mack Richards had a statue of Terri Miller placed in the lobby of the Voice of Adams building. The first thing a visitor noticed upon entering was the fire in her eyes that the statue so vividly portrayed. The second thing observed was the small vase built into the statue's base and the single red rose that Mack Richards placed there every morning.

The Constitution of the United States of America was not only returned to its place of honor at the National Archives, but also to its rightful position as the law of the land.

It had all come about because of the courage of an

uncommon few who dared to challenge and defy a growing tyranny over a free people. Yet, the entire nation unknowingly owed a huge debt of gratitude to one man who had given up everything, including making the ultimate sacrifice, to sound the alarm in anyway he could. Like other revered patriots before him, his selfless courage had saved his nation.

As Brad Jackson arrived at his usual stop in the train station next to the school, he stepped onto the platform. Immediately he noticed a familiar, yet now very surprising sight. There on the wall, written in a red fluorescent paint were the words:

**"It does not take a majority to prevail. But rather an irate, tireless minority keen to set brushfires of Freedom in the minds of men."** They were the words of Sam Adams.

Suddenly Brad realized that Harold Riggers had somehow survived the attack by Vito. This was his way of letting the world know that the Graffiti Bandit was still alive to experience his victory.

Hoping to see his friend again, Brad smiled and said to himself, "Thatta boy, Harold. Thatta boy," as he headed off to his classroom and a new day of teaching real history.

# Note from the Author

Nearly every detail in this book actually exists in public policy. Of course I have taken some liberties for the sake of certain dramatic depictions, and my characters are fictitious. But much of the dialog is taken verbatim from actual events, as are several of the scenes I describe. I created Edgar Thornton as one man, but he lives inside several hundred such power mongers who use fear and deceit to destroy our society. They have many tools and tactics throughout the education system, our churches, the Internet, business and government to impose their vision for our future.

And yes, electronic books can be changed in just the way I have described to erase any message deemed undesirable or dangerous. Tyrants of old had to burn books to eliminate a nation's past. That's so messy and draws the attention of the masses. Electronic books can eliminate such messages with just the touch of a button. It's the same way votes at the ballot box can disappear. Just because we can do it doesn't mean it should be done. Technology designed to make our lives easier can also be used for evil intent in the wrong hands. That makes it a potential danger in a free society that must be controlled at all costs.

Our nation is being changed before our eyes in much the way I have described. And, just as I've presented, there are dedicated patriots racing to stop it. They are outmanned and over-powered. They are ridiculed and accused of spreading conspiracy theories. Some are now threatened with arrest simply for disagreeing with government policy – many of the same policies I have described in this book. In fact, the freedom fighters exist and so do the policies they oppose.

To preserve freedom it is the duty of every American to learn and understand these dangers. That is why true education, in particular the teaching of history, economics and philosophy is so vital to preserving a free society. It is why ballot boxes should be protected at all costs. It is why business and government should not mix, but stay independent of each other. And it is why the pulpits of the nation must be independent of government overreach.

Now you have read ERASE. And now you know how evil forces can secretly manipulate us all to blindly accept their version of truth to change our world and destroy your freedom. That information in your hands is dangerous to their plans.

**Watch your back!**

The first step in liquidating a people is to erase its memory. Destroy its books, its culture, and its history. Then have somebody write new books, manufacture a new culture, invent a new history.

Before long the nation will
begin to forget what it is and what it was.
The world around it will forget even faster.

The struggle of man against power is the struggle of memory against forgetting.

*From the book Laughter and Forgetting*
*by Milan Kundera*

# Acknowledgements

I awoke one Sunday morning with the basic idea for this book rattling around in my head. The day before I had read an article about how the contents of e-books could be manipulated and how the producers could monitor what was being read. In that way, said the report, publishers could produce more of what readers wanted. ERASE was born.

I immediately created an outline for the book idea and fired it off to my good friend **Michael Chapman**. He is an expert on the national education situation and we sometimes travel the nation together giving talks on the subject. Michael's fertile mind started working and he wrote back with several plot ideas that really started the story moving. This book would not be the exciting story that I believe it is without his input.

Next, **Carolyn DeWeese** listened to me for hours discussing the story and she added more creative suggestions. She invented the idea of Harold Riggers. Of course she saw him as a handsome romantic figure and hated the name I gave him!

My good friend **Rick Hamm** was a career soldier who now contracts with Homeland Security. He provided invaluable details for the scenes dealing with the military. **Steve Welch**, also a veteran of the Department of Defense offered more insight.

Then came the enthusiastic support and the imagination of **Debbie Barth**. She is a fellow activist and radio host who fully understands the issues I was dealing with and how to present them in a more dramatic fashion. When I was stuck all I had to do was talk to Debbie and we solved the problem.

My old friend and colleague **Dr. Bonner Cohen** and his knowledge of history provided me with the solution for how the Graffiti Bandit was able to cover so much territory in one night. I am equally grateful to my special lady, **Danyal Guerrieri**. She didn't actually know she was helping me with the book when she gave me a birthday present – a flash drive on a key chain. The idea helped me solve how the hidden report could be seen without trigging the ravages of Vito! Thank you, Danni, it was a key element to the whole story!

And then there was the invaluable work of **Debby Englander**. She's a professional in the publishing business and spent an entire day going over the book line by line, showing me where I needed to flesh out the background of several characters to make them more interesting. With each edit I could feel the book getting better.

The editing was finished to perfection through the dedicated effort of my long time friend and associate, **Kathleen Marquardt**. She has actually read the book more times than I, because she again went through it line by line, finding all of the typos and English imperfections I had created. I told her that if she cleaned up all the typos then people wouldn't believe that I had actually written it. They are my trademark, I argued. She fixed them anyway!

And finally I must thank **Kelly Reed** for his magnificent cover art. He was a joy to work with and a truly creative mind. This is just the beginning Kelly.

Thank you all. This book could not have been written without you!

Made in the USA
Middletown, DE
20 October 2022